The
Inn on
Bluebell Lane

BOOKS BY KATE HEWITT

KATE HEWITT

The
Inn on
Bluebell Lane

bookouture

Published by Bookouture in 2023

An imprint of Storyfire Ltd.
Carmelite House
50 Victoria Embankment
London EC4Y 0DZ

www.bookouture.com

ISBN: 978-1-83790-299-6
eBook ISBN: 978-1-83790-298-9

To the lovely editors of The People's Friend, Hilary Lyall and Shirley Blair, who gave me my very first opportunity to be published. I'll never forget it!

CHAPTER 1

ELLIE

It started raining as soon as they passed the sign for Wales.

"Cro-ee-so I Gym-ru," eight-year-old Josh sounded out slowly, taking his time with the unfamiliar syllables, his dark hair sliding into his face, his eyes screwed up in concentration. "What does that mean, Mommy?"

"I don't actually know," Ellie admitted with a slightly embarrassed laugh. "Daddy never taught me Welsh."

"I never really knew much Welsh," Matthew responded with a laugh. "Besides *bore da pawb*. That meant 'good morning, everyone' and you had to say it every day in assembly. I can't remember much else, to be honest, although I suppose I should." He glanced over his shoulder to smile at his younger son. "But I do know the one on that sign. It means 'Welcome to Wales.'"

"So, we're almost there?" This was an excited squeal from four-year-old Ava as she bounced up and down in the back seat, pigtails flying, blue eyes alight with anticipation as she craned her neck to get a better view of the scenery—vivid green hills, now awash with rain, a gloom of grayness hanging over the whole, admittedly perfectly pastoral, scene. It was the same thing they'd been seeing for some time, but it was certainly lovely. Ellie couldn't remember the last time she'd seen such lush grass, and such a vivid jewel tone of green. Probably, she realized, the last time she'd been to Wales.

"Cut it *out*, Ava," Jessica snapped irritably as she shifted away from her younger sister and stared out the rain-streaked window from the other side, dark hair in a tangle around her face, which was determinedly averted from her siblings crammed together in the back seat. They'd been in the car for over three hours, all the way from Heathrow, and she'd refused to say a word the entire time, maintaining a stubborn silence that had infuriated and saddened Ellie in turns. At thirteen, Ellie feared her oldest daughter would have the hardest time adjusting to her new life in a tiny Welsh village.

Although, actually, Ellie acknowledged, *she* might be the one to have the hardest time. After fifteen years of marriage and a lifetime in the suburban US, Ellie wasn't at all sure she was ready to embrace country life in all meanings of the word— living deep in rural Wales, and in a foreign country to boot, where they spoke another language. What did *bore da pawb* mean again?

After several years of toing and froing about whether they would ever make the move, how the children would cope, Ellie was now wondering how *they* would cope, or more to the point, how she would. After twenty years in the States, Matthew was as American as Ellie was—or almost. He liked a latte as much as she did, certainly, but he seemed to have embraced the idea of moving with more enthusiasm and alacrity than she had. But then, he was going back to where he'd grown up, the comforts of childhood, the familiarities of youth, whereas she was just going somewhere that felt strange.

Six months ago, they'd finally pulled the trigger—or perhaps the more apt analogy was the plug. Their life in Connecticut had been going down the drain, financially speaking anyway, thanks to Matthew's unexpected redundancy, and so they'd decided to move to Wales and help Matthew's mother with her struggling bed and breakfast. Ellie had done her best to be on board with the move, knowing how much Matthew wanted and even needed the change, but right now, as the car turned down a lane that seemed far too narrow, with high hedgerows on either side blocking the view of the gorgeous, green hills, Ellie found herself longing for all the conveniences of her old suburban life in Connecticut—wide roads, easy parking spaces, sunshine, and a Starbucks on almost every street corner. What she wouldn't do for an iced caramel macchiato right now, while sitting out on the terrace with her friend Joanna, comparing their Labor Day plans...

"We've got about another forty-five minutes left of the drive, Ava," Matthew called from the driver's seat, his tone as upbeat as ever. "Until we get to Granny's house, that is. But at least we're in Wales."

Yes, at least they were in Wales, Ellie told herself, trying to summon the kind of cheerfulness that seemed to come so easily to her husband. It really was ridiculously beautiful—the gently rolling hills, the little stone cottages nestled in valleys, and when the sun came out from behind a cloud for a brief moment, the whole world glinted. It made her spirits, if not quite lift, then at least flicker a bit. She knew it was going to be hard to adjust to this new life, but she really was going to do her best to try.

Still, she could admit, at least in the privacy of her own mind, that she'd never been all that thrilled about the prospect of moving. Upending her whole life, leaving her friends, her family, and as paltry and shallow as it might have seemed, the *convenience*... When Matthew had told her that the nearest grocery store was thirty minutes away, she'd thought he'd been joking. How had she never realized that, when they'd visited his mother before? She supposed because it hadn't been relevant to her real life, back in Connecticut... the life that was now gone.

Trying not to feel as dispirited as her eldest daughter, Ellie turned to look out the window at the impossibly green country-side. The sun had slipped behind a bank of violet-tinged clouds once more and a few raindrops spattered the windshield. She'd agreed to this move, Ellie told herself, because, well, it had seemed *fair*. Matthew had spent twenty years in her home country; she could spend a little while—length still to be determined, as she kept reminding herself—in his.

But right now, she was fighting a deep-seated terror at the prospect of this new life of theirs, never mind the beautiful, misted hills that rolled on to the horizon, dotted with sheep; the woolly creatures looked almost as if they'd been strategically placed, as props. You could take a photo of the scenery, put it on a postcard along with the—what was it again? *Croeso y Cymru.* But it didn't necessarily mean you wanted to *live* there.

Eleven-year-old Ben let out a bored sigh as he ran a hand through his sandy hair—he really needed a haircut, Ellie realized—and kicked the seat in front of him, which happened to be hers. She managed to suppress a grunt as his foot connected, through the seat, with her tailbone. "Why is this car so *small*?" he demanded. He'd had a growth spurt this summer and was now to Ellie's chin, and a good foot taller than Josh, who let out a yelp of complaint as Ben elbowed him in an attempt to get more comfortable—or perhaps just to annoy his younger brother.

The rental car was decidedly smaller than the eight-seater minivan—people carrier, they called them in Wales, didn't they?—that they'd had back in the US, and had recently sold, much to Ellie's reluctance. "We could keep it," she had suggested wistfully to Matthew at the time. "It's only got forty thousand miles on it..."

"Keep it?" Matthew had looked puzzled. "What for?"

Ellie hadn't quite been able to look him in the eye. "You know," she'd half-mumbled. "Just in case..."

"In case of *what*, Ellie?" Matthew had challenged with a good-natured smile, but a rather steely look in his blue eyes. They'd already gone through all the pros and cons of this move, and the pros had outweighed the cons, if only by one or two—one by Matthew's standards, but two by Ellie's, since no Targets or Walmarts had been an acceptable con in her mind.

"I think we could benefit from a life with a little less super-store in it," he'd said to her, to which Ellie had not been able to think of a suitable response, or at least one that wasn't rude.

"This is a new start, Ellie," he'd told her. "We need to embrace it." His tone had suggested that since they'd already had that discussion, there didn't need to be another one.

Embracing, Ellie had come to realize, was different than accepting. She'd just about got on board with the latter—which had meant selling their house, their car, and most of their belongings. Okay, fine, Ellie had told herself, trying to be brac-ing. She wasn't attached to possessions. She didn't want her children to be attached to them, either. She'd always said as much, believed it, and yet right now, in the admittedly small confines of the rental car, she realized she wanted to hold onto something familiar, and it felt as if there was nothing left.

But she needed to have a good attitude about all this, espe-cially if she wanted her kids to have one, as well. Jessica was already decidedly dragging her heels about leaving her friends, and the words "ruin my life" had crossed her lips more than once. Ben wasn't that far behind her in the reluctance stakes, and Josh, at eight years old, her most thoughtful child, was innately cautious and therefore a little nervous about every aspect of this move—from whether Granny would have the kind of crackers he liked for a snack to whether anyone in his new school would like Lego. At four, Ava didn't really understand what it was all about, but Ellie was bracing herself for the moment when her youngest daughter suddenly realized this move was permanent, and that her pink canopied bed hadn't accompanied them across the ocean.

All her children, Ellie knew, needed shepherding, bolstering, protecting—none of which she could do if she was busy sulking about a move she and Matthew had decided on together. She'd been telling herself that all along, but she certainly needed the reminder now, as they drew closer and closer to their destination, with all its unknowns.

"How about we play the alphabet game?" Ellie suggested in her brightest voice, turning around to face the children. They'd played it three times already on the motorway from Heathrow, but a fourth round surely wouldn't go amiss.

Jessica let out a long-suffering sigh—she hadn't participated in any of the earlier rounds—and Ben didn't even bother to reply. Josh and Ava agreed to at least give it a try, and so, with rather beady determination, Ellie scoured the very few road signs visible along the rural roads.

"I see an A in Abergavenny!" she called out as cheerfully as she could.

"B in Brecon!" Josh exclaimed excitedly, a few minutes later.

"C!" Ava cried. "C in something. Mommy, I can't *read*."

"There's a C in Brecon too, sweetheart," Matthew said with a smile, his blue eyes glinting with good humor. "Good job, knowing your letters. We'll have to go to Brecon someday. It's lovely." He glanced at Ellie and placed a hand on her knee. "The Brecon Beacons. Have I told you about them?"

"No," Ellie replied, and then, fearing her voice sounded too flat, added quickly, "Beacons—what are they? Lights?"

"No," he answered, "although that's a good guess, considering their name. They're actually mountains. Well, hills really, I suppose, about half an hour from here. Beautiful place to hike."

"Oh..." She wasn't sure what else to say, as they'd never really been a hiking family, and fortunately at that moment, Josh called out "D in Cardiff" and she was able to turn her attention back to the game.

Maybe she should have known what the Brecon Beacons were, she reflected as the game continued around her—E in Brecon, F in Cardiff. She had been to this little corner of Wales a couple of times over the course of their marriage and, who knew, they might have trekked to the Brecon Beacons at some point during one of those stays. They'd done a few walks certainly. Ellie knew she needed to stop feeling so touchy, so raw, as if every mild remark of her husband's was some kind of criticism of her.

It wasn't. At least, she hoped it wasn't. But she suspected he was well aware of her reluctance to live in Wales, which deepened with every mile they traveled. She'd do her best to be cheerful for the sake of her family, but it didn't mean it wasn't hard.

"G in Abergavenny!" Josh called out, his voice rising in competitive excitement. So often when he played a game, he lost to his older brother, so the possibility of beating Ava held some satisfaction. "H in Hospital!"

"No fair!" Ava wailed. "I don't know what comes after H!"

"I, darling—"

"I in Cardiff!" Josh cried.

Ellie closed her eyes.

Thirty-five laborious minutes later, they were only at M, just as Matthew pulled into Bluebell Lane, the quaintly named rutted track that was devoid of any flowers on this late August afternoon, the rusted gate half-hidden by long grass and hanging off its hinges. Bluebell Inn, as the farmhouse where Matthew had grown up had been named once it had been turned into a bed and breakfast over twenty years ago, was on the edge of the village of Llandrigg. With a population of twelve hundred, it comprised little more than a village green, a primary school, and a couple dozen houses.

Ellie had been to her mother-in-law's house only three times before: once after they'd got married, and then a big trek across the Atlantic when Jess and Ben had both been small—those two weeks had passed in a slow, sleep-deprived blur of jet lag and culture shock. The third and last time had been around three years ago, a long-awaited visit, and the one that had made Matthew wonder if they should move back.

"It's a slower pace of life, less materialistic," he'd proclaimed, while Ellie had noted the teenagers in black hoodies loitering by the bus stop, vaping and scrolling through their phones, just like they did back in America.

In any case, more frequent visits over the years had never seemed all that practical, since Gwen preferred to visit them in America during the down season, when she had fewer guests, while in spring and summer the house she operated as a bed and breakfast was often booked, so there was no room for Ellie, Matthew and the children to stay. She'd always made that very clear, as Ellie recalled.

Except, now, of course, there was plenty of room, because a few months ago Gwen had decided she couldn't manage the B&B on her own, and so Matthew had had the idea of renovating the house, with the plan of eventually taking over the running of it... hence the push to move.

"Here we are!" Matthew called out as they pulled up to the rambling stone house that looked simultaneously charming and as if it had seen better days. The whitewash was flaking off the walls and the ivy climbing across the front looked as if it was completely obscuring the upstairs windows. A few slate tiles were missing from the roof, and the garden, Ellie could see under the now steadily falling rain, that it definitely needed some serious maintenance; it was a wild tangle of bushes, with a few chickens pecking among a patch of grass.

Well, she told herself bracingly, that was why they were there. That was why they'd completely uprooted their lives—to help Gwen out, to give Matthew a focus after being made redundant at the midlevel banking job he'd never really liked. They were here to experience new things, to have an adventure, to come together as a family... She'd spun it a dozen different ways to her children and friends, as well as her own abject parents missing them being stateside, but right now all of it rang horribly, clangingly false.

She didn't want to be here. That was the thorny truth that she kept thrusting aside, pretending she didn't feel it burrowing inside her, deep enough to draw blood. And, she really had to stop thinking like that, for the sake of her husband and children, her family's wellbeing, and frankly, her own. It didn't help matters, considering they were already here, and here they would have to stay, at least for the foreseeable future.

Taking a deep breath, Ellie checked her reflection in the side mirror—her face looked pale, the expression in her hazel eyes set a little grim, and after an exhausting day of travel, her dirty blond hair was limp and flat. Never mind. She'd have a shower later, and in any case, she wasn't trying to impress anyone, not even her mother-in-law.

Squaring her shoulders, she climbed out of the car.

"Come on, guys!" she called to her four children, who were still in the car, every single one of them eyeing the house with wary uncertainty. Ellie wasn't sure if they even remembered the last time they'd come; Ava and Josh certainly didn't, anyway. "Let's go and see Granny!"

With determined cheer, she flung open the door to unbuckle Ava, who, at four, was at least one member of the family eager to begin this new chapter, for now. When Ellie broke the news about her pink canopied bed... well, that was bad news for tonight, she supposed.

Now, Ava scrambled past Ellie, pelting toward the house as she yelled, "Granny... *Granny!*"

Over the roof of the rental car, Ellie met Matthew's gaze, and a sympathetic smile quirked his mouth.

"It's going to be okay," he said quietly, and while Ellie appreciated the sentiment, she wondered how on earth he could know whether it would be good or not, or even somewhat okay. Still, at least he had acknowledged, in a roundabout way, the validity of her concerns, which she had admittedly verbalised to him on several—somewhat heated—occasions, and she was grateful for that.

"Come on, Ben, Josh, Jessica!" Ellie called.

Silently, her children trooped out of the car and toward the house—Josh reaching for Matthew's hand, Ben bounding ahead, Jess slouching behind. Ellie gave them all bolstering smiles before falling in behind Matthew.

"How long has it been since we were last here?" she asked. "Three years, right?"

"Three years last May," he confirmed. "But it was a short visit... not even a week. Ava was just a baby."

"And Josh was five, Ben eight, Jess ten," Ellie recalled with a not-so-mock shudder. Ellie had been *so* tired that trip. None of the children had done well with jet lag, and Ava had been teething the whole time. Just as before, the whole trip had felt like an exhausting blur.

"Well, they're practically all grown up now," Matthew replied with a teasing smile, seeming practically buoyant now that they were finally here, at his family home. After months of tension and uncertainty surrounding his unexpected redundancy, mounting bills and increasing worry, Ellie was glad to see him looking more cheerful, even if she still couldn't help but feel anxious. Her one pervading memory from that trip three years ago, besides the complete lack of sleep, had been her mother-in-law's decided chilliness toward her.

With her curly, gray hair, wide smile, and warm Welsh accent, Gwen Davies should have been the kind of easy-going, relaxed mother-in-law anyone could get along with, especially since Ellie prided herself on being able to get on with just about anyone. Yet somehow, when it came to Gwen, it had never worked out that way.

Every time they'd interacted, it had been in fits and starts, jolts and shudders. Ellie made a suggestion, and Gwen's mouth pursed up like a prune; her mother-in-law made a comment that made Ellie wince and bite her tongue. Even when they were simply chatting about the weather, the conversation seemed to turn tense. Ellie recalled a time when she'd remarked on the rain and Gwen had replied, rather acerbically, that it had actually been sunny all week.

She was left with the feeling she could never get it right; her mother-in-law had long ago decided she was too outspoken, too loud, too American, perhaps. And she, Ellie could acknowledge fairly, had decided likewise about her mother-in-law. She was too reserved, too disapproving, too... *Welsh*, she supposed, although she didn't really know what a Welsh person was like, despite the fact she was married to one.

Yet now they were going to be living in Gwen's house for the foreseeable future.

Ellie had, some months ago, suggested renting in the village, at least while they settled in, but Matthew had completely dismissed such a suggestion.

"Why on earth would we do that? It would cost us a fortune and Mum has the space. Besides, she's looking forward to being with the children."

With the children, Ellie had thought, not with *her*. Not that she'd ever say as much to Matthew. He was under the impression, as she imagined many husbands were, that she got along just fine with his mother—and really, she *did*. They'd never fought, or even argued; Gwen was always friendly in her own way, and interested in the children. When it came to the mother-in-law stakes, Ellie might not have won the lottery, but she hadn't complete lost out, either. But that didn't mean she was relishing the prospect of actually living in her mother-in-law's house, sharing her kitchen, trying to follow her rules.

"Come on, Ellie!" Matthew called, smiling back at her, as he waited for her by the front door, surrounded by a broken trellis weighed down with large, late-blooming roses, releasing their heady scent and browning at their edges.

The children had all gone inside, save Jess, who was lingering behind; Ellie turned to give her an encouraging smile.

"Coming, Jess?" she asked, and her daughter nodded morosely before slipping past her into the house.

With Matthew next to her, Ellie paused on the threshold, taking a deep breath, willing herself to embrace not just this moment, but this new life. Then, squaring her shoulders, a smile firmly planted on her face, she headed inside with her husband.

CHAPTER 2

GWEN

Gwen rose from her seat at the kitchen table as she heard the crunch of tires on gravel from outside. They were here. After four hours in the car, twelve hours of transatlantic travel, *years* of her waiting for her son and his family to arrive... they were finally here.

She took a steadying breath, pressing one hand to her chest where her heart had started to beat with hard, painful thuds. She felt strangely nervous, considering she was seeing her own child. But then, of course, she hadn't seen Matthew like this, with him about to catapult into her life, take over her house, transform the business she and her husband, David, had built with so much love, thought and care... And, of course, there was Ellie and the children to think about, too.

Gwen heard the door creak cautiously open, and then light footsteps. She really ought to move toward the front door, but for some strange reason, she felt as if her feet were stuck in concrete.

It's Matthew, she thought, annoyed with herself for being so silly, and yet somehow, she still couldn't move.

"Granny..." A child's piping voice floated into the kitchen. "Granny?"

Finally, Gwen managed to walk toward the door, and as she rounded the corner into the entrance hall, she nearly crashed into her smallest grandchild, blinking in surprise at the sight of her.

"Goodness!" Gwen exclaimed, one hand still pressed to her chest. "Can this really be *Ava*? You've shot up since I last saw you."

She'd last seen them in Connecticut, for American Thanksgiving, nine months ago. Ellie had made all sorts of dishes Gwen had never heard of—green beans absolutely swimming in a rich cream sauce, and sweet potatoes with brown sugar and marshmallow topping, the sugariest dish she'd ever tasted. Who had ever heard of such a thing?

"I'm four now," Ava told her proudly. Sporting two curly pigtails and a lovably gap-toothed grin, she barreled right into Gwen's middle, making her let out a startled *oof* even as she laughed and put her arms around her in a hug.

"Yes, I know you're four. Do you remember we had a video call on your birthday?"

But Ava was already off, racing toward the kitchen. "Daddy said there was a dog..."

"Yes, his name is Toby." Gwen pressed one hand to her middle as she followed Ava back into the kitchen. The others hadn't come in yet, and she wondered nervously what was keeping them. "He's in the garden now, lying in the sunshine. He's quite old, I'm afraid. He doesn't like to play much anymore." She wasn't sure if she said this as a warning or an apology; she didn't want to disappoint Ava, but neither did she want her granddaughter harassing poor old Toby, who deserved his quiet time, dozing in the sun.

There were more people coming into the house now, and

she turned again, taking in the crew of gangly grandchildren who were crowding in the hallway and seemed very... big.

Gwen had lived alone, save for her guests who came and went, for nearly twenty years, since David had died of a heart attack when he'd been only fifty-four; Matthew had just finished university, about to head to America, and his sister Sarah, two years older, had been working in Cardiff at the time. The bed and breakfast that had been her and David's shared idea and joy had only been running for three years. It had been a terrible shock, to be suddenly plunged into loneliness, along with grief, to have to soldier on alone when she'd anticipated decades together still. All these years later, she'd told herself she was looking forward to sharing her space with her family again—of *course* she was—but right now she was conscious of both their size and presence, the strangeness of them, their silence. No one had said a single word.

"Goodness, Josh. Ben. Jessica. How you've all grown!" Gwen's voice rang out a bit too jolly and she laughed and shook her head. These were her *grandchildren*, and she'd been desperate to have them here with her for so long. Jess was so tall and slender now, her dark hair pulled back into a ponytail, her expression doleful. Ben was almost as tall as she was, with shaggy blond hair in desperate need of a haircut, but fortunately a ready smile for his grandmother. Josh was much smaller, with dark hair and eyes and looking decidedly wary.

Gwen hugged and kissed them in turn, which they submitted to politely, the way you would with a stranger; she knew she was nicknamed Faraway Granny, which stung, even though she'd told herself it shouldn't.

If she was painfully honest with herself, she knew their relationship had always been one based on good manners rather than real affection, unlike that with Ellie's parents, who had been intimately involved in all their lives from the moment each child had emerged, squalling, into the world, or so it seemed to

Gwen when she ventured onto social media to see the many photographs of their holidays and family dinners together, candid snaps of them playing in the garden, decorating a Christmas tree, watching fireworks.

But that was going to change now, she reminded herself. Finally, it was her turn to be the one on hand, close by, *there*, just as she'd wanted to be, even if it felt a little odd at the moment.

Matthew and Ellie were coming in now, Ellie hanging back a little as Matthew strode toward her, arms outstretched.

"Mum!"

"Oh, Matthew." Unexpected tears pricked Gwen's eyes as her arms closed around her son's familiar form. "It's so good to have you here."

"It's so good to be here, Mum. I can't believe we've left it so long."

"It doesn't matter now." Gwen stepped back, brushing at her eyes. "It's just so lovely to see you. *All* of you," she added, making a deliberate effort to include Ellie, who was looking as if she'd rather not cross the threshold.

Typical, Gwen couldn't keep from thinking a little sourly, and then told herself to banish the thought, along with the emotion. She was going to make a real effort with Ellie now that they would be living together. She'd never felt that they'd managed to get along properly, all these years, for one reason or another. They'd never fallen out, never had a cross word, even, but somehow the tension had remained between them, like a thickness in the air.

Gwen knew she was most likely too prickly with her daughter-in-law, just as she recognized that, for whatever reason, Ellie was somewhat stiff and standoffish with her. It had started, really, before she'd even met Ellie; when Matthew had rung her from New York, where he'd been doing his MBA, and told her he'd met the most wonderful girl—an *American* girl—and Gwen had clutched the receiver to her ear, one hand pressed to her middle, and thought, *Oh*.

When Ellie had flown over to meet her a few months later, already sporting a sparkly engagement ring, Gwen had *meant* to make an effort, but somehow it had all felt rather hard. Ellie had found everything impossibly quaint and said so repeatedly, and after a while Gwen had felt herself start to bristle at her loud, American ways, how she exclaimed over everything like it was all so ridiculously old-fashioned and *cute*. She'd used that word a lot—Gwen's garden, her pride and joy, an acre of neatly tended vegetables beds, raspberry canes, and great, big blooming hydrangeas, was *cute*. Her kitchen, a large, pleasant room, once the bustling heart of her house, was *cute*. Even her jumper was *cute*.

Gwen had started to hate that word—just as she'd hated how Ellie had made it abundantly clear that she and Matthew would be staying in America. For Ellie, the idea of moving to Wales—or even Great Britain—clearly wasn't even to be thought of, never mind discussed. If Gwen had suggested it, she feared her soon-to-be daughter-in-law would have simply laughed and said what a *cute* idea that was.

By the end of the week-long trip, Gwen had felt winded, *wounded*, as if a whirlwind had blown through her house—her whole life—and then left again, without remotely realizing the devastation it had wrought. She'd managed, over the next few months, to come to grips—more or less—with the idea of Matthew marrying Ellie, and even of them living in America. She'd always tried to have a game face on when chatting with Matthew via video call, and at their wedding she'd been the dutiful mother of the groom, staying in the background, being quietly supportive. Yet she and Ellie had never really got past that first stage of finding each other rather... different.

With their infrequent meetings and formal visits, they'd never managed to move past those initial reactions, but now

Gwen knew they would have to. Or at least try to. And she wanted to—of course she did. Really.

"Come into the kitchen," she urged them all. "I've made Welsh cakes and I'll go put the kettle on. Then I can show you all your rooms..." She glanced at Ellie, to gauge her reaction, and saw her daughter-in-law force a smile. She looked strained, her blue eyes tired, her light brown hair pulled back into a limp ponytail... but then they had been on an overnight flight.

"That sounds lovely, thank you, Gwen," she said, a response that should have gratified Gwen but didn't, perhaps because her tone was so... dutiful.

"Come through," she instructed, firmly now, and led the way into the kitchen.

The children gathered silently around the big oak table, the same table Matthew and Sarah had eaten so many meals at—full English breakfasts, and hearty soups for lunch, bangers and mash for tea, night after cozy night, when the house had been full and the home happy. It had been a long, long time since those days; most evenings, Gwen took her supper into the sitting room and ate while watching the telly or doing a crossword.

"It's lovely to have children in the house again," she told her grandchildren. "I've always felt this was a house made for children."

These children, however, were looking decidedly nonplussed, as they took in the room's shabby comfort—an ancient Aga, a Welsh dresser crammed with odds and ends of dusty china, a lumbering fridge that wheezed every so often and had been on its last legs for about three years.

Perhaps she could tempt them with food.

"Look, here are some Welsh cakes I made just this morning," she said brightly.

With a little flourish, Gwen took the plate of sugar-dusted cakes from the dresser and put them in the center of the table.

They'd been a teatime favorite with her guests and had won the local Women's Institute's baking competition back in the day.

The four children stared at them on the plate, not one of them going forward to take one. Gwen kept her smile firmly in place.

"Mommy," Ava finally asked in a loud whisper, "do those have raisins?"

Gwen saw Ellie bite her lip, casting her an anxious look before glancing back at her daughter. "I think so, yes." Another questioning look to Gwen. "They do have raisins?"

"Yes, they're *Welsh cakes*," Gwen replied, far too stiffly. "Of course, they have raisins."

"They're a bit like a flat scone," Matthew explained as he nicked two from the plate and scoffed one of them in a single bite. "I'm sure you've had them before, Ellie, when you've visited? They're scrummy. Try them, you lot."

Ellie's mouth twisted as she let out a funny little laugh. "You're already sounding so much more British," she remarked. "I don't think I've heard you say scrummy before, or call us 'you lot'."

She did not, Gwen thought, sound entirely pleased about it.

Matthew raised his eyebrows as he swallowed the second Welsh cake. "I *am* British. Well, I'm Welsh, in fact."

And no one, Gwen noticed with an inward sigh, said anything to that.

It was the first day and it already felt as if it was going wrong, or at least it wasn't going *right*. Not as right as she longed for it to. Her grandchildren looked out of place, and Ellie was already seeming aggrieved—and what had she done wrong? She'd made cakes, that was all, but apparently in her daughter-in-law's book that was an offense.

"Jess, Ben, Josh," Gwen tried again, her tone a tiny bit too commanding. "Do have a cake."

Silently, they all took one, holding them in their hands

without taking a bite. Gwen watched them in dismay, feeling as if they were all here on sufferance. She turned to the kettle, as much to hide the hurt she feared was on her face as to make tea. As far as beginnings went, this was not the one she had wanted.

Still, Gwen told herself, surely things could only improve. She squared her shoulders as she began to make the tea. She would simply have to make sure they did.

CHAPTER 3

JESS

Jess woke up in one of the attic rooms at four o'clock in the morning, dawn light filtering through the curtains and the birds making a noisy racket like none she'd ever heard before. This house was so *weird*. Everything in Wales was weird.

On another morning, in a different life, she knew she might have been charmed by the early sunrise, the dawn chorus, but, as it was, she lay in bed, the duvet drawn up to her chin, and felt her stomach clench hard as realization sank in. She'd moved to *Wales*... and her life was basically as good as over.

Blinking back tears, Jess rolled onto her side and tucked her knees up to her chest, the way she used to do when she'd been little and feeling sad. Back then, she'd had baby problems— someone hadn't shared a stupid toy, or something like that. She'd never had problems the way she did now, at thirteen, with absolutely everything going wrong. Her life was a *disaster*.

Yesterday had been awful from start to finish—the endless car journey, the relentless rain, her little sister being so noisy and annoying, Ben unable to sit still for so much as two seconds, and Josh picking his nose. Gross.

Then they'd finally arrived, and that had been even

worse. She had never felt as if she'd known Faraway Granny, not the way she knew her Grandma and Grandpa back in Connecticut. They only lived an hour away and they often came over for a weekend visit or went on vacations with them. When she'd been nine, they'd taken her and Ben to Disney World, a special treat for the "big kids." Jess had had the *best* time.

But Faraway Granny was totally different. Jess only saw her once a year for a couple of days, if that, and she always stayed on the edges of things, speaking in a polite way that made Jess feel nervous, like she was talking to a stranger, and basically, she was.

Yesterday, her grandmother had looked sniffily at them all as Jess had forced herself to choke down one of those horrible Welsh cakes. She didn't like raisins either, but she wasn't four years old like Ava and so she'd had to eat it, swallowing every stupid bite.

Just as she'd had to say thank you—her mom had given her *that* look—when Granny had shown them their rooms, up on the top floor, where it was stifling hot and smelled like dust and mothballs. Who on earth would want to sleep there?

"I hope you'll be comfortable," her grandmother had said in her stiff way. "I thought it best to put you up here since we'll be renovating the guest rooms on the floor below. It'll be a building site for a while, and at least you'll have some peace and quiet, along with some privacy."

Jess had thought it was her grandmother who wanted the privacy—and why were they living in the *attic*, for heaven's sake? Wasn't that where you hid crazy old wives and stuff? They'd read *Jane Eyre* in school this year, although she hadn't totally understood it, but her grandmother's house seemed just as creepy as Mr. Rochester's.

Still, she hadn't said anything more than thank you to her grandmother, because the truth was, in that moment she didn't trust herself not to cry. She hated it here already, just as she'd known she would.

Jess had fought against moving when her parents had first floated the idea past her and her siblings, back in February. In the grip of a New England winter, Connecticut had been icy and unforgiving, and her dad had seemed completely taken by the prospect of moving to his homeland—not that he'd been there in, like, forever, and he didn't even know Welsh, not really. He'd certainly never spoken back home.

"You'll love it, Jess," he'd assured her, his smile so warm and hopeful that Jess almost didn't want to disappoint him, but... *Wales.* No one in her class had even heard of the place. "It's so peaceful and beautiful," her dad had told her. "Green hills as far as you could see. We'll watch the rugby together! We can finally get the dog you wanted..."

She knew the dog was just a sweetener, because she'd been asking for one for forever. But hills and rugby? Did her dad think she was actually interested in either of those things? She didn't even like American football, never mind the British version of the sport. It had all sounded incredibly boring to Jess, as well as alarming. She didn't want to be stuck in the middle of nowhere, knowing no one. She didn't want to leave her friends, particularly her best friend, Chloe, with whom she did literally *everything*.

She liked her bedroom back in Connecticut, which she'd only decorated last year, in blues and greens, having finally convinced her mom to change it from babyish pink and purple. She liked her weekly ice-skating lessons, too—next year, they were going to have a big gala performance—as well as Saturday lacrosse club, neither of which were apparently available over here. Her mom had told her the nearest ice rink was in *Cardiff*, which was, like, a million miles away, and lacrosse wasn't even a thing here. No one had probably even heard of it. Her mom had said something about netball, but what on earth was that?

None of that had mattered to her parents, though, who had relentlessly forged ahead with the move, even when Jess had resorted to threats of never speaking to them again because they'd ruined her life, and how she would need therapy for years because of this, and who was going to pay *that* bill?

"Jessica, you're thirteen," her mother had said in that pseudo-patient voice that Jess knew came right out of some parenting book. "You've barely *begun* your life, so I don't think it can be ruined just yet. Besides, you might appreciate this change later on, the opportunities you'll have..."

"What opportunities?" Jess had demanded. "The village where Faraway Granny lives is *tiny*. There is, like, literally nothing there except a couple of houses."

"There are bigger towns nearby," her mom had answered with a sigh. "And please don't call her Faraway Granny. It's not very nice."

"But it's not like *here*," Jess had insisted, trying to sound angry despite the tell-tale break in her voice. "I have opportunities here, Mom. Good ones. Really good ones." And more importantly, good friends. Or at least a friend, singular. What would she do without Chloe? They'd started *kindergarten* together, holding hands on the first day. Jess had never been without her, *ever*.

Her mom had softened a little then, but that hadn't made it any better. "I'm sorry," she said, her tone gentle, regretful even, but also implacable. "I know this is hard, and there will be a lot of challenges, but this is something we have to do as a family."

"I *hate* you!" Jess had shrieked, knowing it was pointless, that her mom would just be annoyed by her melodrama, and yet unable to keep herself from it. She'd run to her room and slammed the door as loud as she could for the same reason, and when there hadn't been any noticeable response, she'd opened it and slammed it again, just for good measure. It had been satisfying, for a few seconds, anyway.

Later, her mom had come up and apologized, trying to explain everything, using that patronizing grownup voice about how there were things she didn't understand, and there was stuff they had to consider that she didn't know about, but Jess just had to trust her. Of course, she wouldn't actually tell her what any of it was, and Jess knew it didn't make any difference, not to her, anyway.

"I know Dad lost his job," she'd fumed as she'd rolled over on her bed, her face blotchy from crying, "but why can't he get another job *here*? And what about my school? My friends?"

"You'll make new friends, Jess—"

Jess had pounded her fist into her pillow. "I don't *want* to make new friends!"

Now, thinking of Chloe, Jess reached for her phone that she'd hidden under her bed. Her mother had a strict rule that phones went on the charger in the kitchen at eight o'clock at night, which was *ridiculous*. Chloe's mom let her have her phone all night long in her bedroom, an argument that had never held any water with either of Jess's parents, who remained firm. Jess had stopped asking about it because she knew there was no point; her parents were *that* strict sometimes.

Last night, after her parents had gone to bed, Jess had crept all the way downstairs, the steps creaking underneath her, once so loudly she was afraid she'd been heard, and rescued it from the charger. She *had* to see what Chloe was up to—and tell her all about this horrible place. At least her best friend would get it, even if nobody else did. Her stupid siblings seemed to actually be okay about living here, even if Josh was kind of nervous and Ava was little and couldn't really understand it. As for Ben, he always just seemed to goofily go along with everything, and just rolled his eyes whenever Jess kicked up a fuss.

But when, in the middle of the night, she'd tried to message Chloe on Instagram, her friend had left her on read—the message received but not responded to, the worst online insult. Chloe was her *best* friend. She *never* did that... except she just had.

Her stomach clenching even harder this morning, Jess opened the app to see if Chloe had responded to her message last night—a long moan about everything here that *definitely* deserved a response. But there was still no reply.

Jess's stomach swooped unpleasantly as she realized how long Chloe had left it—*seven hours*. Why? She'd promised she'd message her every single day when they'd left. She'd seen Chloe just two days ago, when they'd had a final sleepover, crying and laughing in turns, staying up late, promising to be BFFs forever. And now she'd left her on read like she couldn't be bothered to reply?

Feeling as if she was torturing herself, Jess clicked on Chloe's story to see what she was up to. A photo popped up of Chloe snuggled up on the sofa with Emily Rhodes, another girl from their class, both of them in matching onesies and fuzzy slippers, a big bowl of popcorn on their laps. *What*? Chloe was having a sleepover with *Emily*?

Jess stared at the picture, hardly able to believe it. Chloe *hated* Emily. Or at least, she didn't like her. Emily was one of the snobby popular girls in the class, the kind who flicked her hair and rolled her eyes while you were talking. Jess and Chloe had always agreed they'd never go after that crowd, never try to be "in" with girls like that, because they knew better.

It looked like Chloe had changed... in just two days. She hadn't even mentioned any plans with Emily when they'd had their sleepover. Had she been lying to her, even then?

Tears stung Jess's eyes and she blinked them away furiously, too angry to cry. *Why* was she in Wales? And why was her best friend bailing on her literally the *second* she'd left?

She flung her phone away from her, not even caring when it clattered onto the wide wooden floorboards, spinning away under her bed. What did it matter if it broke? It was an old and cheap phone, anyway, one of her dad's castoffs, because her parents refused to buy her a new one, like everybody else in her class had, claiming they weren't necessary and were too expensive. She was practically the only girl in her entire grade who didn't have the latest phone. It was *embarrassing*.

"What was that noise?" Blinking sleep out of her eyes, Ava sat up in the bed opposite Jess's, blond curls tumbling over her shoulders. Her blue eyes widened as she saw Jess's phone under her bed. "Do you have your *phone*?" Her voice was filled with the sisterly glee of getting a sibling in trouble. Even though she was only four, she knew the rules about no phones at bedtime, and she'd make sure their mom knew when they'd been broken.

"Go back to sleep," Jess told her irritably. "It's only five o'clock in the morning."

Ava turned to look out the window, a sliver of sunlight filtering through the chink in the curtains. "But it's so bright out."

"That's because the sun rises at about midnight here," Jess replied. And the birds started up with their stupid chorus at crazy o'clock, she thought to herself. "Go to *sleep*, Ava."

Of course, she had to share a room with her four-year-old sister. Back at home, she had her own bedroom, with cool stencils on the wall she and her mom had done together, of dolphins and seahorses, with an ocean-colored carpet and pale green walls, and a canopy over her bed made from this cool sea-blue gauze her mom had found at a fabric store. She'd made one for Ava too, in pink, and Ava had had a meltdown last night when she'd realized the canopy wasn't coming to Wales, crying and kicking her feet while their mom had looked on wearily.

Jess wasn't about to cry about it, but she missed her old room now, almost as much as Ava missed her stupid canopy. She missed *everything*, even the things she hadn't liked so much, like having to re-lace her ice skates when her fingers were freez-

ing, or the gross broccoli and cheese casserole her mom made
her eat sometimes, or even the way her dad had been so gloomy
these last few months, since he'd lost his job. He'd kept saying
he was going to do something like paint the basement or mow
the lawn, but then he'd never actually do it. Her mom had kept
getting annoyed and trying not to show it.

All right, maybe she didn't miss *that*, but she missed a lot. A
lot. And if she had her way, she'd hop on a plane that very
morning to go back to Connecticut, to real life. She'd ask to live
with her *other* grandparents, or maybe even with Chloe. If Jess
went back, Chloe wouldn't hang out with Emily anymore,
would she? She and Chloe could be like sisters; Emily's mom
might let her stay with her family. They had a guest bedroom,
after all, and plenty of space. Jess would make sure not to be any
trouble...

A sigh escaped her as the futile dream evaporated. Her
parents would never let her do something like that. Not yet,
anyway. As it was, Jess knew she was going to have to wait... and
figure out a way to make her family move as soon as possible,
back to where they belonged.

CHAPTER 4

ELLIE

Ellie couldn't sleep. Even though her body was jet-lagged, her brain was racing ahead, around sharp corners and down blind alleys. Would the kids settle in their new schools? Ben was starting a new school in year seven, its entry year, but Jess would have to go into year nine, the lone new students. And what about Josh, who had adored his second-grade teacher? And Ava, who was starting reception at just aged four, a year younger than she would have had to start kindergarten, back at home?

Home. When would she stop thinking of Connecticut that way? How long would it take? And would Matthew really enjoy renovating the bed and breakfast? Ellie knew he needed a project, but he'd never been that into DIY. What if it wasn't financially viable? And what would *she* do here, away from everything she knew? She couldn't even find a job, not yet, because of the limitations of her visa. Would she spend her days doing nothing more than trying to keep out of Gwen's way? What a thought...

At quarter to five, she slid out of bed, doing her best not to wake Matthew, who, in any case, was snoring pretty loudly, and headed downstairs, hoping to have a little alone time before the day started, with all its expected needs, hassles, and complaints.

Yesterday had not been easy. Gwen had been about as welcoming as Ellie had feared, coming over all stiff and formal, which made Ellie instinctively act the same, even as she tried to find a friendly tone, an easy smile. Why did it have to be so *hard*?

And it *had* been hard, all the way through the interminable evening, beginning with the Welsh cakes the children had all dutifully nibbled under Ellie's beady eye and Gwen's gimlet stare, her faded blue eyes unblinking as she'd watched them all. None of her children liked raisins, and Ellie had tried not to flinch as they'd all choked them down; even little Ava had at least managed a bite. Then Gwen had shown them their bedrooms, up in the old attics on the top floor, all of the rooms cramped and baking hot in August, with sloping ceilings that Ellie had cracked her head on twice.

Ellie had understood the reason to cram them all up there, of course she had. Matthew was intending to renovate the whole place, doing as much of the work himself as he could. The five bedrooms on the lower floor were positively dire, the decoration from the 1980s, everything shabby and dated. Business, Ellie knew, had been dropping off for years.

So, yes, of course they all needed to be out of the way while Matthew went about his business, tearing up old carpets and ripping out sinks. Still, it felt a *little* bit like they were unwanted guests, stuck all the way up in the attics, or perhaps even the hired help.

Not, of course, that she wanted to think that way, but it was hard not to, especially when Jess had looked at the room she had to share with Ava—two narrow beds crammed side by side, with a single dresser for both of them—and given Ellie a look that was full of both misery and accusation.

"Do you think we should rent something in the village?"

Ellie had asked quietly when she and Matthew had been getting ready for bed. She'd known he'd vetoed her suggestion before, but it was different now they were here, and even their suitcases barely fit in the bedrooms. "Just to make things easier on everyone," she'd continued, "especially at the start. If Jess could have her own room—"

"What? No." Matthew's tone had been definitive as he'd shaken his head. "That's not the point of all this, Ellie. Mum wants us here, and in any case, you know we need to save money."

"Surely it wouldn't be that much, just for a month or two?" she'd pressed. "Just until we all find our feet, that's all." She'd almost suggested buying a place, if they really were going to live here, but she hadn't wanted to mention something so permanent, and she still hadn't been sure what Matthew expected... Perhaps he was thinking they'd stay at Bluebell Inn forever? They'd never made a plan past moving and renovating the B&B. What life might look like in the long-term hadn't been something Ellie had really wanted to discuss, anyway, but maybe she should have.

"It'll be *fine*," Matthew had assured her firmly, and Ellie tried not to resent the fact that it all seemed so easy for him. He hadn't lain next to Ava for an hour that evening, willing her to fall asleep, or listened to Jess's tearful diatribe as she'd accused her parents of ruining her life... yet again. He'd been downstairs, drinking coffee and catching up with his mother, while Ellie had assured an anxious Josh that he would make friends in his new school, and wrestled the iPad off Ben, who had complained that there was nothing to do *but* play the latest online gaming craze, which seemed to involve shooting aliens that exploded on screen in a mess of green goo. Lovely.

She loved all her children to pieces, she absolutely did, but sometimes their needs felt as if they might overwhelm her... especially when she was having to deal with them all on her own. Not, Ellie had told herself, that she begrudged her husband a catch-up with his dear mother. Of course not. And, she'd reminded herself, Matthew had been a very hands-on dad after he'd been made redundant—offering to do school pickups, kicking the soccer ball with Ben for hours in the yard, making up for lost time after working so many hours, when he'd missed bedtimes and dinnertimes and baseball games. She'd appreciated the effort, so much so that she'd missed it rather keenly just then.

As Ellie had finally closed their bedroom doors, breathing a sigh of relief that her children were mostly asleep, she'd heard laughter drift up the stairs and, for a second, she had considered going down and joining Matthew and his mother. Showing her face, at least, because she had a feeling it would count against her if she didn't, at least in Gwen's eyes. But she hadn't been able to face it—Gwen's sniff when she remarked that she'd never had to coddle her children to sleep, or words essentially to that effect, and how she'd read an article about the dangers of online gaming while Matthew gave her meaningful looks, as if to say *See? They're going to do so much better here*. No thank you, to any and all of it. And so, her body aching with fatigue, she'd simply gone to her bedroom and read her book until Matthew had come up, a whole hour and a half later, looking, to his credit, somewhat apologetic.

"Sorry, I didn't mean to drop you in it with bedtime," he'd said as he'd shucked off his clothes and changed into his pajamas. "I just wanted to catch up with Mum, especially about the B&B. I think she's feeling a little cautious about some of my proposals, but she'll get there." He'd paused as he'd poked his head through the neck of his T-shirt. "Did the kids get to sleep okay? They were probably all exhausted from the jet lag."

As she was.

Ellie had closed her book. "It took a little while," she'd replied, and heard how stiff she sounded.

"We're all going to have an adjustment period," Matthew told her. "It might feel tough for a little while, but I really do believe this was the right move to make. For all of us." He'd smiled at her, and kissed her cheek, and Ellie had just about managed a nod before they'd gone to sleep.

Now, in the fresh dawn light of a new day, she was determined to find the optimism that usually came so naturally to her back in Connecticut. It was a beautiful morning, the pale blue skies looking freshly washed, the sun sending lemony yellow rays across the kitchen floor. Bluebell Inn was a lovely property, she acknowledged, if in need of some TLC. Maybe she could help Matthew with the renovations... or even Gwen. Modernize things just a little bit, without losing the place's charm... How would her mother-in-law feel about such a suggestion? Ellie wondered. Somehow she didn't think Gwen would welcome changes to a house that still looked like it was stuck circa 1987, especially if they came from her.

With a small sigh, Ellie filled the kettle at the deep farmhouse sink and plonked it on top of the Aga. As she waited for it to boil, she gazed outside at the bucolic view of rolling meadow, a rich, velvety green, the whitewashed buildings of Llandrigg visible beyond. In the distance, she could see a milk truck trundling over a little stone bridge; it looked like something off the set of one of those BBC historical dramas she and Matthew watched sometimes, where everybody knew everybody else, and they were all smiling, cheerful and friendly. How could she *not* be happy in a place like this?

Things would go better today, Ellie decided as she spooned coffee granules into a cafetière. Toby plodded into the kitchen and nudged her with his muzzle, his tail thumping on the floor, and Ellie smiled down at him. He was a lovely, old springer spaniel, brown and cream, with long, droopy ears and kind, tired eyes. They'd always wanted a dog, but they'd been waiting for Ava to get a bit older before going down the puppy route. Now they didn't have to.

Now they'd stepped into this amazing life—a beautiful house, a lovely village, a friendly family dog. And a grandmother. What wasn't there to like? It was all going to work out perfectly, Ellie told herself, knowing it was far from the first time she'd tried to bolster her flagging spirits. This time, though, she would make sure it did.

Today, she decided, she'd make a real effort with Gwen. She always meant to, but, somehow, every time she'd tried, it had felt too hard. Gwen's seemingly innocent remarks always caught her on the raw, and everything that came out of *her* mouth made Gwen's purse up like a prune. Maybe it was a cultural difference—two countries separated by a common language, as it was said, although Wales of course had its own language, as well—or perhaps just a generational one. Gwen was only in her late sixties, but she'd lived in something of a time warp, as far as Ellie could see, spending all of her adult life here in rural Wales.

Not, of course, that there was anything wrong with that. She needed to stop thinking negatively about her mother-in-law, Ellie knew, even in the privacy of her own mind. They were sharing a house now, a kitchen, a life. She really needed to make this work, and she was going to, starting today.

Maybe she'd take the children on a tour of the village later; they could see the school, and the play park Gwen had said was across the green. Maybe they'd even meet a few people who could become their friends. Find their feet, as it were.

Gwen had invited Matthew's sister, Sarah, who lived five miles over, in the next village, for dinner, and although Ellie hadn't seen much of her sister-in-law or her family over the years, as Sarah had never visited them in the States, she was determined to make a friend of her now. Sarah's children, Owen and Mairi, were just a little older than Jess and Ben and so they could all finally be friends, and not just distant cousins. The children could start putting down roots, which they desperately needed to do. Once this felt more like home, it would be easier for everyone. They had family here, after all. They could find a way to belong. They *would*.

Smiling determinedly at the thought, Ellie took the kettle off the range and poured boiling water into the cafetière, inhaling the pleasing scent of the freshly brewed coffee.

"Oh," came Gwen's voice behind her, sounding a bit taken aback. "I usually save that coffee for guests."

CHAPTER 5

GWEN

As soon as Gwen uttered the words, she knew they were wrong. Yes, she saved that fancy coffee for the guests, but there weren't any guests at the moment, and there wouldn't be for months, while Matthew renovated the place. She hadn't needed to say anything. Last night, Matthew had said something about Ellie missing Starbucks, of all things, and so clearly a cup of instant coffee was not going to be up to scratch for her daughter-in-law.

Gwen saw how Ellie had stiffened when she'd spoken, and she cursed her clumsiness. Why had she not *thought* before she'd said something? And why did Ellie make her prickle so much, feel defensive and irritable, even though she didn't want to be? She'd wanted things to be different this time, now that they would be living together, but she had a feeling the close proximity was only going to make it all worse. Last night, she'd been waiting for Ellie to join them after putting the children to bed, hoping they might finally have a chance to chat, or even bond, but her daughter-in-law had gone to bed without even coming downstairs to say goodnight. Gwen didn't think it had been meant to be a snub, even if it had felt like one.

"It doesn't matter," she said quickly, as she came into the

kitchen. "I only meant that I usually use instant, myself." She saw Ellie's mouth tighten and knew she'd said the wrong thing, *again*. "But instant isn't very popular in America, is it?" she continued, feeling as if she were digging an even bigger hole for herself to fall into, and there would be no way to climb back out. Nothing she said sounded right, judging by the look on Ellie's face. Gwen let out an unhappy, little sigh before continuing resignedly, "But, of course, you must feel free to use whatever you want." Her smile was forced, as if some invisible hand was pushing up the corners of her mouth into a terrible rictus grin. "What I mean to say is, you must think of this as *your* home now, Ellie. That's what I want you to do."

Ellie did not reply, and Gwen couldn't really blame her. No matter what she'd just said, the truth was, she wasn't sure she actually *wanted* Ellie thinking of this as her home, even if it would be so for the foreseeable future. She supposed Ellie didn't want to, either.

'Would you like some coffee?' Ellie asked after a moment, her voice carefully, coolly polite, without any edge, and yet Gwen felt it, deeply. She suppressed another sigh.

"Yes, please. Thank you."

"I can make you instant, if you'd rather?"

Now there definitely was an edge.

Gwen took a careful breath. "What you've made looks lovely, thank you. Smells lovely, as well. We should use it up, especially as there are no guests around!" Somehow, she managed a laugh. "Don't want it to go to waste."

Ellie gave a stiff little nod and poured the coffee while Gwen got the milk out from the fridge.

This was her favorite time of day—the pale dawn light, the quiet, save for the pleasant twitter and chirp of the birds, the sense of solitude and peace that wrapped around her like a comforting blanket. Unfortunately, right now, the palpable tension in the room felt both unavoidable and unwelcome. The first day in, and she already missed her quiet mornings.

"You're up early," she remarked as she poured milk into the coffees and then took her cup to the kitchen table.

Ellie picked up her own cup and leaned against the counter, cradling it between her hands. "I couldn't sleep," she confessed.

"I thought the jet lag traveling in this direction went the other way...?" Gwen remarked, and Ellie just shrugged. Should she apologize for the coffee remark again? Somehow she couldn't quite make herself do it. Last night had been stilted, to say the least—the children had all picked at the supper she'd made—toad in the hole—one of Matthew's favorites and a childhood classic—yet not for her grandchildren, it seemed.

"I'm sorry, we don't normally eat sausage," Ellie had said when Ava had folded her arms, refusing to try even a bite of the Yorkshire pudding, perfectly golden, hiding succulent bits of meat.

"You don't?" Gwen had been startled. Who didn't eat sausage? "You're not all *vegetarian*, are you?" She had tried not to sound appalled; she knew loads of people were vegetarian these days, or even vegan, and she'd cooked breakfasts to that regard for her guests, but she'd never really understood something she viewed as little more than a fad.

"No, no, not at all, we just... don't eat *sausage*." Ellie had shrugged helplessly, seeming to think Gwen should have grasped this distinction.

"People don't really eat sausages in the States, Mum," Matthew had chimed in cheerfully. "Except at breakfast, and then it's usually doused in maple syrup and served with pancakes."

"Maple syrup!" Gwen had been truly taken aback. "You never have sausages for tea?"

"Tea?" Josh had said in surprised disgust. "You have sausages in *tea*?"

"Tea is the evening meal," Matthew had explained easily. He seemed to find it all so amusing, all the cultural and linguistic differences nothing more than amusing points of conversation, while Gwen struggled not to feel dismayed and, worse, hurt, by all the surprises she was coming up against. Of course, she should know these things by now. She'd visited Matthew and his family in the States quite a few times over the years, she wasn't completely unfamiliar with Ellie's ways, with *America's* ways, and yet... not in her house. Her *home*.

"I suppose," Gwen said to Ellie now, determined to put last night's awkwardness behind them, "this is all bound to feel a bit... strange." She was conscious of how much Ellie had given up, moving to Wales, even if her daughter-in-law didn't realize she understood. Even if, Gwen acknowledged, she didn't act as if she did.

"Yes, it is," Ellie admitted after a moment. She tried to smile, and almost managed it, but her lips wobbled a bit and Gwen felt a sudden, sharp shaft of sympathy for her. She'd known this would be hard for her, of course she had, but perhaps not quite as hard as it actually was. How much of that was her fault? She knew—of course she knew—she could have made it easier for Ellie. "But," her daughter-in-law continued staunchly before Gwen could say anything, although, in truth, she didn't know what she would have said, "we'll all get used to it in time, I'm sure."

She made it sound as if they all had to gird their loins and grit their teeth, to get used to something so very difficult and unpleasant.

"I hope so," Gwen replied after a moment, trying to moderate her tone to something upbeat, but she feared she sounded the tiniest bit skeptical, even though she hadn't meant to.

Ellie gave another stiff little nod. "It's very kind of you to have us here."

"It's no trouble."

What dreadful chitchat they were having, Gwen thought rather miserably. Their sentiments sounded formal and forced and, worse, not entirely sincere, and after another agonizing few seconds, they both lapsed into silence, and Gwen wished she could think of something more to say. Something friendlier, *warmer*.

"Matthew mentioned some of his renovation ideas to me last night," she finally ventured. "They seem quite... ambitious."

In fact, Gwen hadn't been at all sure about half of them—en suite bathrooms for every bedroom? Whirlpool bathtubs and infinity showers, whatever those were? When she and David had first started the B&B, back when Matthew had left for university, they'd only had the one shared bathroom in the hall. They'd put another one in the following year and thought *that* had been a luxury, but now Matthew was talking as if he was going to turn this admittedly rather ramshackle house into some sort of high-end hotel. It all sounded terribly expensive, as well as a bit, well, *ridiculous*. It would take a lot of money and effort to turn the Bluebell Inn into anything remotely close to a five-star establishment, and that wasn't what she or David had been going for at all, anyway.

"He's really excited about it all," Ellie replied as she took a sip of her coffee. "I'm glad he has new a project to focus on." She paused before adding quietly, "It's been a difficult few months, in that way, since his redundancy."

"Yes, I'm sure." Gwen didn't know all the details of Matthew's redundancy six months ago; he'd brushed it all aside when she'd asked him last night, assuring her everything was fine, and she hadn't wanted to press, but she suspected it had all been harder and more damaging than her son liked to admit. "He seems as if he can't wait to get started."

Last night, he'd talked about wanting to start ripping things out as early as today, which had alarmed Gwen. She'd been thinking about a fresh lick of paint, *maybe* some new carpets. But her son seemed to have a different, and far grander, vision entirely, one that required planning permission and business loans and goodness knew what else. Why hadn't he mentioned any of this before? Although, Gwen knew, even if he had, she would have most likely gone along with it, because she'd wanted Matthew back here, with her, and she'd known he needed a project.

"Yes, I think he is champing at the bit to get started," Ellie agreed. She didn't sound entirely thrilled by the prospect, and Gwen couldn't blame her. She had four young children to look after, while Matthew immersed himself in renovations. It wasn't going to be easy, even with Gwen's help—if her daughter-in-law even accepted it. Ellie paused before saying rather brightly, "I thought I'd take the kids to look around the village today, help them to settle in. They'll start school in just a week, and I'd like them to feel as if they know their way around here. And I don't actually know *my* way around, either. It's been a while since we've last been here, and I think I've forgotten where everything is."

Three years, Gwen thought, but didn't say. And only twice before that, in all their years of marriage. It had been expensive, of course, to come over, and when the children had been babies, there had been concerns about the travel, the jet lag. Still, the lack of visits had stung.

"That's a good idea," she told her daughter-in-law as diplomatically as she felt she could. "I'm sure they would enjoy having a nose round."

Ellie took a breath before asking carefully, "Would you like to come with us?'"

Gwen felt it cost her daughter-in-law something to invite her along, but she still appreciated the effort, and wished, rather desperately, that she could accept her invitation. Refusing wasn't going to bring them closer together, but in this case she had no choice.

"I'm so sorry, Ellie," she told her, her voice laced with genuine regret, "but I can't today. I'd love to have joined you, but I have an appointment." Instinctively, her gaze moved to the letter tucked in its envelope on the toast rack she'd used to hold post since Matthew and Sarah had been small. She'd tried to move the date of the appointment when she'd learned of Matthew and the family's arrival, but it hadn't been possible, not without waiting months for another one, and she knew that wasn't a good idea, even if she dreaded it.

"Oh, right." Ellie looked discomfited, a mixture of relieved and disappointed, which was, Gwen suspected, exactly how she felt.

"Perhaps you could go with Sarah?" she suggested. "I know she's looking forward to welcoming you all to the village."

Although, Gwen had to admit, her daughter hadn't said as much in so many words. She was a very busy woman, on half a dozen committees, as well ferrying fourteen-year-old Mairi and twelve-year-old Owen to their horse riding and football events respectively. Gwen had always been a bit intimidated by her oldest child's fearsomely accomplished manner, the way she scheduled every second of her family's busy lives, and all the activities Mairi and Owen participated in, far more than Sarah and Matthew ever had when they'd been young. Gwen had a suspicion that Sarah and Ellie wouldn't be natural friends, but perhaps that was being pessimistic.

"Maybe..." Ellie agreed dubiously, looking less than thrilled; Gwen knew Ellie and Sarah had spent very little time together, but maybe this would be a good opportunity to improve their relations. After all, they were all living close together, *finally*. They would all have to learn to get along... and hopefully it wouldn't be too onerous a process.

"Do you have her phone number?" Gwen asked. "You could send her a text, ask her along."

"I might," Ellie said slowly, before rising from the table. She didn't ask Gwen for Sarah's number, and Gwen doubted Ellie had it. "I'd better go get dressed, before the kids all come down demanding their breakfasts. I'm sorry about the coffee." Her tone had turned scrupulously polite, which saddened Gwen. "I'll use instant next time."

"Really, there's no need—" Gwen began, but Ellie was already walking out of the kitchen.

With a sigh, Gwen slumped against her chair, feeling as if every conversation with her daughter-in-law was doing the opposite of what she wanted and intended it to. When would things get better? *How?*

If David were alive, he'd smile and pat her hand, tell her to give it time. Matthew, she suspected, would look entirely bemused by the idea; she doubted he even realized the problem existed. He'd always been so easy-going, happy-go-lucky, care-free. This redundancy of his might have been a blip, a bit of a bump, but already he was throwing himself into the next project with enthusiasm.

And as for Sarah? Sarah would shrug and say something dismissive. *The two of you are different people, Mum. What does it matter? You don't need to be best friends.*

Maybe not best friends, Gwen allowed, but it *did* matter, because she wanted to get along with Ellie. She wanted to be close to her, as well as to her grandchildren. She'd babysat Owen and Mairi a bit back when they were little, but they were so busy now, with all their activities—and Sarah seemed to have an allergic reaction to asking her own mother for help—that Gwen felt as if she hardly ever saw them. Here was a chance to bond with Jess, Ben, Josh, and little Ava... if only they would let her. If only she could figure out how.

Another sigh escaped her, as slowly, inexorably, her gaze

moved back to the letter lying so innocently in the toast rack, where it had been for several months, since Gwen had first received it.

When, she wondered despondently, was she going to tell Matthew and Sarah about *that*?

CHAPTER 6

ELLIE

"Of course, you *can* get your uniform from one of the high-street shops, but the ones the school sells through its online shop are much better quality, as well as being environmentally sustainable, which, of course, is *very* important, and five percent of the profit goes back to the school, so, really, it's worth doing." Sarah's briskly capable voice carried down the empty street as she and Ellie walked, the children trailing behind them, toward Llandrigg's village green.

"I'm sure," Ellie murmured, trying not to feel overwhelmed by the constant monologue of information her sister-in-law was imparting. She hadn't particularly wanted to text Sarah to join her and the kids on the tour of the village, despite Gwen's good intentions. When Ellie had first married Matthew, Ellie had felt as if Sarah had sniffily examined her and found her wanting, and her sister-in-law's opinion hadn't seemed to change much in the following fifteen years, although, admittedly, they hadn't seen each other all that often. Still, Ellie had felt it, in the way Sarah tilted her head back every time she looked at her, how every time Ellie said something, she replied with "yes, but..."

At the beginning, Ellie had tried a little harder with Sarah.

She'd sent Christmas presents for Owen and Mairi, and they'd Skyped every so often, although Matthew and Sarah had done most of the talking. But somehow, as the children had all got older and life had seemed more busy, it had been easy—and something of a relief—to let their relationship dwindle to Christmas cards, the occasional WhatsApp message or video call.

Now, however, everything was different, because they were here in Wales. Matthew had thought it was a wonderful idea for them to go out together when Ellie had mentioned it, and he had texted Sarah himself, on Ellie's behalf, before she could tell him not to, or at least to wait and let her think a little. Prepare, at least. Meanwhile, he would be spending the day drawing up renovation plans and contacting builders and plumbers, whistling while he worked. It had been understood, without needing to be discussed, that Ellie would be on childcare duty all day, which was *fine*, she loved her children, after all, but...

Really, Ellie thought determinedly, there was no *but*. She was just jet-lagged, emotional, and more or less out of sorts. That morning's coffee debacle with Gwen hadn't helped matters, but she needed to get over it. Get over everything. She was here, she would be happy about it, *end of*. She was going to learn about life in the village, and embrace it all.

"Do you intend to join the PTFA?" Sarah asked in that same carrying voice, and Ellie forced her mind back to the present, giving her sister a bright smile.

"Is that the British version of the PTA?" she questioned, meaning to tease, but Sarah wrinkled her nose, her eyes narrowing just a little.

"I suppose that's what you call it in the US," she remarked, and Ellie heard, or rather *felt*, the slight note of censure in her voice. *You're not in Kansas anymore, Dorothy.*

"Right. Yes, it is." Ellie nodded, determined to move on. "So it's the PTFA here. Well, to be honest, I haven't thought about it yet, but maybe in time? I think I'll probably have my hands full, helping the kids settle in for the first semester—"

"We don't have semesters. We have *terms*. Three of them, actually."

"Right. First term, then, I guess." Ellie tried to keep her voice cheerful. Had that correction, along with a dozen others so far that afternoon, really been needed? She was American. She didn't speak British English, despite being married to a Brit for fifteen years. Maybe she should start trying, even if she feared it would feel forced, and worse, sound fake. But, still. PTFA. Terms. She could remember that.

Sarah had been giving them a tour of Llandrigg for the last hour, talking the whole time, while the children had followed on, looking depressingly disinterested. Ava had held Ellie's hand at the start, skipping along, but she had little legs and was tired from their travel, and after a while Ellie had had to hoist her on the hip, which Sarah had noticed and clearly disapproved of.

The truth was, she was more than a little intimidated by Sarah—she was tall and poised, with her dark auburn hair, the same color as Matthew's, pulled back into a neat ponytail, dressed in immaculate Hunter boots, a waxed jacket and skinny jeans, looking like she belonged on the cover of *Country Life*. Everything about her radiated calm confidence, slight superiority... or maybe Ellie just *felt* inferior, since Sarah seemed to know so much and Ellie so little.

Her sister-in-law hadn't faltered once in her recitation of all Ellie needed to know about life in Llandrigg—so far, she had heard about organic veg boxes, after school cricket club, how the Rainbows had lost a leader and just wasn't the same, and the dangers of the new skate park by the river, which included broken glass and teenagers who vaped.

Her mind was seething with information, as well as worry and frustration about all that lay ahead. Not one of her children, save Ava, who had asked if Llandrigg had a toy store, had said a single word during this whole interminable tour. If Ellie had nurtured hopes they'd bond with their cousins—and to be honest, she hadn't, not really—those had not materialized in the least. Four preteens and teens mooched behind her and Sarah, doleful in the extreme. Sarah, however, who was busy telling Ellie all she needed to know, hadn't seemed to notice.

Maybe, Ellie reflected wearily, she should have given them all a day simply to be before she'd launched them into their new lives, but mooching around the B&B, with Gwen always skulking in the shadows, hadn't felt like the best use of their time, either.

And so, she'd followed Sarah, the children trooping behind, from post office shop to church to primary school and now to the green, listening to her sister-in-law inform them on every aspect of village life, too tired to keep hold of any of the information that Sarah seemed to deem so important.

They reached the village green—a swathe of lush, if rather overgrown, grass with a tiny, dilapidated play park at one end. Ellie thought of the state-of-the-art playground back in Connecticut; it took up half an acre, with slides, swings, tunnels, trampolines, and sprinklers for summer. It was a far cry from this—a couple of swings, a rusty, old roundabout, and a broken seesaw.

Sarah surveyed the offerings with a beady look before she prodded Owen between his shoulders. "Go on, then, Owen. Show your cousins the play park."

With a decidedly unwilling glance for said cousins, Owen walked off, followed by Mairi, and after an awful second's hesitation, Ellie's children trailed morosely behind, Ava letting go of Ellie's hand to follow her siblings toward the playground.

"There," Sarah said with satisfaction as they retreated to a bench on the side of the park, Owen kicking the tufty grass and Mairi scowling into the distance, clearly too cool for Jess, who was a year younger. Ellie's own children were wandering around, seeming disconsolate. "They'll get along eventually. Children always do, don't they?"

With "eventually," Ellie thought, being the operative word. Still, she knew a friendship could not be forced. The cousins would have to sort it out for themselves.

"It really is a cute village," she offered as she glanced around the village green, surrounded on two sides by quaint little cottages, and on the third and fourth sides by the Norman church and a pub. The pub's colorful sign, indicating the three crowns of its name, swung in the summery breeze.

"*Cute*," Sarah repeated, with that little nose wrinkle Ellie was beginning to recognize—and dislike.

"Quaint, I mean," she corrected. Did Brits view cute as an insult? Well, Sarah couldn't argue with *quaint*. Everything about Llandrigg was impossibly quaint and so different from suburban life in Connecticut, with its giant parking lots and box stores and general lack of charm, outside of a small designated historic area that had swanky boutiques and independent stores. But their slice of suburban Connecticut also had multiplexes and playgrounds ten times the size of this one, three outdoor pools, tennis courts and ice-skating rinks, not to mention restaurants of every cuisine imaginable, as well as drive-through banks, pharmacies, and the ever-essential Starbucks, all within a five-minute drive of their house, and no need to leave the air-conditioned sanctuary of their car if they'd rather not.

Ellie had never thought of herself as being particularly materialistic, but right now she felt a sweep of homesickness for the *convenience* of her former life, the utter ease of it. The nearest shopping center, Sarah had informed her, was forty minutes away. Not that Ellie even wanted to go shopping, but *still*. She wanted just one thing to be familiar and easy. Sitting here on this bench, looking at the church and the pub, she felt as if she might as well have been dropped down on Mars. She imagined her children, especially Jess, would feel the same, only more so. Still, she told herself, they'd get used to it. Eventually.

"What about a pediatrician?" Ellie asked Sarah now. Since her sister-in-law seemed determined to be the font of all parental wisdom, Ellie decided she might as well drink from her ever-flowing waters. "Is there one in the village?"

"A pediatrician?" Again, Sarah wrinkled her nose. "How very American of you! Children just go to the regular GP in the UK, Ellie. They don't have special doctors unless there's something wrong. There's a GP in Abergavenny, but there might be a waiting list."

Ellie didn't think Sarah *meant* to sound patronizing, but she did. "How far is Abergavenny from here?" she asked, knowing Matthew had told her, but she'd forgotten.

"About thirty minutes, give or take a few."

Half an hour to the nearest doctor...! Okay, fine. Ellie managed a quick smile and then drew a steadying breath, casting an eye to her beloved brood. Ben was pushing Josh on the roundabout, which normally would have warmed her heart, but she was experienced enough to know he'd probably push him too fast and Josh would start to cry. Jess was standing by herself, arms folded, looking furious because she'd been forbidden from bringing her phone. Owen and Mairi had taken over both swings and were flying high, legs pumping, while Ava looked longingly on. *Eventually*, she reminded herself. It felt like a prayer.

"And what about a dentist?" she asked Sarah, deciding to get it all over with at once.

"Abergavenny." Sarah sounded amused, as if this should have been glaringly obvious, and considering the size of Llandrigg, perhaps it should have been. The takeaway from all this, Ellie thought, was that everything convenient was at least thirty minutes away, which made it decidedly *inconvenient*. "But you'll most certainly have to go on a waiting list for that, I'm afraid," Sarah continued. "Dentists are difficult to come by on the NHS in this area. You could always go private if you wanted, but, of course, that's expensive."

Ellie drew another breath. Fine. It was all going to be fine. She knew it was. She'd make the phone calls; she'd get on the waiting lists. It wasn't that different from America, where finding a doctor or dentist who took your health insurance could be a challenging feat, indeed.

It was just this all felt so *foreign*, from the names of the villages and towns as well as the television shows to whole swathes of life she didn't understand. Matthew really had lost his Britishness when moving to the States; he'd never talked about any of this stuff... and Ellie realized she had never asked. She'd never needed to know, or even considered that she might need to know. Now he seemed to have rediscovered his roots, while she was... flailing.

She stared blindly ahead as Sarah started talking about boots, and it took Ellie several minutes to realize she meant a shop called Boots, not footwear. And when she'd laughingly explained her confusion, hoping for at least a *small* bonding moment, Sarah had wrinkled her nose—*again*—looking politely confused, as if she didn't understand why Ellie might have misunderstood such a thing, because they were *obviously* two totally separate concepts. And yes, Ellie actually *had* heard of Boots, so maybe she was just being a little slow. There'd been one in the airport. She'd bought some travel sickness pills there, for Ava.

"Anyway," Sarah continued, cutting across Ellie's vain attempt at finding the humor in the situation, "you can get some minor treatments at Boots, if you don't want to go to the GP." She gave a little sniff, while Ellie tried not to sigh.

Ellie honestly thought Sarah meant well, just as Gwen did, in giving her all this information—she *knew* they did—it was just they all kept *missing* each other somehow. Perhaps it was a cultural difference; Ellie hadn't realized how much of a difference there was between the UK and the US until she'd married Matthew and, even then, it had seemed negligible, because by the time she'd met him he'd been living in New York for a while and had become used to American ways, seemed to enjoy them. How many times had he extolled the virtues of drive-through convenience, or the enormous portion sizes at the local Applebees?

It had only been when she'd met her mother and sister-in-law, and so infrequently, that she'd had to acknowledge, with a funny little jolt, how different they were, how different *she* seemed to them. Every time she'd visited—or when Gwen had visited them in America—Ellie had come up a little short, startled by the way they seemed unable to get along, without anyone raising their voice or even an eyebrow. It was all so very *civilized*, and yet it left Ellie feeling unsure and out of sorts. When they'd lived in Connecticut, she'd been able to shake it off and move on. But now that she was actually in Llandrigg? The cultural difference was smacking her right in the face. Repeatedly, and she couldn't even get out of the way.

"Well, I'm sure I'll learn the ropes in time," Ellie said with a little laugh, still determined to be optimistic, and Sarah smiled at her.

"Oh yes," Sarah assured her. "I'll help you."

Ellie glanced back at the children—Ben now spinning the roundabout while Josh was screeching to get off, Jess folding her arms and still glowering, Ava standing in front of the swings, pouting as she watched Owen and Mairi sail higher and higher.

Looking at them all, Ellie wished just one thing could be easy, or at least *easier*. These kids were cousins; why couldn't they get along, or even *try* to get along? Why couldn't they all be tramping through the bushes, making dens and giggling excitedly, as she'd pictured in an admittedly hazy way before Sarah had swooped in with all her well-meaning advice and air of superior knowledge?

Or was Ellie just being super-sensitive, because of Gwen, because of the strangeness of this new world, because she felt so raw and homesick and if someone had asked her if she wanted to go home, she'd be halfway to Heathrow if she could?

Well. That wasn't going to happen.

"Ben, slow down," she called, and with a shrug, Ben gave the roundabout one last shove before walking away. "We should probably get back," Ellie told Sarah, a note of apology in her voice. She had a feeling her children were at the end of their tether, or maybe she was. "Thank you so much for... everything."

Sarah gave a complacent nod. "You will let me know if you need anything?" she asked as she rose from the bench and called to Owen and Mairi. They jumped off the swings, with Ava diving out of the way. "Any questions... I'm happy to help, Ellie. Really." Sarah gave her a sympathetic smile. "I'm sure this all seems incredibly strange to you. I can't imagine relocating to Connecticut!" She let out a little laugh as she shook her head. "Really, it would be bewildering... as bewildering as it must be for you to move here. But, whatever you need, I'm here for you." She smiled, seeming sincere, and Ellie was unexpectedly touched.

"Thank you, Sarah," she replied. "I'm sure I'll have tons of questions. I just have to figure out what they are." She smiled humbly, feeling guilty for thinking uncharitably of her sister-in-law when she was so clearly willing to help.

Sarah seemed to have her entire life under control, making organic meals from scratch, volunteering on umpteen committees in the community and school, and holding down a part-time job as a chartered accountant besides. Next to her, Ellie felt like a ditzy mess. Even back in Connecticut, she'd struggled to keep on top of the laundry. Maybe she needed to take a few pointers from her sister-in-law, even if something in her resisted the notion.

To her surprise, when they reached the gate at Bluebell Inn, Sarah gave her a quick, tight hug. "I know this must be difficult," she murmured as she released her. "Chin up."

Chin up. If that was all it took...

"Thanks," Ellie murmured, meaning it. Sarah had taken the time to show her and the children around, and that had been a kind thing to do, no matter how some of her comments might have chafed. "I appreciate... well, everything." At least she was trying to.

With a parting smile, Ellie beckoned to her brood, and they all trooped back to the house.

From upstairs, Ellie heard the sound of a drill and winced. She'd thought Matthew was meant to be phoning the handymen today, not starting the work himself, but clearly the renovations had begun.

"Where's Daddy?" Ava asked as Jess unplugged her phone from the charger in the kitchen, checking the screen with the sort of avidity that saddened Ellie. Her daughter's life was still very much back in Connecticut, and most likely would be for some time. She certainly understood the feeling.

"He's working upstairs, sweetheart," she told Ava. "Have you heard from Chloe, Jess?" She'd kept her voice light, but Jess scowled at her and turned away.

"Yeah, course I have," she muttered, before grabbing a banana from the fruit bowl. Ellie knew she needed to check with Gwen about what food the kids could freely eat; otherwise, they'd be like a plague of locusts, descending on everything in the kitchen and gobbling it up in no time.

She supposed she should do her fair share of food shopping and cooking, as well, although she had a feeling Gwen wouldn't want her taking over her kitchen. More minefields to navigate, she thought with a sigh, and then, after giving the children permission to plug into their various devices for a little while, she headed upstairs to check on her husband.

Matthew was in one of the four guest bedrooms on the house's second floor—or *first* floor, Ellie reminded herself, in British terms. The room was an absolute shambles—wallpaper hanging from the walls in shreds, the carpet half-pulled up, and a sink half-falling off the wall while Matthew wrestled with a wrench.

Ellie glanced around, trying to hide her skepticism about the whole project, as she pinned a bright smile on her face. "How's it going?"

"Good!" Matthew wiped his forehead with the wrist of one hand while he rested the wrench on top of a chest of drawers with the others. "I know it looks an absolute wreck," he told her with a wry laugh. "I just wanted to have a go at something today, really. Get my hands dirty. Not much rhyme or reason yet, but there will be."

"Right." Now, Ellie knew, was not the time to remind her husband that his DIY skills were merely passable, or that they'd discussed hiring an architect or at least some capable workmen who knew what they were about. She folded her arms and then uncrossed them, afraid she looked aggressive. "So, what's your thinking, then?"

"Well." Matthew looked around the room. "I want to get these rooms down to their bare bones, I suppose. Then we can get an architect in to think about en suites and that sort of thing. They're good-sized rooms, and if we can take out the bathroom in the hall, there should be space for every room to have its own en suite, at least with a sink and shower."

"And a toilet, presumably."

He let out another laugh. "Yes, and a toilet. That's a must."

He lapsed into silence and so did Ellie, because she wasn't sure what to say. *Do you really know what you're doing?* was definitely not helpful, but it was what she felt at the moment.

Matthew could do the basics—wire a plug, plaster a wall—but anything more wasn't, Ellie felt, strongly in his skill set. Not enough to be getting bedrooms down to their *bare bones*, at any rate. But what did she know? Besides, she wanted to be encouraging.

"How was your day?" Matthew asked, and something about the way he asked it—as if it was entirely separate from himself and his own hopes and plans—annoyed her.

"Pretty good," she replied, trying to suppress that little sting of irritation. It was a perfectly innocent question, and it deserved a perfectly innocent reply. "Got the lowdown from Sarah on life in Llandrigg, but I'm not sure how much I can actually remember."

"I'm sure she has loads of helpful information."

"She *is* terrifyingly competent," Ellie agreed dryly, which was the gist of what Matthew had said many times in the past about his only sibling, but now he gave her a slightly reproving look.

"Give her a chance, Ellie," he stated quietly, like a rebuke.

"What!" She stared at him, surprised and more than a little hurt. "Matthew, I *am*. I spent the whole afternoon with her, after all."

He sighed as he picked up the wrench. "That's the kind of thing I mean," he told her as he began to work again at the sink.

Ellie stared at his back, wondering how and when this distance had come between them. She didn't think Matthew would have given such a response before they'd moved to Wales, or at least before they'd started *thinking* of moving; she was honest enough to admit that from the first time they'd started talking about it, things had sometimes—and only sometimes—become a little tense. But that wasn't entirely her fault, was it?

They'd used to laugh at things, but she knew that being made redundant had changed Matthew, on a fundamental level, or at least knocked him back. He'd tried to be upbeat about it all, seen it as a second chance of sorts, but when he kept sending his resumés out and not getting interviews, his determined cheerfulness had started to flag—and that had been hard on both of them.

She opened her mouth now to make some defensive retort she knew would come across as childish, and then closed it again. "Do you think you might want to spend some time with your children?" she asked instead, which, unfortunately, she realized also sounded childish and petulant, but she meant it. He'd been AWOL all day. His children needed him. She did too, but she'd settle for him hanging out with their kids for an hour or so, and giving her a bit of a break.

"Of course I want to spend some time with my children, Ellie," Matthew answered, a definite edge to his voice. "What kind of question is that?"

"What kind of *answer* is that?" Ellie fired back, amazed they were actually arguing. They never argued; Matthew was too laidback, Ellie too cheerful. When they'd bickered in the past, it had usually ended up with both of them laughing at the sheer silliness of it.

Not now. Not for a while, Ellie knew. Not since Matthew had been made redundant and they'd started talking about Wales and everything had become laden, fraught, because they'd realized, even if they'd never said as much out loud, that for the first time in their married lives, they might have wanted different things.

Matthew put down his wrench again. Ellie waited, tensed, poised to fire back once more, because she didn't think she was being that unreasonable. They'd been at Bluebell Inn for twenty-four hours and Matthew had been doing his own thing pretty much the whole time. What about *start how you mean to go on* and all that?

"Ellie..." Matthew began, staring down at the floor. It

sounded like a warning. Then he shook his head, heaved himself up, and, to Ellie's surprise, considering she'd thought they were on the cusp of a serious argument, he came over and put his arms around her. She stiffened in his embrace for a few seconds before she let herself relax into it. "I'm sorry," he said. "I've been a bit stressed about getting started on all this. Mum can't afford to keep the B&B closed for more than a few months, and I want to show her I can do it."

"She can't?" That was news to Ellie, although she supposed she shouldn't be surprised. It wasn't as if Gwen talked to her about finances—or anything else personal, for that matter.

"She told me as much last night, and so I felt like I needed to get started ASAP. And," he added with a rueful little sigh, "I just wanted to *do* something. To feel productive. I've been sitting on my hands for six months, and..." He blew out a breath as his arms tightened around her. "It was good, to feel like I was accomplishing something, even if it was just ripping out a sink."

"I understand that." Ellie pressed her cheek against his shoulder and closed her eyes. "I'm sorry for being so prickly," she told him in a low voice. "I'm jet-lagged and emotional; I'm sure things will settle down soon. Once the kids start school..."

And I somehow learn how to get along with Gwen, she added silently.

"Yes, they will," Matthew agreed, with more certainty than Ellie felt, no matter what she'd just said. "How about I kick a soccer ball around with Ben and Josh for a bit?"

"You mean a *foot*ball?" Ellie returned wryly. "Yes, that would be great."

Matthew gave her one last squeeze before heading downstairs.

Ellie stood there for a moment, looking around the wreck of the room. She was glad, truly, that Matthew had found some purpose and satisfaction in starting the renovations, but she couldn't keep an unease from creeping through her all the same, because she couldn't yet see how any of this—*all* of this—was going to work. Would Matthew be able to finish the renovations, considering the grand scale he was envisioning? Would they live in the attics the whole time, and what about when the B&B reopened, with paying guests? Where were they meant to live then?

It had only been one day, Ellie reminded herself. Twenty-four hours. They had plenty of time to figure things out, see how it all went, find their stride. She just had to take each day as it came, and not worry too much about the next.

"*Mo-meee!*" Ava's wail echoed through the house, making Ellie glad that Gwen hadn't yet returned from her appointment, whatever that had entailed. She hadn't been very forthcoming about it, and Ellie hadn't felt she could ask, as there had been something repressive about Gwen's attitude, but then there often was. "Ben won't let me play soccer with him!" Ava shouted, sounding very put out.

Squaring her shoulders and straightening her spine, Ellie headed back downstairs. "All right, you two," she called, thinking that they might have moved to the other side of the world, but some things never changed.

CHAPTER 7

GWEN

"Gwen Davies?"

Gwen looked up from the magazine she'd been staring at rather blankly for the last twenty minutes to catch the nurse's kindly smile.

"That's me." She rose, smoothing her skirt, trying to still the nerves that fluttered in her tummy and up her throat. Her GP had assured this was little more than routine... sort of. *Let's check, just in case, Gwen, especially at your age...*

That was routine, wasn't it?

"Come this way, please," the nurse said, and Gwen followed her down a corridor to a consulting room.

The procedure, she'd been told, was not too invasive and would only take twenty minutes. She'd be back home within the hour; Ellie and Sarah might not have even finished their walking tour of Llandrigg. Maybe she'd even have time to bake something for all of them before they returned—nothing with raisins, obviously.

Gwen envisioned herself baking chocolate chip cookies, back in her comforting kitchen with the smell of sweetness in the air,

Toby lying at her feet at his usual place in front of the Aga, plumed tail beating the floor. The thought steadied her as she perched on the edge of the examining table, the paper crinkling loudly beneath her. In an hour, she would have put this all behind her. Hopefully.

Several minutes ticked by and Gwen kept reminding herself of all that, trying to keep calm. She wasn't normally a nervous person. David had used to call her unflappable. "*My unflappable Gwen,*" he'd say with an affectionate smile. "*What would I do without her?*"

The memory made Gwen's eyes sting. Goodness, she wasn't usually this emotional, either. David had been gone for twenty years now, although sometimes it felt like the blink of an eye, and she'd fight a wave of surprise that he wasn't there in the armchair in the sitting room with the paper and a cup of tea when she turned around, or lying next to her when she woke up in the morning, blinking the sleep out of his eyes. But, mainly, over the years, she'd just got on with things—the house, the B&B, the grandchildren and chickens, a vegetable garden and village life. And she had so much to keep her busy and to be thankful for, she knew that, truly.

Perhaps it was having Matthew back, along with Ellie and the children, and now having this... *concern* that made Gwen feel as if life had suddenly become very precious, very fragile, like a bubble that could so easily pop from just the lightest touch. A single brush of a fingertip and it was gone, forever. She didn't want to let the little things get in the way of enjoying all that life had to offer—right now, waiting for a consultant to come in, her tense little confrontations with Ellie seemed silly indeed. At least this was putting them into perspective, she thought, grateful for small mercies. She wouldn't make any more silly remarks about the coffee, or anything else, from now on, she promised herself.

"Gwen?" A woman with a sandy bob and smiling eyes

poked her head around the door. "I'm Anne Jamison, and I'm going to be doing your biopsy today."

Gwen swallowed hard as she nodded.

Ms. Jamison looked at her notes. "I believe you've been briefed on the procedure?"

"Yes, I think so." She knew so, but somehow, she couldn't say as much. Her throat had gone very dry, and her heart was beating far too hard.

"It's a needle biopsy, and it should take around twenty minutes," Ms. Jamison explained. "I'll numb the area with a local anaesthetic before I take the sample. Depending on how it goes, I might need to put in a single paper stitch, but most likely no more than that. You can go back to work right away, but I always advise patients to take it easy for the rest of the day, just because." The smile she gave Gwen was full of kindness and humor. "Be kind to yourself, because, why not?"

"Okay," Gwen murmured. She wasn't exactly sure what being kind to oneself entailed. She just wanted to be home, in her kitchen, Toby at her feet, the kettle on the boil... that sounded like heaven, right about now. Maybe *that* was being kind to herself. It felt like it, at any rate.

"Right. Let's get started, shall we?" Ms. Jamison continued briskly. "Do you have any questions?"

She should, Gwen thought, but right now her mind was completely blank. Silently, she shook her head.

"Then I'll have you sign this consent form and we'll be on our way."

Taking a steadying breath, Gwen took the pen she was offered.

As good as the consultant's word, twenty minutes later it was all over. Gwen had a single paper stitch, a slightly tingly numb area near her shoulder, and a promise that she'd have the results of the biopsy in a week or two.

A week or *two*? Gwen couldn't help but think that second week would go very slowly, if that were the case.

Still, she tried to stay optimistic as she drove back to Llandrigg. When she'd found the lump several months ago, her GP had advised a biopsy "just to be on the safe side." She hadn't said the dreaded C word right away, but, of course, she was thinking it, and so had Gwen.

"Even if it is cancer," she'd told Gwen at the end of the visit, after Gwen had had a very little wobble, "it is very treatable. Breast cancer has a terrific five-year survival rate—five out of six women."

Yes, Gwen had thought, but somebody had to be that lonely one out of six, and in any case her GP was only talking about five years. What about after that? Gwen was only sixty-eight. No spring chicken, certainly, but she'd hoped to have more than five years left, certainly. A few more than that, anyway.

She pushed those thoughts to the back of her mind as she turned down the lane toward Bluebell Inn. Just a precaution, her doctor had said. And, anyway, she'd know what was going on in one—or two—weeks.

Back at the house, Matthew was making a racket upstairs; he seemed to have got every tool from the shed and was operating them all at once. She hadn't expected him to get out the power tools quite so soon; she'd wanted to think things through carefully before making any decisions, but last night Matthew had been full of determination and excitement, and knowing what a difficult few months he'd had, she hadn't been able to bear dampening his enthusiasm in the least.

Now, already fighting a tension headache from the stress of her appointment, Gwen winced at the noise as she switched on the kettle. She'd have a cup of tea and order her thoughts, and then she'd go see what Matthew was up to, maybe offer a gentle word of caution if she could.

A sudden, bloodcurdling shriek had Gwen tensing even more.

Ben ran into the kitchen, grinning gleefully, with Josh following behind, scowling and fighting tears.

"Give them *back!*"

"Don't you know they're for babies?"

Ben danced around the kitchen table, holding something above his brother's head, pushing his shaggy hair away from his face as he grinned tauntingly.

"Give it back!" Josh fairly screamed, fists clenched, face red. He reminded Gwen a little bit of Matthew at that age, slender and small but so very determined. And, right now, making a lot of noise.

"Boys," Gwen protested faintly, overwhelmed by the noise, the *chaos*. "Boys..."

"Give it *back!*" Josh screeched again. "You're always so mean, Ben! I want my card!"

Gwen only just managed to keep from putting her hands over her ears.

"Boys!" she said again, louder this time, her voice rising to a shout, knowing she should handle this better, but in the moment unable to. "Boys, boys, this won't *do!*"

Just then, Ellie came into the room, so, unfortunately, it was Gwen's near-screech, not Josh's, that she heard. Her eyes narrowed and Gwen suppressed a weary groan. Of course, Ellie was going to think the worst of her now, that she was being cross and unreasonable toward her children behaving like, well, children.

"What's going on?" Ellie asked in a voice that sounded rather dangerously neutral. "Ben? Josh?" Her narrowed gaze swung to Gwen. "Gwen?"

"I don't know," Gwen replied wearily. "Something..." She

gestured to the boys, unable to explain, or maybe simply too tired. "They were bickering about something. I don't know what."

The kettle switched off then, and Gwen moved gratefully to make herself a cup of tea, her back to the boys and Ellie, but she felt her daughter-in-law's frustration and impatience, and she suspected it was directed primarily at her.

"Ben, why don't you tell me what's going on?" Ellie asked in that same neutral voice.

Briefly, Gwen closed her eyes. She wanted to go lie down in a dark room, preferably somewhere very quiet, but now Matthew had started up what sounded like a circular saw and Josh had, inexplicably and with no further provocation, burst into noisy tears.

"*Ben.*" Ellie put her arm around her younger son as Gwen turned around, clutching her cup of tea to her. "What did you do?"

"I didn't do anything! You always blame me, just because Josh is such a baby—"

"I'm not!"

"I don't," Ellie said, sounding exasperated. "But why is Josh crying?"

Ben blew out a breath, looking annoyed. "How should I know?"

"Ben—"

"It was something about a card." Gwen blurted the words, mainly to get everyone to stop *shouting*. Her head was beginning to ache abominably. "Josh wanted some sort of card back."

This earned her a sulky, resentful look from her older grandson, and, belatedly, Gwen realized she'd essentially become a telltale. Oh, this was all so difficult.

"Ben?" Ellie asked quietly. "Did you take his card?"

In reply, Ben flung the card at his brother, so it fluttered to the ground, while Josh whimpered and sniffed, scrambling onto his knees to clutch at the precious paper.

"It's my best one," he said, fighting more tears, and Ben shook his head and rolled his eyes, clearly dismissive of the cards, whatever they were.

"You're *such* a crybaby," he sneered, and Josh let out another whimper.

"That's enough, Ben," Ellie said severely, her voice close to snapping. "You're off electronics until tomorrow."

"*What?* That's not fair—"

Ellie straightened, giving her son a level look, while Josh half-hid behind her and Gwen looked on wearily. "You heard me."

Gwen thought she sounded rather tired. Perhaps it was just jet lag... or something more? She wished she could think of some way to help, but she always felt as if she were more of a hindrance to Ellie than anything else.

Ben scowled and stomped out of the kitchen, slamming the door behind him.

Goodness. She took a much-needed sip of tea.

"Josh, go on, now," Ellie said more gently. "Put your Pokémon cards away and stay away from Ben for a bit. He's not in a good mood, as you can see. Next time, you don't need to get so upset, all right? Just ask for it back—"

"I did," Josh replied, sounding aggrieved, and Ellie sighed.

"All right, then come and get me instead. Okay?" She smiled at him, giving his shoulder a pat, before, still clutching his card, Josh slipped out of the kitchen. The silence that followed, with just Ellie and Gwen in the room, didn't feel as peaceful as she might have hoped. Gwen tried to think of something to say, but after the events of the day, her mind felt completely blank.

Ellie heaved a large, gusty sigh. "I'm sorry about that. My children aren't usually *quite* this badly behaved."

"It's a new situation," Gwen murmured. Her head was really pounding now, and she wanted only to lie down. "They're bound to find it difficult, especially at first."

"Yes..." Ellie looked as if she wanted to say something more, but Gwen wasn't sure she was up for hearing it now. It was unfortunate that whenever an opportunity came for them to have a proper chat, something else was going on—noise, children, headaches, the fear of *cancer*. But she couldn't think about that right now.

Ellie was simply standing there, looking rather exhausted, and Gwen didn't feel she could slip off for a nap. Despite her headache, she made herself ask as brightly as she could, "Cup of tea?"

"Oh..." Ellie looked startled, and then, rather touchingly, grateful. "If it's not too much trouble. Thank you. That would be lovely. I'm sorry for all the noise."

"Which noise?" Gwen asked wryly as Matthew continued to clatter about upstairs. "I think my son is the loudest of them all, and that's not your fault." The saw had been replaced by some hammering. What was he *doing*?

"He does seem keen," Ellie agreed with a sigh. "I'm glad he has something to focus on. It's been a while since he's felt like he's had that." She spoke cautiously, as if she didn't know how much Gwen knew, or maybe had guessed, and the truth was, Gwen wasn't sure she knew, either. Matthew had been decidedly—and, Gwen thought, deliberately—vague about everything that had happened. She'd known he'd been made redundant, but he'd glossed over the details, and she hadn't felt she could press. She doubted her son would have been forthcoming even if she had, but, in any case, she'd decided he would tell her when he was ready... whenever that was. But, meanwhile, he was ripping out her bedrooms, and that was more than a bit alarming.

"Yes, I suppose so," Gwen agreed after a moment. She made

Ellie a cup of tea, sinking down into her seat with her own, with a small sigh of relief.

"Are the children looking forward to school?" she asked.

Ellie made a face as she took her cup of tea and sat opposite Gwen. "Ava is, I think, at least. The others are pretty nervous. It's always hard to start a new school or workplace, isn't it, especially when you're Ben or Jess's age, and it feels as if everyone has already made all their friends."

"Yes, I would think so," Gwen agreed, "but Llandrigg is a friendly place." She smiled, brightening her voice, because Ellie looked so worried. "I'm sure they'll have a whole group of new friends before too long. Children usually manage to get along, don't they?"

"I hope so." Ellie didn't sound convinced, and Gwen couldn't really blame her. Starting over had to be hard, especially for Jess, at thirteen—not an easy age, regardless of one's circumstances. Still, she felt her daughter-in-law needed some cheering up, and so she continued with more enthusiasm than she felt.

"Sarah showed you the sights, then? She knows so much, more than I do, I'm sure."

"Yes," Ellie agreed, after a pause, her tone sounding a tiny bit flat. "She does."

Oh, dear. Gwen knew she wouldn't be entirely surprised if Sarah and Ellie didn't become the best of friends themselves; they were such very different people. Sarah was so officious and efficient, and Ellie... wasn't. But that, perhaps, was a problem for another day, if at all. Right now, her head was throbbing, and she was doing her best not to wince and cringe and show how much she was struggling to Ellie, although she feared she gave herself away when her daughter-in-law looked at her in concern. As much as she'd been trying to take this morning's appointment in her stride, clearly, she hadn't quite managed it.

"How was your... appointment?" Ellie asked.

Gwen thought of the waiting room, the needle, as her head continued to pound. "It was fine," she replied, and she knew from her tone that she'd been a bit repressive, even off-putting. Ellie looked a little offended, although she tried to hide it. Gwen forced a smile as she finished her tea. "All fine," she said again, more firmly this time.

CHAPTER 8

JESS

Jess glared at her reflection—pleated gray skirt, boring white buttoned-up blouse, a forest-green sweater and actual knee socks. Who wore those, like, ever? She looked like such a *nerd*.

"Why do they have uniforms here?" she'd complained to her mother when they'd bought all the clothes online a few days ago. "Why can't you just wear your normal clothes, like back home?"

Home. Jess had been in Wales for almost a week, and she still wanted, *so* badly, to go home. The place just got worse and worse—it had rained for the last three days, it was only August and it was already *cold*, and she'd decided she really didn't like her stuck-up cousins. Even when they'd come over for dinner, they'd barely talked to her. Mairi was crazy about horses and seemed to think Jess was weird for never having gone horseback riding. No one in her old school had ever even *been* on a horse, but the way Mairi talked, everyone here had their own pony. Just another way she was going to stand out and seem weird. And now this uniform, having to go to the comprehensive in Abergavenny, walking into a huge school where she knew absolutely no one...

She couldn't count on her cousin Owen, who was in the year below her, or Mairi, in the year above. Owen had literally not said one word to her during dinner, although he and Ben had kicked a soccer ball around in the yard, which had made her mom think they were practically best friends. Or, as her Aunt Sarah had remarked with that tinkling little laugh, "you mean a football, darling, don't you? In the *garden*." Whatever. She didn't even want to speak the way everyone else did. She'd do her best to make sure she didn't.

It wasn't any fun being in this boring house either, where everything was creaky and dusty and old—her dad was making a total racket, and he was too busy to actually *do* anything with them, and her mom always seemed hassled and stressed, while her grandmother always looked nervous around her. Ben and Josh were always fighting, and Ava was little and whiny and boring.

Tears pricked Jess's eyes and she blinked them back angrily. If only she was back in Connecticut; they'd started school yesterday, and she'd scrolled through all the first-day selfies—no stupid uniforms, just cool outfits. Chloe was even wearing lip gloss, which had been forbidden last year, but her mom was way cooler than Jess's, so maybe she'd allowed it for eighth grade. If she and Chloe had been starting together, they would have coordinated their outfits, lent each other clothes, done each other's hair... it would have been *epic*.

As it was, Jess's stomach had clenched when she'd seen Chloe and Emily standing shoulder to shoulder in front of the big yellow school bus, arms linked, both of them grinning wildly. *What?* Chloe hadn't posted any photos since that sleepover one, and Jess had half-convinced herself that it had been just one of those weird things, like, maybe their moms had insisted on the sleepover, or whatever. They'd had a really good text chat two nights ago, when Jess had snuck her phone upstairs again, but Chloe hadn't mentioned Emily and Jess hadn't wanted to ask. And then she'd seen that second photo with Emily, and she'd wondered if her friendship with Chloe was all fake. Did Chloe even miss her?

It had been enough to make Jess Snapchat her last night, *Is Emily your new BFF or what?* Thankfully, Chloe had replied immediately: *No way! As if I'd forget you.* With several hearts and kissy face emojis that had made Jessa feel a *little* bit better.

I just want to come home, she'd texted.

Any chance of that???

Not yet.

Just be really bad, Chloe had advised. *Act out in school and stuff and then they'll have to send you back here. You could live with me!*

That had been such a wonderful thought that Jess had almost laughed out loud with the sheer delight of it. If she really showed her parents how much she hated it here, would they agree to send her back? How bad would she have to be?

"Jess!" her mom called up the stairs. "The bus is coming in ten minutes from the village green. We should get going."

Jess gave her reflection one last unhappy look. She really did look like a nerd. Was this how everyone else was going to look? What if it wasn't? She had no idea of the styles and fashion in Wales. During the summer back home, everyone she knew wore sports tops and shorts, but Mairi had shown up at dinner in flared jeans, which *no one* wore back home, and a sparkly top. Jess had felt sloppy and underdressed in her sporty clothing, and she was afraid she was going to stick out today, which was the *last* thing she wanted starting a new school.

With a sigh, she grabbed her backpack and headed downstairs, resigned to her fate... at least for today.

"You look amazing!" her mom enthused as Jess came into the kitchen and she rolled her eyes.

"I do not," she stated flatly.

"I think the uniform suits you. It's like something out of Enid Blyton."

Jess stared at her, nonplussed. "Who?" Whoever she was, she sounded lame. Who was named Enid anymore?

"I'll explain later," her mom said with a laugh. "They're stories for children. British children read them, but I did too, actually. That's one cultural reference I *can* make." She let out another laugh, this one with a little bit of an edge, and then grabbed her travel mug of coffee. "Come on, I'll walk you to the bus stop."

Ava and Josh were sitting at the kitchen table, still in their pajamas, while her grandmother leaned against the counter, sipping tea and looking kind of spaced out, like she wasn't even aware anyone else was there. Ava and Josh didn't have to leave at ridiculous o'clock to get the bus. Their school day at the local elementary school started a whole half-hour later and was only a five-minute walk away. Why did her school have to be a whole half an hour away? Back in Connecticut, it had been a ten-minute bus ride, *tops*.

"Ben!" her mom called up the stairs, clearly trying not to sound aggravated and, Jess thought, failing. "Come on! I don't want you and Jess to miss the bus!"

Her brother thundered down the stairs, and a few minutes later they were walking toward the bus stop, Jess dragging her feet, even though her mom kept telling her they'd be late, and it was twenty minutes to Abergavenny, so she wouldn't be able to drive them, what with Ava and Josh needing to get to school, too. Her mom sounded seriously hassled, and Jess felt like snapping, *try starting a new school, in a frigging new country. That will make you stressed.*

She didn't, though. She just sighed, quite a few times, heavily enough that her mom would know how she felt, as Ben loped ahead totally unaware. *Boys.* Her brother didn't look stupid in his uniform, and he would probably make friends with the first kid he played soccer with, because that's what he always did. He was oblivious to the social strata of school, while Jess already knew she was going to struggle to fit in. Girls just didn't welcome a new person in, the way boys seemed to. Even worse, everyone else in her grade had already been in the school for two whole years; every girl in her class was going to have a best friend already, and they were *not* going to be interested in making another one.

As they approached the bus stop, Jess saw with an awful sinking sensation just how absolutely wrong she'd got everything. No one's parents were there, for one. She was entering year *nine* and she was being treated like a little kid, her mom marching her to the bus stop. Plus, she realized, with a swirl of dread in her stomach, no girl was wearing navy blue knee socks, despite the uniform guidelines; it was all tights or little white ankle socks that barely covered their heels, and slip-on shoes, not these clunky brogues. No one—absolutely no one—had their stupid socks hiked up to their knees like she did. Everyone's tie was knotted so it was half the length of Jess and Ben's, and the girls all had leather shoulder bags for their books rather than stupid sporty backpacks like she did, because that was what everyone had back in Connecticut. Back *home*.

Jess felt as if she were shrinking inside herself with every step she took toward the bus stop, with many pairs of prying eyes trained on her for an excruciating second before they all looked away, utterly indifferent, or worse, smirking. She saw two girls exchange looks and roll their eyes, and everything in her both burned and cringed with shame, with awful, *awful* humiliation. She hadn't even started school yet, and she'd completely messed up.

"Bye, darling," her mom began, and Jess jerked away from the actual hug her mom had been about to give her, furious with her mother for getting it all so wrong, even though she knew it wasn't really her fault. It *felt* like it was, though.

"Bye," she snapped, and stalked off to the other side of the stop, away from her mother and Ben, who had joined a group of boys with easy obliviousness.

As Jess stood there alone, she willed with every fiber of her being for the bus to come so she could slide into a seat and do her best to disappear.

CHAPTER 9

ELLIE

Half an hour after dropping Jess and Ben off at the bus, Ellie watched Ava trot happily into her reception class after getting a little cuddle from the teacher, Mrs. Baggins. Llandrigg Primary seemed like a lovely little school, with less than thirty pupils in each year, far smaller and friendlier than the large elementary school Josh and Ben had gone to back in Connecticut, with three classes in each grade.

Even so, Ellie had to swallow past the sizable lump in her throat as she watched Ava go inside. If they'd stayed in Connecticut, Ava wouldn't have gone to school for another year. She would have had her at home for lazy mornings and afternoons of crafts or playdates, for midday snuggles and a companion in the grocery store. She hadn't been ready to let go of her youngest, to have the house empty—although, of course, it wasn't. Matthew and Gwen would be home with her all day, although she suspected her husband would be consumed with DIY and as for her mother-in-law? Ellie had no idea.

Across the schoolyard, Josh was standing by himself, observing the happy chaos around him with a quiet, studied air, as boys in year four chased each other and girls huddled in gossipy little knots. He'd always eschewed rowdy groups for the company of one good friend, and Ellie prayed he'd find one here. She hoped they all would, herself included.

She'd smiled at several mothers who had met her eye as she'd come through the school gates, and they'd smiled back, but no one had made one of those overwhelmingly friendly overtures that Ellie desperately craved, asking her if she was new and telling her they'd have to go for a coffee, get to know each other.

She felt too tired and fragile to make the first move this morning, but, judging by the way parents were greeting each other with easy familiarity, laughing as they exchanged summer stories, she'd most likely have to. Nobody was taking any notice of her, but all the same Ellie didn't think she had it in her to manage a simple conversation without bursting into tears, and that was not a good start to any potential friendship. Waving a clearly miserable Jess and an indifferent Ben off on the school bus this morning before taking Josh and Ava had just about finished her off. Everything was so new, so strange, and she had a horrible feeling Jess was going to have a bad day—simply because part of her contrary daughter seemed as if she *wanted* to have one—and there was nothing she could do about it, no way to help smooth the way. Ben, she felt, would probably be okay, but Josh was already looking a little lost, and Ava was so *little*. How could she let them all go?

Matthew would no doubt tell her she was being silly; Sarah, too, and probably even Gwen. They wouldn't be all weepy and emotional, the way she was, at seeing her youngest child off to school.

Josh was heading into his class now, and parents were drifting away in groups, their laughter floating on the air, glad to have their time back to themselves. Ellie struggled not to feel desperately alone.

Now she had to go back to Bluebell Inn and face Matthew,

who was ripping up old carpets with gleeful abandon, and Gwen, who was still stepping around Ellie with the stiff formality she hated, even as she reciprocated it, without really knowing why.

She'd told Matthew last night, when they'd been getting ready for bed, that she needed to have a talk with Gwen about divvying up housework and meals. For the last week, she'd been feeling like a somewhat unwanted guest, and she didn't think she could take Gwen cooking and cleaning for her and her family. Besides, it wasn't fair on Gwen. Matthew, however, had looked boyishly nonplussed.

"Why? Hasn't she been managing all right?"

"Ye-es, but *I* need to do something, Matt," Ellie had said, trying to be patient. Why did men revert to little boys when they went back home? After fifteen years of training, to make him put his dirty socks in the hamper and his dishes into the dishwasher and not just on top of the counter, her husband had started leaving socks on the floor again, dishes for his mother to clear up. "It's not fair on Gwen to cook for seven people every evening," she'd told him, "Or pick up after us." Yet when Ellie had hesitantly offered to cook last night, Gwen had looked both surprised and a bit appalled. She was not a woman ready to relinquish her kitchen.

"I doubt Mum minds," Matthew had said with a shrug. "She wants to spoil us."

Spoil you, maybe, Ellie had thought with a sigh. The trouble was, it seemed Gwen *did* mind, although not enough to let Ellie use the kitchen, which left them in an unhappy limbo... something she was determined to tackle today. They would have to get to the bottom of this tension, somehow, even if it was difficult, and most likely excruciatingly awkward. Besides, Ellie needed something to do, now more than ever with the children at school, even if it was just making dinner. Her visa didn't allow her to get a job yet, but she could still make herself useful.

Trying not to feel too lonely, Ellie headed back toward Bluebell Inn, alone amidst the little groups of parents still chatting as they walked along the high street. She felt too dispirited even to meet someone's eye, not that anyone was even looking at her, and so she walked quickly, her head down.

Halfway back her to the house, her phone pinged with a text, and her heart lifted when she saw it was from Elise, her best friend from Connecticut. *Just wanted to wish you well on the first day of school. Meet a nice mom!*

If only.

Isn't it about three in the morning there? Ellie texted back.

Yes, I set my alarm. Couldn't let it go by without something from me!

Tears stung Ellie's eyes and she blinked them back. She missed her friend. She missed her house. She missed the *weather*; today was gray and chilly, but back in Connecticut, according to the weather app on her phone, which she checked far too much, it still felt like summer, sunny and warm, with families spending their weekends at the beach. The truth was, a little over a week into their Great Welsh Adventure, Ellie still missed *everything*.

Back at the house, Matthew was continuing to make alarming sounds from upstairs, hammering and ripping and generally causing mayhem. Ellie had steered clear of the four guest bedrooms he seemed to be renovating simultaneously; she was not a DIY person, and, in any case, Matthew seemed to be doing fine on his own. *Too* fine, it sometimes seemed, although perhaps she was being a bit petty.

He'd emerged from whichever bedroom he was working on whenever she asked him to, to play with Ben and Josh, or read Ava a story—Jess seemed to prefer her own company these days —but she still had to ask, and that was starting to annoy her.

He'd been so good with the kids back in Connecticut. Even before he'd been made redundant, he'd been an active, interested father, albeit one who worked a lot of hours. When he'd lost his job, he'd tried to see it as an opportunity, but his optimism had definitely begun to flag long before the move to Wales. She was glad he seemed to be getting his mojo back, but she'd still like him to do things without being asked. To think of doing them himself first.

Ellie ventured into the kitchen, bolstering her courage when she saw Gwen sitting at the table, a cup of tea cradled between her palms.

"School drop-off went all right?" she asked in a too-bright voice as Ellie sat down across from her.

"Yes, I suppose so... I felt a little emotional, to tell you the truth." She tried to smile but felt her lips wobble. She did not want to cry in front of Gwen.

"I remember I cried when I dropped Matthew off," Gwen reminisced with a small smile. "I didn't with Sarah—I had Matthew at home, and I think I felt too exhausted all the time. But with Matthew..."

Ellie smiled and nodded, because she'd always suspected Gwen had a soft spot for her youngest child. It was nice to hear a little bit about how Gwen had been with Matthew, back then. "It's strange, to think they'll always be at school now," she remarked. "A certain period of my life is over." It felt like grief, but she wasn't sure she could explain that to Gwen.

"Anyway," her mother-in-law continued in a brisker tone, demonstrating that typically British stiff upper lip, "I'm sure they'll be fine. I think children are always ready for school, more than the mummies are sometimes!"

She was definitely not going to share now how she felt as if she was grieving. "You might be right." Ellie took a deep breath. Now was as good a time as any to tackle the thorny topic of sharing a kitchen. "Look, Gwen," she began, "I wanted to talk to you about something."

Her mother-in-law was immediately alert, her gaze wary. "Oh?"

"It's just, we're going to be here for a while, aren't we?" Ellie said, trying to pitch her voice as friendly, easy, light. "And it isn't good for anyone if we feel like guests, and you feel put upon."

Gwen bristled a little, drawing herself up. "I hope I've not given the impression that I've been *put upon*," she returned rather stiffly.

"No, no, not at all," Ellie assured her. "You've been wonderful, absolutely amazing, and I'm sure you'd carry on the same way. The truth is, I'm mentioning this for me as much as for you. I miss my own home. My own kitchen. And I want to have something to do."

"That's understandable..." Gwen murmured after a moment, still looking wary.

"So, I was hoping we could share the cooking, shopping, housework, all that," Ellie continued determinedly. "I want things to be easier for you, but I'd also like to be involved. I feel a bit purposeless at the moment, to tell you the truth. I always thought I'd go back to work when the kids were all in school, but that's not possible now, with the visa situation." She tried to smile, but Gwen simply stared at her, silent.

Ellie braced herself for a polite rejection. *That's very kind of you to offer, Ellie, but...* What would she do then? Drift around like a guest in her mother-in-law's home, she supposed. Maybe she could find some volunteering to do. She'd worked for a literacy charity, before she'd had the kids. Maybe she could find something similar here, in a volunteer capacity.

"Very well," Gwen said after an uncertain pause. "If that's what you want. It makes sense, I suppose. Shall we draw up a... a schedule?"

"Oh." Ellie couldn't keep the surprise from her voice. She

realized she really hadn't been expecting Gwen to agree, but she was glad she had. Very glad. Perhaps now they'd finally find some common ground. "All right, sure, that would be great."

"I'll get a piece of paper." Gwen rose from the table and hunted through one of the drawers of the Welsh dresser, her movements slow and laborious, her head bowed.

Ellie watched her uncertainly, half-wanting to take it all back. She'd succeeded in her mission, but somehow, as she watched Gwen's slumped figure, she didn't quite feel as if she had. She felt as if she'd taken something from Gwen and hadn't actually gained anything herself—but it didn't have to be that way, surely? They could make this work?

These were growing pains, she told herself. This was progress. They just had to get used to each other... if they could.

CHAPTER 10

GWEN

Gwen gazed down at the schedule she and Ellie had made—
Ellie would cook supper on Mondays, Wednesdays, and Thurs-
days, and Gwen would do Friday fish and chips and a Sunday
roast. Saturday was takeaway, and Tuesday leftovers. They'd
split the shopping between them, as well as the housework.
They'd worked it all out with a surprising and encouraging
amount of cooperation; Ellie had been very careful not to
presume, yet Gwen had still felt as if she had no choice but to
acquiesce. Still, she couldn't fault her daughter-in-law, not at all,
and really, it was all eminently sensible... considering her own
situation. It might even come as a relief, no matter that Gwen
had been a bit taken aback by Ellie's suggestions.

She took a sip of tea, deliberately trying to empty her mind
out. Ellie had gone upstairs to tidy up, and Matthew was still
busy working on one of the guest rooms. Gwen had been
relieved to realize he wasn't sledgehammering his way through
walls... yet. So far, he'd just ripped up old carpets and taken out
all the basins, getting ready for the grand plan of adding
adjoining bathrooms.

"It might be a bit much, don't you think?" she'd asked

faintly when he'd shown her the plans he'd drawn up with one of those online design sites. "Every bedroom with a bathroom..."

"That's how it's done these days, Mum. No one will settle for less anymore." Matthew had sounded so certain, but what did he know about the B&B business, really? They'd started it up when he'd been at uni, and he'd never involved himself during his holidays back home.

"Won't they?" she asked. She wasn't really ready to commit to such a huge change, but she couldn't bear to disappoint her son. And, she admitted, her bookings *had* dropped off a bit in the last few years, and the guests who did come tended to be long-time visitors or young people on a shoestring budget.

Besides, there was every likelihood she might not be able to manage even the simplest of renovations, depending on the result of her biopsy. It was sensible to let her son take control, and yet she couldn't keep from issuing a warning of sorts.

"I'm not aspiring to be the Ritz, you know, Matthew."

"Trust me, Mum, this isn't the Ritz. It's just what everybody else is doing." His smile had taken any sting out of the words, and when he'd shown her website after website of upscale B&Bs, with king-sized beds and beautiful marble bathrooms, Gwen had let herself be reluctantly convinced, even as she wondered if she really wanted to do any of this. What if, with her health concerns, she couldn't manage the B&B at all? Would Matthew be willing to do that, after he'd completed the renovations? Would Ellie? The future felt fearfully uncertain.

"As long as you know what you're doing..." she'd said, trying to smile.

"I don't know everything, but I can hire people who do," Matthew had replied cheerfully. Like Ellie had said, he was happy having a project, and he seemed enthused about what he was doing, so she supposed that was all to the good.

Now Gwen gazed unseeingly in front of her, as, despite her

attempts not to think about it, she recalled the voicemail she'd listened to that morning.

This is the Oncology Department of the Royal Gwent Hospital. If you could ring us at your earliest convenience...

She'd listened to the brief message three times, and then she'd deleted it, and decided not to do anything about it, at least for the morning. She wanted one morning, a few hours, of not knowing. Not thinking.

Except, it seemed she was thinking anyway.

With a sigh, Gwen rose from the table and went to the garden. Now early September, it was past its most glorious bloom, but there were still late-fruiting raspberries to pick, and the old, knotted tree at the back was laden with apples not quite ready to harvest.

All her guests had loved this garden, its deliberate, artful wildness, although, admittedly, this summer it was less artful and more just wild. She simply hadn't had the energy to keep it up this year, although she had tried, at least a little.

Gwen had also tried to entice her grandchildren out here—she'd had vague visions of them feeding the chickens and building dens in the bushes—but only Ava and sometimes Josh had been interested, and mostly in the old rope swing, which needed replacing. The flat wooden seat had rotted right through, without Gwen realizing. She really had let so much of the place's upkeep get away from her in the last year or two.

Now she sat down on the wrought-iron bench David had given her for their twentieth anniversary, just a few years before he'd died. They'd spent many a happy evening sitting companionably out there together, watching the sun set. It was quieter at the back of the garden, so Gwen could hear the birdsong, the cluck of the chickens, even the whisper of the wind through the trees.

If only she could stay like this forever. Not wondering. Not worrying. Not *knowing*.

Because, of course, she *did* know. The oncology department didn't ring when it was good news. They sent a letter, with the relevant bits filled out. A phone call was always bad news.

Or could she hope it wasn't, just a little bit, that this phone call was nothing to worry about, just a box they had to tick? Life could go on, the same as always...

Except, of course, it couldn't, because it never did. "Everything you have in this world is just borrowed for a short time," she remarked softly, an old Welsh proverb David had loved to quote. And, in truth, things were already changing. The homely bed and breakfast that had been her and David's dream simply wasn't viable anymore. She had known that, even before Matthew had come in with his sledgehammer and saw and his ambition. Already, all the fixtures and fittings they'd lovingly laid down were being ripped up and discarded like rubbish.

Gwen understood it had to change, of course it did. She wasn't so sentimental or foolish not to realize that the furnishings had been more than a little dated. And yet... it still hurt, because life felt so precious and fragile and fleeting right now, and she still had to ring the hospital and find out what they had to tell her.

She glanced around the garden, just past its height of summer beauty, the leaves starting to curl at the edges, the bright color beginning to be leached from them. There was a tang of autumn in the air, the scent of change. Usually, Gwen loved this time of the year, the crisp nights, the first frost, but today she felt only the pang of sorrow for the loss of summer, the changing of seasons and the turning of the years.

"All right, enough maudlin wool-gathering," she told herself.

She was just getting up from the bench when an almighty racket came from the upstairs, a most alarming, crashing sound, as clouds of dust flew from the open windows and billowed above the garden.

Gwen hurried back toward the house, her heart starting to pound as Ellie appeared in the back doorway, her face shocked and pale, her eyes wide.

"I think—I think the roof might have fallen in," she exclaimed. "There's plaster and dust everywhere, and I'm scared to go in the bedrooms. Gwen... I called up for Matthew and he didn't answer!"

CHAPTER 11

ELLIE

Ellie sat on a hard plastic chair, staring into space, a paper cup of cold coffee cradled in her hands, forgotten. It had been an hour since Matthew had gone into surgery after being rushed to hospital. An hour of worry and waiting and wondering *what if*.

"He'll be all right," Gwen said quietly, although her face was pale and drawn and she hadn't drunk her coffee, either. "And at least... at least it's only his arm. Not... not his head, or anything like that."

Ellie just nodded, unable to summon the energy for more of a response. They'd had the same brief conversation three times already, since the paramedics had found Matthew in the rubble of the guest bedroom, the floor of Ellie and Matthew's attic room in jagged pieces all around him.

They'd dragged him unconscious from the mess, plaster dust in his hair, making him appear even more lifeless, like a statue—or worse, a corpse—and frightening Ellie so much she'd only been able to stare, frozen in shock, before she'd started to tremble violently. *Matthew...*

Fortunately, on the way to the hospital, he'd woken up and started speaking, and the doctors weren't as concerned about his head as they were about his right arm, which she'd seen had been at a horribly awkward angle. Ellie still didn't like to remember how it looked.

In the hospital, the doctors had informed Ellie and Gwen that Matthew needed surgery on his elbow, and Ellie had numbly agreed. Now she was waiting. Hoping that, despite everything, it was all going to be okay, although she wasn't even sure what that looked like, anymore. Gwen's house was a complete mess, if not a downright ruin; her husband had, at the very least, a broken arm... It wasn't a total tragedy, she *knew* that, but right now it felt like more than she could bear.

"Mrs. Davies?" The surgeon stood in the doorway of the waiting room, smiling tiredly, as both Ellie and Gwen stood up.

"Yes—" they said at the same time.

The surgeon looked from one to the other, and Gwen sat down, blushing.

"Sorry," she murmured, and Ellie wondered what she thought she was apologizing for. They both were worried to hear what the man had to say. And they both loved Matthew. And, she thought wryly, they were both Mrs. Davies. Maybe *that* was really the issue between them, not that that sort of thing mattered now.

"Is Matthew... is he out of surgery?" Ellie asked.

"Yes, and he did brilliantly." The surgeon smiled briefly before turning serious once again. "It was a very nasty break, unfortunately, but we've secured the bones with a pin, and as long as he takes it easy and keeps it as immobile as he can, it should heal well. It's in plaster and will need to be for the next six weeks, at least. We'll see him in two weeks, just to check on the progress."

Six weeks in plaster.

But her husband was all right, his arm was going to be all right, and suddenly Ellie had to sit down because her legs were shaky, and she felt faint with relief. Too much had happened in too short a space of time, and her brain was just catching up with it all, sending out all the panic signals a little too late.

She took several deep breaths before she smiled at the consultant.

"Thank you," she managed to murmur. "Thank you so much."

Gwen smiled at her and touched her hand, a gesture of support.

Ellie smiled back, or tried to. She felt alarmingly close to tears, even though it had been good news. She really must have reached her limit. She was grateful for Gwen's concern, especially when she knew her mother-in-law had to be just as worried as she was.

"Thank you," she murmured, touching Gwen's hand briefly in return, before she turned to the surgeon. "May I see him?" she asked when she trusted her voice.

"Of course. He's out of recovery and is being brought to a room on the ward. The nurse will tell you where it is."

"Thank you," Ellie said again, and the surgeon smiled and nodded before turning away.

"You should go first," Gwen offered. "You'll want some time alone, the two of you."

"No, no," Ellie replied, although part of her did want that, very much. She wanted to put her arms around her husband, gently of course, and hold him close. Even so, she knew she couldn't deny Gwen a chance to see her son, especially when she'd been so worried. "Let's go together."

Gwen's eyes lit up as she smiled uncertainly. "Are you sure?"

"Of course," Ellie replied firmly. "We're both worried, and we want to see him."

Together, they followed a nurse to a room where Matthew lay in bed, his poor arm in plaster, his expression still a bit sleepy from the general anesthetic he'd been given.

He gave Ellie a sheepish, lopsided smile as he caught sight of her. "Aren't I daft," he half-mumbled, and she couldn't keep from letting out a small, choked cry.

"Yes, you are," she managed as she leaned forward and gently kissed his cheek. "You *very* much are."

"Sorry, Mum." Matthew turned tired eyes to Gwen. "I haven't done this whole renovation thing very well, have I? Stoved your ceiling in. What a palaver."

"Never mind all that." Gwen sounded brisk, but Ellie saw her discreetly dab at her eyes, and her heart twisted in sympathy. Poor Gwen. This had to be so hard on her. "I'm sure the ceiling was a danger, anyway, since it fell in like that, without any warning. It's a good thing you spotted it."

Matthew let out a huff of laughter and closed his eyes. "That I did."

Gwen and Ellie gave each other rather watery smiles, and Ellie felt another surprising surge of affection for her mother-in-law.

"The surgeon said your arm is going to be all right," she ventured after a moment. "As long as you keep it immobile and don't do anything too silly."

"Six weeks in plaster." Matthew opened his eyes as he grimaced. "I won't be up to much, unfortunately, that's for certain."

"We can all pitch in," Ellie replied bracingly, although DIY was most definitely not her speciality, or, for that matter, their children's. Still, they would make it work. Maybe it would help them all to bond, or feel more at home at Bluebell Inn. "It'll be fun," she insisted. "And we should probably hire contractors for the big bits anyway." At least they wouldn't be having *that* argument again.

"Yes, I think we should have hired a contractor at the start," Matthew agreed wryly. "I was just having a prod of the joists... I had no idea that would bring the ceiling down."

"I'm just glad you're all right," Gwen said. "Really, Matthew, that's all that matters."

"How is the house?" Matthew asked. "Is it liveable? Are we all going to have to move out till they fix the floor? I'm so sorry, Mum, this is the last thing you need—"

"Nothing as dire as that," Gwen replied with an attempt at cheer. Ellie had heard her earlier ringing John, the local DIY man she said she'd used over the years, and Gwen had told her that he'd looked through the house while they'd been waiting at the hospital. He'd made temporary repairs as needed and told her that besides the two rooms that had been affected, the rest of the house was perfectly stable and could be used. Considering everything else that was going on, that had been a big relief... and yet two rooms was two rooms—her and Matthew's bedroom as well as the guest room beneath.

"Still," Matthew said. "It's a big mess."

"Messes can be cleaned up," Ellie told him firmly. "And nothing was actually broken or wrecked, besides the ceiling and your elbow. It could have been a lot worse." Considering the middle of her bedroom had caved in, she was grateful her possessions hadn't ended up broken beyond repair. She glanced at the clock above Matthew's bed with a worried frown. "I'm sorry, I'll have to leave to get the kids from school in a minute." It felt too soon to go, and yet she couldn't be late, not on their first day. She was aching to see them, to reassure herself that they were okay.

"Let me do it," Gwen said. "You'll want to stay here with Matthew."

Ellie bit her lip. "Oh, but it's their first day..." She so wanted to be there, to see Ava and Josh come out of the school doors. She wanted to hear all their news, every last bit of it, and sweep Ava into her arms and ruffle Josh's hair. She wanted to be home to greet Ben and Jess, with snacks and smiles and whatever else they needed. And yet it felt wrong to leave Matthew so hurriedly.

"They'll be fine, I'm sure." Gwen gave her an uncertain smile. "I'm happy to fetch them, Ellie, honestly. I've been wanting to help out, now that you're living with me. Let me do this for you."

Ellie hesitated, torn between wanting to see how her children had fared on their first day, and sensing she should be with her husband. Besides, Gwen looked like she really wanted to get the children herself, and Ellie didn't want to deny her that.

"All right," she said at last, pushing any lingering uncertainties aside. "Thank you, Gwen. That's very kind."

"Good." Gwen looked both pleased and relieved, and Ellie squashed the pang of sorrow she felt, that she wouldn't be there. There would be plenty more days to pick them up, she reminded herself. "I suppose I should get going, then," she remarked, and Ellie nodded.

"Thank you for getting them."

Gwen stooped to kiss Matthew's cheek. "Take care of yourself," she said, and then she left the room.

Ellie settled herself in the chair next to Matthew as an uncertain silence descended. Now that his mother was gone, Matthew didn't look as wryly cheerful. In fact, he looked quite despondent.

"Matt...?" Ellie ventured. "Can I get you something? A drink of water or a cup of tea?"

"No, I'm fine." He closed his eyes and turned his head away from her, and Ellie tried not to feel stung.

"You're tired," she said quietly, patting his good shoulder. "I'm sorry this all happened."

"So am I." His tone was almost bitter. "What a cock-up, eh? A week in and I mess everything up. Again."

Again? Ellie eyed him uncertainly. His eyes were open now,

but he was still averting his face from her, staring determinedly
at the wall.

"Matthew, it could have happened to anyone..."

"I was such an *idiot*." He sighed. "Maybe this whole move
was a mistake. Uprooting everyone, thinking I could manage all
the DIY, do up the whole house..."

What?

"Matthew, don't say that," Ellie protested. "We just got
here. There's bound to be all sorts of growing pains, for all of
us." She could hardly believe she was the one spurring him on
now, and yet she meant it. She hadn't realized he might need a
talking-to, just as she sometimes did. She touched his shoulder
again, gently. "It's going to be okay."

He closed his eyes. "I'm tired," he said, and it was clearly
the end of the conversation.

Ellie leaned back in her chair with a sigh. Part of her felt
like being furious. *If you had so many doubts, why didn't you
share them with me?* But another part felt only sad. Somehow,
they'd already grown apart in all this, and she wasn't even
sure how.

CHAPTER 12

GWEN

Gwen stood in the schoolyard by herself, watching the young mums gather in tight little knots, chatting away merrily. She wondered if Ellie had felt so alone this morning, and a shaft of sympathy went through her. None of this was easy.

It had been a long time since her own days as a young mother in this schoolyard, chatting with friends, feeling busy and content. She couldn't remember the last time she'd been here; Owen and Mairi had gone to the primary in their village a few miles away, and in any case, Sarah had rarely asked her to pick them up.

Gwen glanced around, looking for the inevitable changes—it had been thirty years, after all—and noted the new play equipment, a bike shed, an outdoor classroom. Vaguely, she recalled a village fundraiser for the shed; she'd made some cakes. She hoped Josh and Ava had enjoyed their day here. Should she have let Ellie pick them up? She'd wanted to be helpful, but maybe she'd been too pushy. It was so hard to know how to set the right tone.

She thought of Matthew looking so pale and worn in the

hospital bed, and her heart lurched within her. At least he was safe. He was *alive...*

Which made her think, unfortunately, of the wretched voicemail she still hadn't returned. She needed to call the doctor's office, and she really didn't want to. But never mind that now, she told herself. She could hardly make the call in the middle of the schoolyard, with her grandchildren about to emerge from the school on their very first day.

Her heart lifted at the thought of them. Wasn't this what she'd wanted all along, to be there for her grandchildren, picking them up from school, plying them with freshly baked biscuits and glasses of milk when they returned home? Never mind the voicemail or even Matthew right now, she told herself. She had this moment, at least, and she wanted to treasure it.

She nodded to a few acquaintances she recognized, who were picking up their own grandchildren, and one woman she knew from the village ventured over.

"I don't usually see you here, Gwen."

"I know, Sue." Gwen gave a self-conscious little laugh. "My grandchildren started at the school today. They've just moved here from America."

"Oh yes, I think I heard about that." Sue nodded thought-fully. "Must be lovely to have them close by."

Very close by indeed, Gwen thought, as she smiled. "Oh yes," she said firmly. "I'm absolutely thrilled."

The classroom doors opened, each class lining up and then trotting out pupil by pupil, reuniting with their parent or, as was often the case, grandparent. Gwen had always felt a bit envious of her friends and neighbors who had grandchildren locally. Of course, she had Owen and Mairi nearby, but Sarah was always so busy, scheduling them with afterschool activities every day, and treating visits to Bluebell Inn like sporadic fly-bys, Gwen had never felt truly involved or needed, not the way she'd wanted to be.

"Granny?" Josh walked slowly toward her, a frown puckering his little brow. Already he looked worried, his gaze darting around the yard. "Where's Mom?"

"She had something to do with your father," Gwen improvised, realizing she should have had an answer ready. "She'll be back a bit later."

"She didn't want to see us right after school?" Josh sounded shocked, and his lower lip wobbled before he quickly looked away. "She said she'd be here," he commented, half to himself.

Oh dear, maybe Ellie really should have been the one to pick them up.

"She did, Josh," Gwen assured him, "of course she did. It was just..." She didn't want to tell him about Matthew's accident, not here among all these strangers. Already, Gwen was starting to feel out of her depth. "Something came up, I'm afraid. I'll explain more when we get home. Now, where do you think Ava could be?" She made a big to-do of looking around, trying to hide her desperation with a jolly tone, a ready smile.

"She comes out the Infants door," Josh said with a nod toward the other end of the school. "I'm in Juniors, Granny."

"Oh, of course. Silly me." She should have remembered that, from picking up her own children, so many years ago. The school hadn't changed *that* much, although, admittedly, it had got a little bigger. Or maybe it simply seemed bigger, somehow, from what she remembered, when she'd been like one of these other mothers, calm and capable, busy and productive. "Right, then, shall we go and find your sister?" Gwen asked Josh as she reached for his hand.

To her disappointment, he sidled away, ducking his head, not looking at her. Gwen tried to push away that needling, stinging hurt. He was only eight, and it was early days. She had plenty of time to get to know her grandchildren, to bond with them. *Hopefully.*

Ava was already waiting, holding the teacher's hand, most

of the other children already collected by parents or grandparents who understood about the two entrances, when Gwen reached the Infants door. Ava looked anxious, her eyes wide, her lower lip jutting out, one pigtail drooping, its ribbon lost. She looked even more anxious when she saw Gwen and not Ellie.

"Where's Mommy?" she demanded.

"She's busy, darling. How was your first day at school?" Gwen gave the teacher, a woman she didn't recognize, a harried, grateful smile as she reached for Ava's hand. Thankfully, the little girl let her hold it, her face lighting up briefly.

"I had chocolate cake at lunchtime! With chocolate sauce!"

"Oh my, that sounds absolutely *scrumptious*, Ava." Gwen smiled at her warmly, relieved to be on surer footing. "Now, where do we pick up Ben and Jessica, do you think?"

"They don't go to this school, Granny," Josh said, looking anxious again.

Gwen managed a light laugh. "I know they don't, Josh, they're far too big, aren't they? I meant the stop where they'll get off the bus. I suppose it's the one on the way back home." She smiled, trying to imbue him with some confidence in her abilities. She did know where the bus stop was, after all. She'd lived in this village for forty years. "Right, shall we set off?"

She navigated the crowded schoolyard, Ava clinging to her hand, Josh sloping along behind, seeming morose. She tried to ask them both more about their days, but Josh didn't seem to want to talk, and Ava was more intent on pulling on her hand rather hard as she skipped ahead. Gwen felt rather exhausted by it all already, along with thinking about Matthew's condition and the state of the house... and that voicemail.

She hadn't even been back yet to see how bad the damage to the house was, never mind John's assurances that he'd "seen worse." At best, there was a hole in the ceiling, and Ellie and Matthew's room was now off limits. And at worst...

She didn't even want to think about that.

The bus from the comprehensive was pulling up to the concrete shelter across from the village green as Gwen approached with Josh and Ava. The children spilled out from the doors in a flurry of coats, bags, and boisterous chatter, but, with a lurch of alarm, Gwen didn't see either Jess or Ben. They had made it onto the bus, hadn't they? What would she do if they hadn't?

Then, finally, when most of the children had already started to wander off, Jess got off the bus, holding her backpack in one hand, her blazer tied around her waist, her skirt rolled up at the waistband several inches. She glowered as soon as she saw her grandmother, and Gwen faltered mid-step.

"Hello, Jess," she managed as brightly as she could as she made herself move forward. "How was your first day?"

"What are *you* doing here?" Jess demanded in a sullen tone.

"Your mum had something important to do," Gwen said yet again. She wished she'd thought of a better response than the one she'd first blurted, but no matter now. "I'll explain when we get home."

"Explain?" Jess looked suspicious, her eyebrows drawn together in a scowl.

Ben came loping off the bus, glancing at them all in almost comical surprise. His hair was a rumpled mess, he had mud all over his school shirt, and his arms were full of both blazer and bag, his tie stuffed into his pocket. Gwen couldn't help but smile at him; he reminded her of Matthew at the same age.

"Hey, Granny," he greeted her cheerfully, and she was gratified by his friendly response.

"You had a good day, Ben?" she asked with a smile. The tie fell from his pocket, and she stooped to pick it up. "You look as if you did."

"Yeah, it was pretty good. Everyone here plays soccer. Not like at home."

"Your dad used to be football mad," Gwen returned. "Or soccer, as you said. I'm glad you had a good day."

"Can we please *go*?" Jess demanded, and Gwen turned to her granddaughter with a small, apologetic smile. Ben might have had a good day, but Jess clearly hadn't.

"Yes, sorry, sorry," Gwen told her. "Let's head back. We can get something to eat..." Not Welsh cakes, though, she reminded herself, or anything with raisins.

Jess stalked ahead, and with Ava still clinging to her hand and Josh lagging behind, Gwen struggled to keep up.

"Ow, stop it, Ben," Josh yelped, and Gwen looked behind her to see Ben ruffling his little brother's hair. Josh ducked away, irritated and already tearful, and Ben laughed. He seemed in high spirits, Gwen thought, but Josh did not appreciate the teasing. Before Gwen could even think to intervene, Josh had shoved Ben in the shoulder and Ben had shoved him back, hard enough to make Josh stumble and fall onto his knees. Josh started to cry, seeming furious with himself for doing so, while Ben called him a baby.

Meanwhile, Jess had disappeared around the corner, and Ava was hopping from foot to foot.

"Granny, I need to pee."

Gwen's head pounded as she gazed at them all in dismay. Why did everything feel so *difficult*? How did Ellie manage it?

"Come on, Ava," she said finally. "We're very nearly home. I'm sure a big girl like you can hold it for a bit."

"I *can't*."

"Ben and Josh, stay away from each other, please, if you can't manage to be civil," Gwen instructed in as commanding a tone as she could manage. Ben followed Jess toward home as Gwen reached out a hand to Josh, who took it as he stood up. "There now, that's not so bad." She glanced at his slightly scraped knees. "I don't think you'll need a plaster."

"I don't like it when he messes up my hair," Josh said on a sniff. "He knows that."

"I'm sure he does," Gwen agreed. "Brothers and sisters always know how to wind each other up, don't they? Your dad and your Aunt Sarah were just the same."

Josh cocked his head, a gratifying gleam of interest lighting his brown eyes. "They were?"

"They certainly were. I could tell you some stories."

"What stories?"

"Let me think of a few as we walk."

Josh fell into step beside her as Gwen started walking briskly, pulling Ava alongside her.

"Let's see," she remarked as they turned the corner. "I remember on one occasion when Sarah wore your dad's new trainers—sneakers, that is. They were the same shoe size for a few years, and he had a brand new pair he was proud of. He was absolutely furious, as I recall. She'd got them covered in mud." She smiled at the memory, even though it had been far from funny at the time.

"Ben doesn't borrow my sneakers," Josh told her. "His feet are too big."

"Then you can count yourself lucky."

"Granny, I really need to pee," Ava exclaimed, dancing from foot to foot.

Gwen gave Josh a conspiratorial smile. "We'd better hurry, then!"

They headed up the lane and into the kitchen of Bluebell Inn, the table immediately covered in backpacks and lunch boxes and shrugged-off jumpers, Ava raced to the bathroom, while Ben was rooting in the fridge for something to eat, and Josh looked around, wrinkling his nose. Jessa had already flounced somewhere with her phone.

"What happened, Granny?" he asked. "Everything's so dirty."

"Yes, it is..." Gwen ran her fingers along the counter and saw the tips were covered in plaster dust. The whole house would have to be cleaned from top to bottom, she thought wearily. "Well, that's what I wanted to tell you about," she told Josh as she turned around. "Something rather exciting happened today. Exciting and a bit scary!"

"Scary?" Josh's eyes widened with anxiety, and Ava peered from around the open bathroom door, still sitting on the toilet.

"What was scary?" she asked.

Ben turned from his perusal of the fridge. "Yeah, it is dirty in here," he remarked, clearly noticing it for the first time. "What happened, Granny?"

"Well—"

Before Gwen could begin, Jess burst into the kitchen. "Why is the top floor sealed off with tape?" she demanded. "And there's dust, like, *everywhere!*"

"Ah, yes," Gwen said a bit weakly. "Well, let me explain about that. There was a bit of a to-do with the renovations, but it's all going to be all right."

"What—"

"What happened?"

"Is Daddy okay?" Josh asked, a wobble in his voice.

"Daddy's fine, Josh," Gwen reassured him. "I'll tell you all about it. First, though, let's have a snack."

Somehow, with an energy Gwen hadn't realized she still had, she managed to wipe off all the surfaces and then settle the children at the kitchen table with glasses of milk and slices of toast with jam, which they seemed to like more than Welsh cakes. The backpacks were piled in the front hall, the cardigans folded neatly away, the lunch boxes rinsed out in the sink. Progress, even if she felt like wilting.

"Aren't you going to tell us what happened?" Jess asked as she munched her way through her second piece of toast.

"Yes, I am." Gwen sank into a chair at the table with a small sigh of relief. She had forgotten just how tiring this all was, although of course when she'd been in the thick of things with small children, she'd been much younger herself. "So, your father was looking at some ceiling joists, I think, and they were a bit wobblier than he thought, and unfortunately the ceiling came crashing down."

"What—" Jess exclaimed. "Is he okay? Is he—"

"Yes, he's okay. Everything and everyone is fine. He broke his arm, but it's in plaster and he should be home soon with your mum." She patted Josh's hand, noting how worried he looked. "Really, it's absolutely fine," she reiterated. She thought of the voicemail on her phone and knew she couldn't actually make any such promises. No one could.

"The *ceiling*," Ben said, sounding impressed. "Wow."

"Is all our stuff ruined?" Jess asked anxiously. "Can I even go in my bedroom?"

"Yes, I think so," Gwen answered. "It was the floor of your parents' room, and the ceiling of the room underneath. John, my handyman, said everything else was stable."

"But the tape—"

"It's just a precaution, I'm sure," Gwen responded wearily. At least that was what John had said. "Now, your mum will be back quite soon, I'm sure, and your father, too." She hadn't heard whether Matthew would have to stay in hospital overnight or not, although she hoped not. "It's all going to be absolutely fine, I promise you. Now, who would like another piece of toast?"

"I'm not hungry anymore," Jess mumbled, pushing her plate away from her. As she got up from the table, Ava began to cry.

"*Daddy*..." she wailed, and Josh patted her clumsily on the shoulder, while Ben grabbed Jess's uneaten slice of toast.

"There's nowhere to go," Jess complained, and then, with a theatrical sigh, she stomped into the living room, slamming the door behind her so the whole house shuddered. As long as no more floors fell through, Gwen thought with a sigh, and turned back to the counter to make more toast.

CHAPTER 13

JESS

Everything about life in Llandrigg was absolutely *awful*, Jess thought as she threw herself on the sofa, her phone clutched in her hand.

School had been absolutely terrible, even worse than she'd feared, and now her dad had a broken arm, and the house was *wrecked* and, who knew, the ceiling might fall on her at any minute... What had her grandmother even meant, about the joists being wobbly? What even was a joist? Just one more thing in her life that *sucked*.

Jess took a shuddering breath before burying her head in her arms. She hated it here. Hated it, hated it, *hated* it. There had to be some way she could get away. Some way she could get back home, because that was where she needed to be. Where she *had* to be...

After a few minutes of struggling not to cry and yet at the same time wanting to give in and have a really good sob, the kind of snotty, full-body gasping cry part of her craved, Jess rolled onto her back and held her phone above her, squinting at the screen. No new Snapchats or Instagram messages from anyone. Nothing from her so-called best friend. Chloe had started school yesterday, and she hadn't messaged Jess even once since she'd begun. All Jess had seen was the public post Chloe had put up of her and Emily by the bus, and her stomach had clenched as she'd scrolled through the comments, all from the coolest people from their grade, the people she and Emily had never, ever been friends with.

What was going on? Why was Chloe suddenly hanging out with the cool crowd, the kind of people they'd both agreed they didn't want to be friends with, because they were so shallow and stupid? Those hair-flicking girls with the fake laughs and the constant selfies? She and Chloe weren't like that. They never had been; they'd *decided* not to be.

But now it seemed as if Chloe had forgotten about her best friend completely, and meanwhile Jess was stuck here in the middle of nowhere, in the worst school in the world, without a single friend and not likely to find one anytime soon, or *ever*...

Tears smarted in her eyes again as she recounted the endless miseries of the day. First off had been looking like a complete nerd when she'd boarded the bus; she'd seen some girls exchange snickering glances and her cheeks had burned with mortification. It didn't matter that she'd quickly pushed her socks down and shortened her tie as best as she could, even though she barely knew how to knot one, or that she'd walked off the bus holding her backpack like a bag instead of over her shoulder, the way all the other girls did. The damage had already been done. Jess knew that full well.

It had only got worse as she'd started school. The well-meaning teacher who was in charge of new students wittered on to Jess's "shadow"—the year nine girl who looked like she was there on absolute sufferance and yet was meant to show her around—making Jess cringe in embarrassment. "Now, Bronwen, I know you'll be friendly to Jessica and introduce her to every-one," the teacher had said in the kind of tone usually used with a six-year-old. "She's come all the way from America, can you imagine?"

Bronwen had given the teacher a flat-eyed glare, utterly unimpressed.

"And," the teacher continued determinedly, "she might have a tricky time fitting in with everyone, so make sure she feels really welcome and that everyone else is kind to her, okay? Can you do that, Bronwen?"

Bronwen had given the smallest, most unenthusiastic nod ever.

Wow, thanks, Jess had been tempted to say to the stupid teacher. Didn't she realize she was making everything a thousand times worse with her comments? Now instead of Jess just feeling like a saddo, she really *was* one—and the teacher clearly thought so, too, judging by all her advice.

Bronwen, meanwhile, had rolled her eyes, sauntering ahead as soon as the teacher had gone, deliberately ignoring Jess as she walked her to the first lesson, and then ghosting her for the rest of the day, not even sparing her so much as a glance.

The result of that had been that Jess had stumbled from class to class, trying to find where her lessons were, late for everything, having to slink into a seat at the back, much to her teachers' annoyance; a few had tried to be kind about it, but others had snapped at her, not caring that she was new, and several times Jess had, to her own humiliation, been far too close to tears.

At lunchtime, she'd tried to pay for her sandwich, drink, and bag of potato chips—or crisps, as they called them here—with the money her mother had given her, and the dinner lady had barked that everything was on a Parent Pay system, whatever that was, no cash allowed. She'd sounded as if Jess had been trying to annoy her on purpose, and she'd made her go back and return all the items she'd wanted to buy to their various shelves or trays. Everyone had stared and some had whispered as Jess had fumbled to do it all and then left the line, trying once again not to cry. Why was everyone so *mean*?

Jess had ended up spending the rest of the lunch break hiding out in an empty classroom, her stomach growling as she'd tried to avoid anyone and everyone, feeling utterly miserable, except then it had gotten even worse. A teacher had poked his head into the classroom and told her, quite sternly, that she shouldn't be hanging about in classrooms and would have to go outside with everybody else.

Outside, all the other students were clustered together in tight knots, and there was no way she was going to be able to speak to anyone. No one was even looking at her, which was both a relief and a deep, dragging disappointment. Ben, she saw out of the corner of her eye, was kicking a soccer ball—*football*—with half a dozen other boys on the field. Why was it so easy for boys, Jess had wondered miserably, and so excruciatingly difficult for girls? At least girls like her.

She'd sat on a bench by herself, trying not to look as if she minded being alone. She knew students weren't allowed phones during the school day—that had been drilled into her in every lesson—and so she couldn't even hide behind a screen, pretending to look engrossed in whatever interesting and important messages someone was sending her. So, she'd sat there miserably for fifteen minutes, staring into space and trying to look as if she were deep in thought, before the bell rang and everyone shuffled back inside.

By the time the day had ended, Jess had just wanted to get home and hide in her bed, the pillow over her head, her duvet up to her chin—and she couldn't even do that, because of the stupid ceiling caving in. She couldn't bear to think about having to face another school day again tomorrow, and the day after that, and the day after that...

It was too, too horrible to contemplate. She couldn't stand it, she really couldn't. She *had* to get out of here. Somehow, some way...

Her phone pinged with a text, and with relief she saw it was from Chloe. Finally.

How was school?

Terrible, Jess texted quickly, thumbs flying across the screen. *I hate it SO much.*

Belatedly, she wondered if she should have pretended she was having a good time, since Chloe so obviously seemed to be, back home with Emily. But why should she have to pretend with her best friend? She already knew her mom was going to be desperate for her to have had a good day, and she'd give her that mingled look of guilt and disappointment when Jess told her she hadn't. Even if she was able to fake it for her mom's sake, which she wasn't even sure she wanted to, she needed to be honest with someone.

Chloe sent a flurry of sad face emojis. *Soorrrry. Miss u.*

Jess felt an ache between her ribs, a physical pain.

How was your first day? she texted back.

Rlly gud! Chloe texted with a bunch of smiling emojis and thumbs up. *Emily and I are in Mrs. Lerner's class. She's so cool.*

Acid churned in Jess's stomach and the pain between her ribs got worse, until she felt as if she might gasp out loud from it. Couldn't Chloe have commiserated with her, just a little? And not mentioned Emily? Mrs. Lerner was the fun, hippyish teacher who all the girls in school loved. Jess couldn't stand the thought of Emily and Chloe sitting together with their cool teacher while she was stuck all on her own with teachers who didn't even know her name and had just yelled at her for being late or in the wrong place when neither was her fault at all. Life was so unfair.

Sorry, got to go, Chloe texted. *Lunch is over.*

Lunch being over... or more important people to message?

Cooler people who actually lived in Connecticut instead of halfway across the frigging world?

Jess tossed her phone away without replying. The tears that had burned behind her lids all day started to trickle down her cheeks. She *couldn't* stay in Llandrigg, she absolutely couldn't, not for another day, another second, never mind a year.

She *had* to find some way to get out of here. And fast.

CHAPTER 14

ELLIE

It was past six before Ellie got back to Bluebell Inn, practically wilting with exhaustion. She'd met with Matthew's doctor and a physiotherapist, and the good news was he'd be able to return home tomorrow morning. The bad news was that, in addition to the six weeks with his arm in plaster, he'd have months of physiotherapy afterwards, something he'd tried to take on the chin, but she could see how down he looked, angry with himself for getting into such a scrape, for being so seemingly stupid. Not, of course, that she'd say anything like that to him, but she still felt it.

If he hadn't been so desperate to prove himself... if he'd been *sensible*, and thought through things, and consulted a professional...

If they hadn't upped and moved to Wales at all...

No, she definitely was not going to let herself think like *that*. At least, not for too long. In the car on the way home, she'd let herself have ten minutes' luxuriating in self-pity, and then she'd shaken her head, given herself a stern talking-to—out loud, even —and thought practically about the future. About her children, who had had their first day at school and she had absolutely no idea how any of it had gone, because Gwen had not texted her, even though Ellie had texted her twice, asking how everything was. The lack of response wasn't entirely unexpected, because her mother-in-law didn't check her phone all that often, but it was still worrying.

"Hello?" she called as she came into the house, trying to pitch her tone bright, even though she felt like curling up somewhere and going to sleep for at least twelve hours. "I'm home!"

"*Mommy!*" Ava hurtled out of the kitchen, tackling her around her waist so hard that Ellie took a stumbling step backward before she was able to right herself. "Mommy, where have you *been*? Where's Daddy? You didn't pick me up from school." The last part was flung at her accusingly, even as Ava wrapped her arms around her waist even tighter, burrowing her head into Ellie's stomach.

"I'm so sorry, sweetie. I wanted to be there more than anything." Gently, Ellie stroked her daughter's soft hair as a pang of guilt assailed her. How could she have missed her children's first day in a new school, a new *country*? She really should have been there; she should have told Gwen she could do it herself. "Did Granny tell you about Daddy's accident?" she asked Ava.

Her daughter tilted her head to blink up at her. "Yes, his arm is broke."

"*Broken.* Yes, but not too badly." Actually, quite badly, for a break, but she wasn't about to explain that to her four-year-old, or, for that matter, to her thirteen-year-old.

"But he's going to be all right, she said," Ava insisted, a fearful, petulant tone creeping into her voice. "She said he would be ab-so-lutely fine." The way her daughter sounded out the syllables made Ellie smile despite her tiredness.

"Yes. Yes, he will, sweetheart." Gently, she untangled Ava's arms from around her waist and held her hand. "Where is everyone, Ava?"

"I'm in here!" Gwen called, and Ellie came into the kitchen. Her mother-in-law was smiling, but she looked tired, standing at the stove, stirring something, her shoulders a little slumped. There was a tub of crayons and a dozen sheets of scribbled-on paper on the table.

"Thank you so much, Gwen, for holding down the fort," Ellie said. "I don't know what I would have done without you."

"It wasn't a problem. I gave the children toast and jam, and they did a bit of coloring. Well, the younger ones, anyway. How is Matthew?"

"He'll come home tomorrow morning, thank goodness. Where are the others? Did they have a good first day?"

"Upstairs, I think, although not on the top floor, yet. I thought you might want to have a look, and there's dust everywhere..."

"I'm sure." Ellie hadn't even thought about the mess that would need to be cleared up. Would she even be able to get her things from her bedroom? "The kids all seemed okay, though?" she asked Gwen.

"Yes, for the most part." Gwen paused. "Jess seemed a bit stroppy, I suppose. She didn't tell me how her day went, but it didn't seem as if it went all that well, if her behavior is anything to go by."

"She was really grumpy," Ava chimed in. "And I almost wet my pants."

"Ava..." Gwen protested, smiling a little in apology. "You didn't."

"I *almost* did," Ava replied, and then stuck her thumb in her mouth. "School's long," she told Ellie, speaking around her finger, so her words were garbled. "And I don't like sitting on the rug for story time."

"I'm sure there were lots of nice toys to play with," Ellie replied, trying to rally, even though her heart had sunk right down to her toes when she'd heard about her oldest daughter. "Is your teacher very nice?" she asked Ava.

Ava shrugged, her thumb still in her mouth. "She's okay. Jess was *really* grumpy." Spoken with relish, like only a younger sibling could.

"I see." Ellie had had such hopes that the first day would have been, if not brilliant, then at least okay. Adequate. She'd so wanted her daughter to find a friend, or someone who could be a friend one day. Or even had a class with an inspiring teacher, or at least liked the food in the cafeteria. *Something.* "And Ben?" she asked Gwen, stroking Ava's hair.

"Yes, he seemed all right. He played football with some boys. That was as much as I got out of him." Gwen gave her a tired smile. "The house is sound, thankfully. John came back and showed me around just now. The two rooms affected have been closed off—your bedroom and the guest room beneath. We took out all your clothes and things, and I've put them in a room downstairs. John says nothing is actually dangerous, as long as we keep out of those rooms."

"That's good to hear." Thank heavens for small mercies, Ellie thought. At least she'd have her pajamas for bedtime. "Thank you for doing that. I'll just go see how the others got on today." She was desperate to check in with the children, find out for herself how they'd managed. Maybe Jess's day hadn't been that bad, after all...

"They didn't really tell me much, I'm afraid," Gwen said, like an apology. "Supper's in a few minutes. Bacon pasta." She smiled at Ava. "Ava, darling, do you want to help me stir the sauce?"

"Thanks, Gwen." Ellie headed into the hallway as Ava ran over to help her grandmother.

As Ellie mounted the stairs, she breathed in the plaster dust still lingering in the air and tried not to cough. It could have been so much worse, she reminded herself, and yet when she dared to peek into her bedroom and saw the jagged, gaping hole in the middle of the floor, she had to acknowledge this was pretty bad. How much would it cost to fix that, on top of the other renovations? When would they be able to be back in their room? Closing the door again, and locking it for good measure, she decided she'd think about all that later, and went in search of Josh, Ben, and Jess.

"Hey, Josh." Her younger son was lying on his bed, reading a *Horrible Histories* book. Ben was on the other, playing on his iPad. Ellie perched on the edge of Josh's bed and smiled at him. "How was school?"

He shrugged, his gaze glued to the book. "Okay."

Okay was better than some of the other words he could have used, Ellie told herself. Josh could be so quiet, so sensitive. When he found something he loved, he was full of enthusiasm, but his first instinct was to hang back, wait and observe. Even in Connecticut, it had taken him a while to make friends, and she worried about him here. What if he wasn't able to find a friend?

"Is your teacher nice?" she tried again, and Josh just shrugged. He clearly wasn't in a talking mood, and she knew there was little point in pushing him. Ellie turned to Ben. "What about you, Ben? Good day at school?"

"Yeah. Okay." He didn't look up from his screen.

"Granny said you played soccer?"

"Football, Mom," Ben replied in a joking, put-on British accent, and Ellie smiled.

"Right, football, darling," she replied in the same sort of voice. "Spot on."

Josh gave a little giggle, and Ellie's smile deepened. It was moments like this one, simple and small as it was, that lightened her heart and made her able to face the next day.

"So you made a few friends, playing football?" she asked Ben, and he rolled his eyes.

"I mean, I hardly know them, but, yeah, I guess."

That was as emotional as he was going to get, Ellie thought wryly, but she was satisfied. She decided to go in search of Jess, beard *that* lion in her den.

"All right, you two," she said as she rose from Josh's bed. "Dinner's in a few minutes and no screens afterward, okay? Ben? Did you hear me?"

"Yeah, yeah, okay," he replied, and she had a feeling he hadn't taken in a word she'd said.

When Ellie went to find Jess, her older daughter was curled up on her bed, her back to Ellie, a pillow clutched to her chest. Ellie's heart ached at the sight of her.

"Jess?" she asked gently as she came into the room. "How was your first day of school?"

"Horrible," she replied in a muffled voice. "I hate everything about it. *Everything*. I don't want to be here. It completely and totally *stinks*."

Ellie hesitated, unsure what tone to take when Jess was clearly feeling so emotional. Sympathetic? Bracing? It was so hard to know sometimes how to pitch it. She sat on the edge of the bed and touched her daughter's back, but she flinched away. "First days are always hard, aren't they," she murmured. Hers hadn't been much better than her daughter's, all things considered.

"As if *you* know." Jess hunched her shoulders further, away from Ellie. "You've never moved halfway across the world, to the lamest place *ever*."

"No," Ellie agreed equably. "You're right, I haven't, at least not before now. But I did start a new school when I was thirteen, where I didn't know anyone, and that was pretty hard." She still remembered the sinking feeling in her stomach, like a pit opening up inside her, when she'd walked into the cafeteria that first lunchtime and seen a sea of tables without a single empty seat. Was there anything more dispiriting than having nowhere to sit in a middle-school cafeteria? Was that what Jess had faced today—or worse?

"It's not the same," Jess said, still clutching her pillow. "It wasn't a different *country*."

"No, you're right, it wasn't." The last thing Ellie wanted to do was seem as if she were competing with her daughter for who'd had it toughest. "Tell me about your day," she invited, gently touching Jess's back again. This time, at least, her daughter didn't flinch away. "Were your teachers nice?"

"No, they were horrible and mean and they *shouted* at me. Teachers in America don't shout the way they do here. They'd probably get sued or something, if they did."

"I'm sure some shout, sometimes," Ellie replied, and Jess let out a harrumphing sound. "Anyway, what about the other kids? Did you meet anyone friendly?" Ellie asked, striving to keep a light, upbeat tone, even though she felt herself wilting inside with every word Jess said. Had it really been as awful as her daughter made it out to be? "In any of your classes?"

"No," Jess replied, "everyone ignored me and acted like I didn't exist. I didn't speak to a single person all day."

"What about lunch?" Ellie knew she was getting desperate now, but surely *something* had gone right, or at least not completely wrong. "Anything tasty in the cafeteria? Pizza? Pasta?"

Jess rolled over onto her back, and Ellie's heart squeezed painfully at the sight of her daughter's blotchy face, the way she was glaring at her. "I didn't even get to *eat* lunch," she spat at her, "because you can't pay with regular money, you have to have some stupid account that *you* were meant to set up before school started, and the lunch lady yelled at me about it and I had to put everything back and it was really embarrassing. Plus, I was, like, *literally* starving."

"Oh, Jess." Ellie looked at her in dismay. Vaguely, she recalled Sarah mentioning something about a lunch account, but she hadn't really taken it in. "I'm so sorry. I didn't realize that. I'll set it up tonight." Did that mean Ben hadn't had any lunch, either? Ellie wasn't about to ask Jess and incur more wrath. "Have you eaten anything since you got home?"

"I had some toast," Jess replied, grudgingly, before rolling back onto her side, her back to Ellie again.

"I'm *so* sorry, sweetie," Ellie murmured, feeling wretched for her part in the misery of her daughter's day. "That must have been really tough, on top of everything else." As well as embarrassing, which would have been far worse in Jess's eyes. "It will get better, though, I promise. I'll set up the account tonight, make sure it's all working." She might have to call Sarah and ask her to help her.

"You can't promise *anything*," Jess replied, her voice muffled again as she buried her head in the pillow. "You don't even get how bad it is. I hate it here. I *hate* it. I wish we'd never come."

At this point, Ellie was wishing the same thing. She knew there was nothing she could say right now to help her daughter through this, although she hoped they could have a calmer conversation later. Time was the greatest healer, after all, wasn't it? At least it could be... if she could figure out what to say to her daughter that would be helpful.

"Dinner will be ready in a few minutes," she said quietly, with one last pat of Jess's shoulder. "It will be good to eat something, at least, and maybe we can think about some... some strategies for tomorrow."

She knew she was offering so little, just as she knew sometimes you had to wade through the sadness, step by soul-sucking step, even when it felt as if there was no end in sight.

CHAPTER 15

GWEN

"Are you sure you don't want to come?"

Ellie seemed uncertain as she looked at Gwen. She was standing in the kitchen doorway, car keys in hand, while Gwen tackled the morning's washing up. It was the morning after Matthew's accident, and she was going back to the hospital to fetch him, and Gwen had already told her she'd stay here. In truth, she was looking forward to a bit of peace and quiet.

"Yes, I'm fine, and I don't think you need me," Gwen told her. "I'll tidy up here, have a bit of quiet. You and Matthew will want some time on your own, I'm sure."

Ellie looked around at the dirty breakfast dishes strewn across the table, cereal-encrusted bowls and crumb-scattered plates, biting her lip. "I'm sorry everything's such a mess. You can leave it and I'll clean it when—"

"It's fine," Gwen assured her. "It's nice to have a busy household."

Even if it was exhausting.

Gwen didn't know if it was the stress of yesterday that had made her so tired, but the children's noise at dinnertime last night had seemed louder than usual, a din of squabbles, teasing, laughter. Some of it had been cheerful enough, but it had been so noisy. Even Jess's sulking had seemed loud, with deliberate, dramatic sighs punctuating the happy chatter every few minutes. And when she'd cleared the table, she'd put the plates in the sink with an almighty clatter and then muttered a rather snarky sorry when Ellie had asked her to be more careful, before sloping off to her room. She supposed Sarah had gone through a similar stage, although it seemed very faraway now... and Sarah hadn't had to move across the world the way her granddaughter had had to.

After that there had been bath time to get through, and homework, and a load of laundry at nine o'clock at night because it turned out there was only one pair of school trousers that Ben thought were comfortable. Gwen remembered how it used to be with young children, at least she thought she did, and yet it still felt so unfamiliar. She wanted to help Ellie, since her daughter-in-law seemed to have her hands more than full, but it was hard. Harder than she'd ever expected.

At least now, after half an hour of mayhem as the four children had readied for school and eaten breakfast, leaving the house in a virtual whirlwind of slammed doors and shouts for missing shoes, Gwen could have some quiet. Enough quiet to sit down and make that phone call she'd been dreading since yesterday morning.

"Go on, now," she urged Ellie. "I'll be fine. I'll have lunch ready for when you both get back. Soup and salad okay?"

"Sounds wonderful, thank you." Ellie hesitated for another second and then, with a smile that seemed gratifyingly genuine, left the kitchen.

At least she and Ellie seemed to have found some points of sympathy, Gwen thought. It was something of a silver lining to the dark cloud of her son's injury.

As the front door closed, she heaved a sigh of relief. Alone at last.

She needed to make that phone call, but she also knew she needed to be in the right frame of mind to do it, so first, dishes. Anything to postpone the inevitable.

Gwen filled the sink with warm, soapy water, enjoying the simple pleasure of a sunny day, the chickens pecking in the yard outside, the leaves on the trees just beginning to turn to russet and gold. The kitchen was quiet and peaceful, a haven after the chaos of the last twenty-four hours, and twenty minutes of work soon set it to rights.

After she'd tidied up, Gwen boiled the kettle and slowly made herself a cup of tea, still trying to postpone that moment when she made the call. Then the phone rang, making her heart lurch with the what if that could be on the other end. Taking a few steadying breaths, she answered it, only to have Sarah's anxious voice strum down the line.

"Mum, I just heard about Matthew. What on earth—?"

Briefly, Gwen closed her eyes. She'd forgotten to tell Sarah about Matthew's accident and knowing how in-the-know her daughter liked to be, Sarah would be hurt, and would hide it by acting all sniffy and stiff. "I'm so sorry, Sarah. With all the mayhem, it completely slipped my mind to tell you what had happened. I was going to call you last night..."

"I saw John on the way back from the school run, and he said the ceiling had *caved in*." Sarah sounded aggrieved. "Is that really true? And Matthew's had *surgery*?"

"Yes, on his elbow, but he's going to be fine."

"And you didn't think to tell me any of it?"

"I'm sorry," Gwen said yet again. She knew how much Sarah liked to be kept in the loop, even if she wasn't as adept at keeping Gwen abreast of her own family's news. When her husband, Nathan, had changed jobs, Gwen had been one of the last to know. It would have been fine, except that Nathan had seemed surprised and a bit hurt when Gwen hadn't congratulated him. "Like I said," she continued, keeping her tone mild, "it slipped my mind."

"I just can't believe it." Sarah sounded dazed, which was better, Gwen supposed, than aggrieved.

"I know," she agreed, "it's all been rather a shock."

"But he's okay? Matthew? You're okay—?"

Again, that voicemail flickered through Gwen's mind. "Yes," she answered firmly. "Yes, we're all okay. I really am sorry I didn't tell you."

"I understand," Sarah replied, but she still sounded a little hurt. "Anyway, what can I do? I'll bring a meal over. A lasagna?"

She knew how her daughter liked to be busy, in control, and needed. Of course she would want to do something to help.

"That would be lovely," she told Sarah. Did Ellie's children eat lasagna? Gwen hoped so. "Thank you."

After the call, she took her cup of tea and the phone to the sitting room and sat down in her favorite chair, across from the one David had always sat in. It was so quiet. Even though it had been some months since she'd had any guests, she'd got used to having them around, reading the paper in the chair by the window, or just moving about upstairs. But right now it was only her, and she had nothing left to do to put off making that call.

Gwen put her cup of tea down and picked up the phone. She took a deep breath and then dialed the number of the consultant, her heart starting to thrum in her chest. Within a few seconds, she was connected, and then put on hold, which suited her fine. She could wait. She could wait a long time for the news she was afraid she was going to receive, even if she had to listen to an endless loop of what to do if you had chest pains.

But then, all too soon, she was put through to the consultant, who spoke in a serious tone. "Gwen? It's Anne Jamison.

Thanks for calling. I wanted to speak with you about your biopsy."

"Yes, thank you." Gwen's voice sounded faint.

"I'm afraid the biopsy has had a positive result," Ms. Jamison said, her voice terribly gentle.

"Positive..." For a second, Gwen's heart leapt wildly with hope. Positive was a good thing, surely.

"For breast cancer, I mean."

"Oh. Yes, of course." It wasn't a surprise, after receiving the voicemail, and yet at the same time, it was completely a surprise. How could she possibly have *cancer*? She felt perfectly well. A little tired, yes, but...

Gwen didn't say anything for a few seconds, and then the consultant continued.

"I know this is difficult news to hear, but it's really not as dire as you might think. Let's make an appointment for you to come in, and we can discuss the treatment possibilities. At the moment, I'd recommend a course of chemotherapy followed by radiation, but we can discuss that when you come to hospital, go through it all slowly. Sometimes it helps to have someone come with you."

"Right." Briefly, surprisingly, Gwen thought of Ellie. "Thank you."

"Are you all right?" Ms. Jamison asked. "Is there someone with you now? I know receiving this kind of news can be a shock, but I did want to get it to you as soon as possible, so we could get started on treatment. Breast cancer responds very well to—"

"Yes," Gwen said, interrupting her because she didn't think she could take any more information right now. "Thank you."

A few minutes later, after making an appointment for the following week, Gwen had put the phone down. Her mind was spinning emptily, thoughts too fleeting and strange to catch hold of. She found herself thinking of Matthew and Sarah when they were little, and how she would rock them to sleep, the only sound the creak of her grandmother's antique rocking chair as she cradled them in her arms, their heads against her shoulder. How long ago it seemed, and yet at the same time so very close. She could still remember the sweet, sleepy smell of them as babies, how she'd brush her lips against their downy heads and breathe them in...

And then she found herself recalling the day of David's funeral, cold and windy and wet, the weather matching her mood. She remembered the hymns—"All Things Bright and Beautiful" was one—and how she'd sat in the front pew and cloaked herself in a disbelieving numbness, to keep from breaking down. That was how she felt right now—numb. Numb was good. At least, it was the best she could hope for, while this news sank in. While it changed everything...

Gwen was still sitting there, her mind drifting between memories, her tea stone cold and only half drunk, when the front door opened half an hour later.

"Gwen?" Ellie called. "I'm back, and Matthew's here. We're home."

CHAPTER 16

ELLIE

Ellie stood on the edge of the school yard as Josh and Ava lined up for their classes. Nearby, a little cluster of mothers were chatting easily, and a burst of laughter floated on the crisp September breeze as Ellie lifted her chin.

It had been a week since school had started, and it had definitely not been one of the best weeks of her life, what with Matthew breaking his arm, Jess having such a difficult start, and Ellie herself still feeling lonely and adrift, despite her best intentions to be friendly and open. At least Ava seemed happy to go into school, she thought with a sigh, and Josh was accepting, if not entirely enthusiastic.

Ben seemed to have settled well too, with a bunch of boys who liked to play soccer—*football*—but Ellie was still anxious for all her brood, as well as her husband, who was definitely seeming restless and a bit down while recuperating at home, and Gwen, who had been a bit distant and out of sorts recently, although she wouldn't say why, not that Ellie had dared to ask her outright, but she'd tried to hint.

She'd thought, or at least hoped, that they'd been starting to get along, but, in recent days, it felt almost like they were back at the beginning. Gwen certainly seemed distracted, and Ellie didn't feel she knew her well enough to ask her about it.

Why, Ellie wondered not for the first time, did everything feel so *difficult*? Was it just a matter of soldiering through, passing time, until it got better? She'd come to school this morning determined to say hello to somebody, but it felt as if no one wanted to meet her eye. She'd thought about calling her best friend Elise from home, but she could only lean on her so much. She was four thousand miles away, after all, and while her cheery texts had been welcome, she wasn't here and never would be.

"Hallo, you must be Josh's mum?"

Ellie turned and blinked in surprise at a cheerful-looking woman standing in front of her. She had wildly curly hair, sandy in color, pulled back from her face with a band.

"Er... yes," Ellie replied cautiously, trying to smile. "And you are...?"

"I'm Zach's mum. Has Josh mentioned...?" She raised her eyebrows expectantly, while Ellie shook her head, afraid she might have missed signing some necessary permission slip, or worse. "I'm sorry, he hasn't really mentioned anyone from school yet."

"They never tell you anything, do they?" the woman answered with a little laugh. "I ask Zach every day what he does at school, and the answer's always the same."

Ellie felt a smile tugging at her mouth. "*Nothing?*" she guessed, and the woman laughed again, deeper this time, making Ellie smile all the more. Goodness, she'd missed even the most basic of social interactions with acquaintances or friends. She was grateful for this woman's kindness.

"Got it in one," she said with a nod. "I'm Emma, by the way. Emma Owen. Zach and Josh are both mad about Lego, as far as I can tell, and I was wondering if Josh would like to come over tomorrow afternoon for a play? He's welcome to stay for tea, if that's all right with you. Nothing fancy—pizza, maybe, or spaghetti bolognaise?"

"Oh…" To her embarrassment, Ellie felt tears sting her eyes. This was the first time someone at the school had made anything close to a friendly overture, and she was so very grateful. And apparently emotional, because she wasn't quite able to blink back the tears that had come to her eyes. "Sorry," she half-mumbled, half-laughed, as she brushed at her eyes, embarrassed. "I'm not a complete basket case, I promise. It's just been a… a challenging time."

"You *aren't* a basket case?" Emma raised her eyebrows, seemingly unfazed by Ellie's little emotional display. "Because I certainly am. I think any mum qualifies." She laid a friendly hand on Ellie's arm. "You've just moved here, haven't you? From the States, by the sound of it?" Ellie nodded. "Well, if you're free now… do you fancy a coffee?"

Ellie let out a wobbly laugh. "Oh yes, *please.*"

Ten minutes later, they were sitting in Llandrigg's one café, a tiny tearoom on the high street with rickety tables and colorful, mismatched cups and saucers. It was quaint and charming in a slightly shabby way, and Ellie loved it. More importantly, she loved sitting down with someone she hoped might turn out to be a kindred spirit, a friend. Emma ordered a hot chocolate with lashings of whipped cream without a qualm or remark about having to watch her weight, and recklessly Ellie did the same. No skinny soy lattes for her, she thought with relish. *That* was a change from America.

"So, you're new," Emma remarked once the waitress had gone, and they were alone, save for an elderly man brooding over the newspaper in the corner of the tearoom. "That's always difficult, isn't it?"

She stated it so matter-of-factly that Ellie felt a rush of relief. Someone *understood.* "Yes," she said. "It is a bit difficult at times."

Emma arched a skeptical eyebrow and Ellie laughed.

"All right, yes, it's been incredibly hard. Much harder than I expected, to be honest, although I'm not even sure *what* I expected. It all seemed to happen so quickly. One minute we were living in Connecticut and the next we were in Wales." Ellie knew it hadn't happened like that really; she and Matthew had had multiple discussions, weighing the pros and cons, but, in retrospect, she felt as if it had sped by, and she had emotional whiplash from it all.

"It always is harder than you expect, isn't it?" Emma agreed with a nod. "Maybe because you can't bear to think through everything before it happens. We moved here three years ago from London—Zach starting year one, my younger daughter Izzy in nursery. Perfect timing, I thought, for them and for us, and my parents are only an hour away. I had this image of living in the country—it involved loads of delicious things bubbling on top of the Aga I don't actually have, because we can't afford one, and joyful tramps through the countryside in muddy wellies, usually with a dog we also don't have." She laughed and shook her head. "The trouble is, I don't particularly enjoy cooking *or* walking in the countryside, and that didn't actually change when we moved here, even though I hoped it would."

"I suppose I had a similar image," Ellie admitted slowly. "Although, underneath that, I was afraid and, to be honest, reluctant. I always knew that, and yet I still wanted everything to fall neatly into place." She grimaced ruefully. "The word idyllic comes to mind..."

"And bucolic," Emma replied, grinning, and Ellie couldn't help but laugh.

"Yes. I don't know why I chose to be so deluded." She shook her head and then their hot chocolates arrived, topped with mountains of whipped cream and marshmallows. Ellie couldn't remember when she'd last enjoyed something so decadent.

"So, what brought you to little Llandrigg, anyway?" Emma asked as they both took sips of their drinks.

Ellie explained about Gwen, and Matthew, and the bed and breakfast.

"That place on Bluebell Lane? It's so lovely," Emma exclaimed. "And I bet it has an Aga."

"It does," Ellie admitted. "Although I'm still figuring out how to use it."

"So you moved to help do the place up?"

"Yes, and because I felt it was only fair—to spend some time in Matthew's home country, after we'd been so long in mine," she explained. "And when he was made redundant..." She shrugged, a soft sigh escaping her, not wanting to go into all the messy details with someone she barely knew. "We were at a loose end, in many ways, and it seemed like the right choice at the right time, for all of us."

"And does it still?" Emma asked a bit shrewdly. "A couple of weeks in?"

"Well..." Ellie let out a shaky laugh. "Yes and no. I feel like we've had a lot to deal with, more than I could have possibly expected. I mean, you try to prepare yourself for the usual things—grumpy kids, culture shock and..."

"What else has there been?" Emma asked, frowning a little in concern.

With a grimace, Ellie explained about the ceiling crashing in—their bedroom, although much improved, with John starting to repair the floor, was still a construction site—and Matthew breaking his arm, having it immobile in plaster for at least six weeks.

"And I don't know why, but I don't feel like I get along with my mother-in-law," Ellie confessed in a semi-guilty rush. "Things had gotten a little better recently—at least I thought they had. But even though she's lovely, truly, we just always seem to... come up against each other. I don't know what it is, exactly. We're very different, I guess." Although not that different, surely, she thought. Not really. Maybe she needed to ask Gwen outright why she'd become so distant, right when Ellie thought they'd been making progress, showing some solidarity with each other.

"Mother-in-laws are always a bit tricky, aren't they?" Emma sympathized. "Even the really nice ones."

"Yes, and I don't suppose you normally have to *live* with your mother-in-law." When they'd been in hospital together, waiting to hear about Matthew, she'd felt, for the first time, as if they were truly on the same page. But since then, everything had got tense and muddled again; last night, Gwen had snapped at Ava for playing too loudly, and when Ellie had offered to make dinner even though it wasn't her turn, she'd been decidedly cool. Ellie really wasn't sure what to do.

"Sounds like quite a list," Emma remarked. "Anything else going on?"

"Well..." Ellie hesitated, not wanting to pour out all her woes on this near stranger, and yet knowing she needed someone, anyone, to confide in. "My oldest daughter is in year nine and seems to hate everything about her life here, including *me*." Ellie let out a trembling laugh. A week of school had not improved Jess's mood in the least, although at least Ellie had sorted out the parent pay for her lunches. She wouldn't go hungry, but hopefully she wouldn't be so lonely, either. "Sorry," she mumbled as she felt her throat thicken. "I actually think I might cry again." She brushed at her eyes, willing it all back, at least for now.

"I wouldn't blame you if you did," Emma said as she gently touched her arm. "It sounds like you've got far too much going on, especially when everything feels so new and strange. But it will get easier, trust me. It will get better. It just takes time, day in and day out, showing up, slogging on. It's hard, and sometimes it feels long, but you *will* get there."

"It already has got better," Ellie told her, smiling through the last of her tears. "I can't tell you how much it's meant to me, just to have someone to listen to me complain for a little while. I think I needed to let that all out, whether I realized it or not." She gave her new friend a watery smile that Emma warmly returned.

"I'm so glad," she said, and Ellie knew she meant it.

"But what about you?" Ellie asked. "I've been moaning about myself for ages. Have you settled into Llandrigg life, without an Aga or muddy walks in the countryside?"

Emma laughed and took a sip of her hot chocolate. "Have I?" she mused as she put her cup down. "Yes, in some ways. I think I'll always miss London, but I wouldn't want to be back there, either. And people are friendly here, once you get to know them. It takes a little while, and I know the schoolyard can be intimidating, but when you keep showing up, they will notice you."

"I'll bear that in mind," Ellie promised.

"Are you thinking of working?" Emma asked. "Now that Izzy is in school, I've thought about going back, but there's not much around here, to be honest."

"What did you do, back in London?"

"BC?" Emma filled in wryly. "Before children? I was an event planner. I did all sorts—parties, weddings, retirement dos. It was on a small scale, but I loved it. Hard to start from scratch here, though, but I've thought about it. What about you?"

"I can't work for a while yet," Ellie replied, "due to my visa. I worked for a literacy charity before I had kids, but it's been ages, and I suppose helping with the B&B might fill up my time."

"Is that something you want to do?" Emma asked, and Ellie considered the matter.

"I think so," she said slowly. She'd been so focused on making sure Matthew had a project, that she hadn't really thought about whether she needed one. But, yes, she would be interested in helping out, if she could find a way to do it that didn't step on anyone else's toes—Gwen's or Matthew's. "We'll see," she added, and Emma nodded in understanding.

"Right now you just need to focus on finding your feet. And I promise it won't take you as long as you think it will!"

Ellie smiled, feeling better already, thanks to their chat. "I'll hold you to that," she warned, and Emma laughed and nodded.

"And so you should!"

CHAPTER 17

GWEN

"Is there anything else I can get you, love?" Gwen asked.

Matthew gave her a wry smile as he shook his head. "You've been amazing, Mum, but I don't need to be coddled. Not too much, anyway." His smile turned into a sigh as he gazed at his plaster-encased arm. "I just want to get out and *do* something. I hate feeling so useless. And I know it's all my fault. I can't believe I was so stupid, acting like I knew what I was doing when I so clearly didn't."

Gwen heard the bitterness in his voice and her heart twisted in sympathy. "It was an accident, Matthew," she told him gently, "and I know it's hard to have to rest, but six weeks isn't that long—"

"And months of physical therapy after?" He sighed and shook his head.

In the week since Matthew had come home from the hospital, he'd been slowly but surely going stir-crazy, just sitting around while John and an able assistant got on with the job of repairing the ceiling. Gwen couldn't blame him; her son had always been the type of person to thrive on activity and busyness, and here he was, stuck reading the newspaper or watching

TV, not even interested, it seemed, in perusing the architectural drawings he'd been longing to show her before the ceiling had caved in.

He hadn't seemed particularly interested in spending time with the children either, Gwen had noticed, much to Ellie's quiet frustration. Admittedly, it was difficult; he couldn't kick a ball with Ben, which was all he seemed to want to do, and Jess wasn't really talking to anybody. Matthew and Josh had done a puzzle together last night, but her son had stopped after half an hour, saying his arm hurt, while Josh had continued alone. Gwen had offered to help, but her little grandson had, politely but firmly, refused.

All their relationships continued to seem fraught, Gwen acknowledged, but she supposed it was simply the pain of adjusting... as well as keeping secrets. She hadn't told anyone about her diagnosis, and with every day she left it, she knew it would be more difficult to finally come clean. Already, Ellie seemed to be noticing something was wrong—asking her if she was okay, offering to make dinner. Gwen appreciated the gestures, but in her defensiveness and anxiety about it all, she feared she sounded irritable to Ellie. She *felt* irritable, unable to settle, longing for things to be different in so many ways.

At least the worst of the damage had been repaired, she reflected as she went back into the kitchen to tidy up. Matthew and Ellie's bedroom was still uninhabitable as they waited for the floor to be finished, but the house was no longer a mess of broken bits and plaster dust, and they could hopefully move on with freshening up the bed and breakfast, although she hadn't spoken to Matthew yet about any of her concerns... not with his intentions for her home, or her own health.

She sighed as she slowly wiped the counter, the weight of her diagnosis settling firmly on her shoulders once more. Sometimes, for a moment or two, she forgot about it, only for it to come back in a fearful rush. Yesterday, she'd had the appointment to discuss her treatment plan. She'd meant to speak to Matthew and Sarah, and Ellie too, before she went, but somehow she hadn't found the words, or maybe just the nerve. She'd told herself it would be easier to talk to them about it once she knew what she was facing—how often her chemotherapy sessions would be, what the effects would be like. Her consultant, Anne, had been reassuringly brisk but also kind, which was exactly the tone Gwen had needed to keep from breaking down completely. She was afraid, she realized, desperately afraid, and she didn't want to admit that to anyone, least of all herself.

But now she was scheduled to start chemotherapy next week and she knew she needed to tell both Matthew and Sarah —and Ellie too—but somehow the moment still never came. Sarah was busy with her children, and Matthew was brooding over the B&B as well as his broken arm. And Ellie seemed busy too, rushing about after the children, doing errands or maybe just trying to stay out of Gwen's way, and considering how touchy she'd been, Gwen couldn't really blame her.

Still, Gwen knew she was just making excuses. She'd had plenty of moments to explain what was going on, she just hadn't taken them. She didn't want to be fussed over or be seen as someone who was nothing but a patient, a problem to be dealt with, a worry to have. And there was so much going on already, the last thing she wanted to do was add to everyone's burdens.

But, she told herself, it really had to be done, because she would probably need some help, once the side effects of the chemo kicked in. She'd read them all in the brochure Anne had given her—nausea, vomiting, fatigue, mouth sores, hair loss...

None of it was particularly a surprise; she'd had friends who had had cancer, and she'd seen their symptoms and side effects, but it still all sounded rather dreadful. Like Matthew, Gwen thrived on busyness—her house, her garden, the bed and breakfast she'd lovingly nurtured. The thought of being too tired or ill to do any of the things she loved both frightened and depressed her.

From the sitting room, she heard the sound of Matthew turning on the telly, and she straightened her spine. Really, there was no time like the present, was there? Ellie was out, giving them privacy, although, of course, she would have to tell Ellie too, or Matthew would. How would her daughter-in-law react? Gwen realized she had no idea, and for some reason this shamed her. She hadn't really ever got to know her daughter-in-law at all, had she? She'd let their differences stand in the way, although she'd felt they'd made progress recently, before the weight of her diagnosis had come crashing down on her.

But her relationship with Ellie, she told herself, was a problem for another day. Her son was home with nothing to occupy him, save for the dubious options of daytime television. If she didn't talk to him now, when would she? What, really, was she waiting for?

Gathering her courage as well as her determination, Gwen went into the sitting room. Matthew was where she'd left him, sprawled on the sofa, watching one of those home improvement shows from America.

"Look at that bathroom," he said as he caught Gwen's eye, his tone an unsettling mixture of despondency and enthusiasm. "Carrera marble. Isn't it *fantastic*?"

"Mmm." Gwen did not particularly want marble bathrooms in her homely guest house, but that was yet another conversation for another day. "Matthew..." She took a deep breath. "Look, love, I need to talk to you about something."

"I know you do, Mum." Matthew pulled a grimacing sort of face as Gwen stared at him in astonishment. Surely he couldn't have guessed? Had he seen the letter from the hospital? Why hadn't he said anything?

"You... do?" she asked uncertainly.

"Yes. To tell you the truth, I've been wanting to talk to you, as well." He turned the television off and laid the remote control on the arm of his chair, giving her a direct, serious look.

Gently, Gwen lowered herself onto the edge of the sofa opposite, her mind spinning. She couldn't believe that Matthew might have suspected what was going on and not said a word. Did Ellie suspect, as well? And Sarah?

"I didn't think you'd realized..." she began slowly, feeling for the words as if through the dark.

Matthew shook his head sorrowfully. "I don't think I wanted to realize. I've been so full of my own plans... but look how they've turned out." He let out a gusty sigh as Gwen tried to work out his meaning. She had a dawning feeling Matthew was not talking about her cancer diagnosis, and his next words confirmed it. "I'm really sorry, Mum, about everything. I've taken on this whole bed and breakfast idea without any thought or consideration for you, or how you felt about all my grand plans. I just rushed ahead as I always do, because I needed to, I guess. Or I *thought* I needed to. And I've made a mess of it."

Gwen let out a little sigh—whether it was relief or disappointment, she didn't know. Matthew hadn't guessed. They were talking about two entirely different things, but she knew this was a conversation they needed to have, as well.

"You've been excited about the project, Matthew," she told him gently. "And I'm happy about that, truly."

"I know, it's just..." Matthew frowned into the distance, his shoulders drooping. "Being made redundant really knocked me for six. I thought I had it all sorted, you know? Good job, nice house, great life. And then, in one fell swoop, it felt as if everything had been taken away from me, and all because I wasn't good enough." He pressed his lips together. "We were about to lose the house, because we hadn't been able to keep up with the mortgage payments. Did Ellie tell you?"

Gwen shook her head. "No, of course not. She hasn't said a word about any of it, Matthew, and I don't think she would."

"Well." He shrugged. "It would have had to go back to the bank, if we didn't do something fast. Ellie was looking for work, as I was, and then moving here seemed the best option. We sold the house in a fire sale... way under the going price, but what can you do?" He shrugged again, his head lowered as if he couldn't bear to meet her eye.

"Oh, Matthew." Gwen shook her head, overwhelmed with sympathy for her son. She'd been so concerned with her own worries, she hadn't realized how badly all this had affected her son. And Ellie too, she realized. No wonder her daughter-in-law had seemed so stressed. "That all sounds as if it has been incredibly difficult, and I'm so very sorry. But you still have a beautiful family, Matthew, and a wife who loves you. That's more than many people have."

He didn't look at her as he answered, his face set and grim. "I feel like I've let them down. Disappointed them with my own failure. Ellie's angry with me, and I don't blame her."

"I don't think Ellie is angry," Gwen replied. "Worried for you, perhaps. But it wasn't your fault you were made redundant. It was a company reorganization." Or so Matthew had told her.

He shook his head as if to deny the truth of her words. "Yes, but if I'd been better at my job, it wouldn't have been cut. I wouldn't have been one of the first to go."

"I don't know about that," Gwen answered, "but life is full of disappointments. Things happens, things that hurt. They can send you reeling, and that's all right—you need to take the time to recover, reassess, which you have. The important thing is to get back up again, whatever way you can, and having your family around you to help you do it is a huge blessing." In case she sounded like she was lecturing him, she added quietly, "But I know it's hard. Very hard—harder than I can imagine." She needed to take the same advice, she knew, in regards to her diagnosis. "Have you talked to Ellie about it?"

Matthew sighed. "Sort of."

What did that mean? Matthew and Ellie hadn't, Gwen realized, spent too much time together since arriving at Bluebell Inn. She'd assumed it was because of Matthew's determination to get going with the renovation, but maybe it was something else. Something deeper.

"Well, I think you should," she said firmly. "She's your wife, and she loves you—"

"She's disappointed in me."

"Has she said so?" Gwen demanded with some asperity. "Or are you projecting that onto her? Don't wallow in self-pity, darling. You've had a setback, but you can get up again, and there are plenty of willing hands around to help pull you back up, Ellie's included." Hands that would help her in time, she hoped, but clearly now was not the time to talk about all that.

"I know," Matthew said. "And I am thankful for them, and you, Mum. I really am." He gave her a quick smile, his eyes still shadowed. "I'm sorry I sound so down. But I'm worried about everything, as well. The children don't seem to be settling in as well as I'd hoped. You think they'd be fine, they're young enough, but Jess seems so withdrawn, and Josh is so quiet. Ben seems okay, and Ava is little enough, but... I don't know. It feels like a lot, more than I thought it would. I know Ellie is worried about them, too, and she's probably angry with me for dragging us all over here. I don't think she's very happy here, to tell you the truth." An unhappy sigh escaped him as he shook his head.

"Isn't she?" Gwen felt another pang of guilt. Her relationship with Ellie felt so fraught and confused sometimes, she kept forgetting how difficult her daughter-in-law must be finding this transition. "It's still early days. Give them all time. And I really think you should talk to Ellie... about everything. She loves you, Matthew, and she wants you to confide in her. I'm sure about that."

"I know, but it didn't help matters that I put a big hole in the ceiling, did it?" He shook his head.

"Perhaps not, but John said there was some rot we didn't know about, so, really, it's a blessing in disguise." Gwen gave him a purposefully stern look, reminiscent of when he'd been a sulky teen. "Now, it's time to stop feeling sorry for yourself, Matthew Davies. You've got an adoring family and, thanks to John, a solid roof over your head. You have much to be thankful for. Start counting your blessings!"

Matthew gave her a sheepish smile, his expression thankfully lightening. "I know, Mum. I will."

"And you'll talk to Ellie?"

"Yes, when we find a moment."

"Let's make sure you do, then." Gwen paused before continuing, her tone softer, "I know this is difficult, and it's so challenging when life... when it doesn't turn out the way you'd hoped." She swallowed hard, thinking of her own situation. "But you've got loads to keep you going, you really do."

"I know I do." He reached out to touch her arm. "Actually, I wasn't intending to go into all of that just now, although I guess it needed to come out. What I really wanted to say was, I'm sorry for rushing ahead with ideas about en suites and a fitness center—"

"A *fitness center*?" Gwen raised her eyebrows. "You hadn't got around to mentioning *that*. Where on earth would we put it?"

"I was thinking we could renovate one of the barns. But the point is, I didn't consult you about any of it. I just took over. I suppose I... I wanted to feel like I had a job again. I wanted to feel in charge of something."

"Oh, love." Gwen squeezed his hand. "Of course you did."

"But this is *your* house, Mum, and the B&B was yours and Dad's dream. I don't want to take that away from you, or turn it into something it's not meant to be."

"You haven't," she assured him. "And you won't. This is something we can do together, Matthew, and that will involve collaboration and compromise. That's what I want."

He smiled and nodded. "I want that, too."

"Good. But, I have to say, there will be *no* fitness center in the barn." She spoke sternly, and Matthew laughed.

"No fitness center," he agreed, and with a smile Gwen rose from her seat.

Now, she acknowledged with an inward sigh, was definitely not the time to mention her diagnosis. But when would she?

CHAPTER 18

JESS

"What are you doing?"

Guiltily, Jess looked up from the keyboard she'd been messing about on. She'd taken to hiding in the music rooms during the hour-long lunch break, just to avoid the sheer awfulness of wandering around alone while everyone in her year clustered in tight little groups, laughing and chatting. Now she looked up as a tall girl with straight, brown hair, glasses, and an uncertain, inquisitive smile came into the room.

"Nothing, really." She turned off the keyboard and hunched her shoulders defensively. "Just messing around."

"Do you play?"

"Not really." She'd had lessons when she was little, but she hadn't practiced and her mom had stopped them after a while, claiming they were a waste of time. Jess hadn't really minded. "Do you?" she asked, and the girl shrugged, hunching her shoulders.

"Sort of. When I can."

This was the most Jess had talked to anyone since she'd arrived at this school. It felt good, but also a little scary. Uncertainly, she moved over on the bench seat. "You can have a turn, if you want."

The girl's face brightened, making Jess smile. "Can I? Thanks." She sat next to Jess and switched the keyboard back on. "I'm really bad," she added self-consciously, like a warning, and Jess found herself smiling all the more.

"You couldn't be as bad as me."

"I'm Sophie," the girl said after a moment, and she smiled shyly.

"I'm Jessica," Jess replied, smiling back, "but you can call me Jess."

"You're new, aren't you?"

The smile started to slide off Jess's face. "Yeah."

"And American."

"How can you tell?" she managed to joke, and Sophie gave a little laugh.

"Oh, I don't know, the accent, maybe? It's cool. Everyone here sounds so... *Welsh*. It's nice to hear something different."

"Is it?" Jess was heartened; her science teacher had made fun of the way she'd said some words, which had made Jess burn with humiliation. She didn't think he'd meant it meanly, but didn't he *know* how kids her age operated? Everyone had mimicked her American accent as she'd gathered up her books, putting on the most over-the-top and ridiculous accents. She knew she didn't sound like that. The only plus about not having any friends was that at least they'd all forgotten about her by lunchtime, so she hadn't had to endure the teasing for very long.

"How do you like it here?" Sophie asked.

Jessa thought of the miserable two weeks she'd spent feeling like she was in an isolation tank, or maybe just invisible, and that was if she was lucky. She'd been counting down the hours and sometimes even the minutes of every single excruciating school day. "It's okay," she said.

Sophie gave a commiserating sort of grimace, as if she'd

guessed at everything Jess hadn't said. "Yeah? It's not so bad, once you get used to it. There are some nice teachers, and some good after-school clubs."

Jess couldn't help but notice Sophie hadn't mentioned anything about the school's students. Did she have trouble making friends too? Was that why she was on her own at lunchtime? She seemed nice enough to Jess, but she knew kids could be cruel. There had been some mean girls back at her old school—girls like Emily. Chloe had barely texted her all week, and she was trying not to mind, even though it hurt, bitterly. Clearly she had a new BFF, one that was way cooler than Jess ever had been.

Turning back to the keyboard, Sophie let her fingers ripple over the keys. "Do you know this one?" she asked and played the opening bars of a pop song Jess had heard on the radio.

Unthinkingly, Jess sang along for a few seconds, and then stopped, embarrassed, tensing in case she was teased. Again.

"You have a great voice," Sophie encouraged, and she played another familiar pop song, raising her eyebrows expectantly. This time, they both sang the opening lines, before bursting into embarrassed giggles, ducking their heads.

"You're really good on the keyboard," Jess remarked. "Much better than me. I took lessons when I was little, but I can only play a couple of chords."

Sophie scooted over, gesturing to the keyboard. "Have a go."

"Okay..."

For the next twenty minutes, they took turns playing the keyboard and singing along to pop tunes. It was the most fun by far that Jess had had since moving to Wales. It felt so *nice* just to chat to someone her own age, to joke around and have a laugh over nothing much. It felt like a million years since she'd done something like this with Chloe, or anyone. She'd been feeling so lonely, she knew she had, but she hadn't even realized how much until now, when she felt as if she'd just taken a big drink of water in the desert. She was refreshed and energized just by a few minutes of joking and chitchat. She finally felt *seen*.

The bell rang for the next lesson, and Sophie rose from the bench reluctantly. "I've got double science now," she said with a grimace. "You?"

"Double math." Jess grimaced too. "Or maths, as everyone says." She grimaced again.

"I like your accent," Sophie told her with a smile. "And the American words." She raised her eyebrows. "See you around?" she asked, an uncertain smile curving her mouth, her voice lilting with hope, and Jess nodded enthusiastically, too pleased with the possibility of a friend to try to seem cool or unbothered. What was the point, anyway?

"Yeah, definitely," she said, like a promise. "See you around."

They left the music room together, and as they walked down the corridor toward the science block, a snide girl's voice called out, "Oh look, it's Snotty Sophie. Has she *finally* made a friend? How *sweet*."

Jess looked over, startled, to see a girl with a high blonde ponytail and narrowed ice-blue eyes looking at them. Sophie's cheeks had started to turn red, but she ignored the girl and kept walking.

Jess did the same, but she felt everyone's eyes on the pair of them and her face started to flush as well. She told herself she didn't care about that stupid girl—of course she didn't—but she realized, uncomfortably, that it wasn't quite true and, in any case, Sophie obviously did. She mumbled her goodbye, not even looking at Jess as she hurried to get her bag left outside the cafeteria, leaving her alone once more.

With a sigh, Jess went for her own bag. For a little while she'd felt as if she'd finally made a friend, and it had been amazing. Now she just hoped it lasted, but she hadn't even seen

Sophie before today. What if they didn't run into each other again?

Jess thought of Emily and Chloe, taking mirror selfies together, tongues sticking out. If Chloe could make a new best friend, well then, so could she. She'd just have to figure out a way to find Sophie again, and make it clear she didn't care about those other girls' teasing. At all.

CHAPTER 19

GWEN

"What would you like to do, Ava?"

Gwen smiled at her granddaughter as they stood in the sunlight-dappled kitchen after school. Ava's uniform looked too big on her skinny, little frame, her eyes wide as she stared back at her grandmother in surprise, it seemed, at being asked such a question. In a busy family like hers, with so much going on, Gwen doubted Ava was asked her opinion very much.

Ellie had gone to pick up Josh from a playdate, and Ben and Jess were due back from school at any moment. For now, Gwen was in charge, and she was pleased to be spending some time with her youngest granddaughter.

"We could play a game," Gwen suggested, "or do a puzzle, or go out and feed the chickens." Ava had enjoyed visiting the chickens, and she'd helped Gwen collect the eggs on several occasions, squealing in delight when she'd found one. "Or Toby could use a brush, if you like." She glanced down at the faithful spaniel, stretched out in front of the Aga. He caught her glance, his droopy eyes lighting up as his tail began a staccato beat against the stone-flagged floor. Gwen knew how much Ava loved Toby—maybe a little too much, sometimes. "Well?" she asked with a smile. "What do you think?"

"Can we bake something, Granny?" Ava asked, her eyes lighting up. "I like baking. Mummy and I used to bake lots, back home, but we haven't since we've come here." She stuck her lower lip out in a pout, and Gwen realized afresh how so much had changed for her grandchildren.

"Of course we can." With a smile, Gwen went into the pantry for sacks of sugar and flour. "What would you like to bake? Biscuits? Or should I say, cookies?" She gave her granddaughter a wry smile. "A cake? Or perhaps brownies?"

Ava screwed her face up in a thoughtful frown. "What about those cakes?" she asked.

"Cakes...?" Gwen repeated, not sure what she meant.

"The ones with the raisins."

"Welsh cakes." Gwen let out an uncertain laugh as she recalled that particular disaster. "I thought you didn't like those, Ava."

"I like them now," the little girl declared. "I didn't know that I liked raisins."

"Didn't you?" Gwen murmured, with a smile. She felt rather ridiculously heartened by the little girl's admission. "Well then, of course we can make Welsh cakes. Or *pice y ar maen*, as they're called in Welsh. That means 'cakes on a stone', because that's how they used to be cooked. We'll make ours on the Aga, though."

"I've learned some Welsh," Ava announced. "At school."

"Oh? What have you learned?"

Ava paused, screwing up her face again, and then said carefully, "*Alla... i... fynd...i'r... toiled!*" She smiled triumphantly, and Gwen let out a laugh.

"May I go to the toilet," she translated into English. "Very good."

"And I know how to say *amser cinio*," Ava told her, and Gwen nodded.

"Lunchtime."

"And *amser chw—chw—*" She paused, frowning, and Gwen filled in.

"*Amser chwarae*? Playtime."

"Yes!" Ava looked both surprised and impressed. "How do you know Welsh, Granny?"

"I learned it when I was little," Gwen told her. "I grew up not too far from here, about an hour north, where lots of people spoke Welsh all the time, back in the day. I spoke quite a bit of Welsh myself, when I was your age, but I've got out of practice."

"I can teach you," Ava offered seriously, and Gwen was both amused and touched by her granddaughter's offer.

"Why, thank you," she said. "That's very kind. You've learned quite a bit of Welsh in just a short amount of time. I'm very impressed."

It occurred to her, as she helped Ava to measure out flour and sugar, that she hadn't actually expected anything to ever change, to be able or even *allowed* to change. She realized, with an uncomfortable pang of guilt, that she'd assumed she and her son's family were all stuck in relational ruts, unable to move or grow or reach out to each other, and yet here she was with Ava, baking on a sunny afternoon, just as she'd once dreamed of—and they were even making Welsh cakes! She never could have imagined such a thing, and it felt like both a blessing and a miracle. She was so very thankful.

Ava scooped out a handful of raisins, clutching them in one chubby fist.

"Can I eat one?" she asked with a cheeky grin, and Gwen smiled.

"Of course you can."

She laughed as Ava crammed the whole handful of raisins into her mouth.

"Greedy goose!" she told her affectionately as she rumpled Ava's soft curls. "Save some for the cakes, or they won't be Welsh cakes at all, will they?"

"Hello?" a voice called from the hallway, and then Sarah appeared in the doorway of the kitchen, holding a casserole dish wrapped in foil. "Isn't this cozy?" she remarked as she surveyed Gwen with Ava. "Are you baking with Granny, Ava?"

"Welsh cakes," Ava said with triumph.

Sarah smiled, but Gwen thought her daughter looked a little discomfited by the pleasant scene, maybe because she hadn't expected it. Gwen knew Sarah had picked up on the tensions between her and Ellie.

"I've brought you dinner," Sarah announced, and Gwen wiped her floury hands on her apron.

"That's very kind, Sarah, but you didn't have to—"

"I was trying to be helpful," Sarah interjected in a slightly injured tone. "What with Matthew's arm—"

"It's not as if he does much cooking," Gwen teased as she took the casserole dish. "But thank you. It's very kind and thoughtful." She knew Sarah needed to feel needed. Sometimes she forgot, because her daughter was so quietly capable, seeming to need no one, and yet right now was a reminder that, like everyone else, Sarah had insecurities. "Ooh, shepherd's pie," she said as she peeked under the foil. She gave Ava, who was still munching her mouthful of raisins, a smile. "One of my absolute favorites."

"I thought it was," Sarah remarked, and then looked around the kitchen. "Where's Ellie?"

Gwen told her about the playdate, and her daughter raised her eyebrows.

"They're all settling in well, then? I've been meaning to ask Ellie over for a coffee, but it's hard to find the time."

"Well, I know how busy you are. I'm sure she'd appreciate it, though."

Sarah shrugged. "I saw her in the café with Emma Lanfer the other day. She seems to be quite busy herself."

Had Sarah been expecting to be Ellie's first, and maybe only, friend? Gwen wondered. If so, Sarah hadn't made much effort toward that end, but then perhaps neither had Ellie.

"Even so," she told Sarah. "It's got to be hard, very hard indeed, to move so far away from home. I'm sure Ellie could use all the friends she can find. You really should invite her over for a coffee. I'm sure she'd appreciate it." She turned back to Ava. "Ready to put the raisins in?"

Sarah watched silently from the doorway, her arms folded, her expression rather closed, as Gwen and Ava finished mixing the dough for the Welsh cakes.

"Can I flip them, Granny?" Ava asked as Gwen put them on the griddle pan on the Aga. "Can I? Can I?"

"Of course you can, if you're really careful. The pan will be hot, and you don't want to get burned."

Sarah continued to watch them for a moment. "I remember when you used to make these cakes with Mairi," she remarked after a moment, her voice turning soft.

"Yes, I did, didn't I?" It had been years ago now, back when Mairi had been Ava's age, and things had felt less busy, less fraught. Now that Mairi was a full-fledged teen, she didn't seem to have nearly as much time for baking with her granny, and Gwen understood that. Mostly.

"Granny, are they done?" Ava asked eagerly. "Can I flip them yet?"

"Yes, darling, you can flip them." Gwen was conscious of Sarah's thoughtful gaze as she helped Ava to flip the cakes, her hand guiding her granddaughter's smaller one.

"I did it!" Ava squealed, triumphant.

"Yes, you certainly did. Well done, Ava."

Bored with baking now, Ava scrambled off her chair and ran after Toby, who had lumbered up from his position in front of the Aga when the baking had started. The poor dog looked alarmed to see Ava bearing down on him with so much enthusiasm, and Gwen suppressed a smile. Ava loved Toby very, very much, and generally he was incredibly patient with her, but he was in his dotage and tired—much like she was!

"Why don't you let Toby out into the garden," she suggested to Ava, "and you can check on the chickens, as well."

With a smile, she watched Ava race outside, Toby trotting in her wake.

As she slid the Welsh cakes out of the pan and onto a baking rack to cool, Gwen glanced up at Sarah, who had a slight frown on her face. "Is everything all right, Sarah?" she asked.

"What?" Sarah came to herself with a jolt and then another little shrug. "Oh. Yes. Fine."

Gwen thought her daughter still looked discomfited, a bit... *sad*, even. "Why don't you bring Mairi and Owen over this weekend?" she suggested suddenly, warming to the idea as she spoke it. "We could have a movie night. I'll make popcorn, buy some fizzy drinks, the works. I'm sure all the children would like to spend time together, and it would be good for them. Fun, I mean."

"Perhaps..." Sarah sounded dubious, and Gwen wondered what was really going on. Something was clearly bothering her daughter, but she wasn't sure what it was, and she had a sense that Sarah might go all prickly if she tried to press. Before she could even think to, however, the front door was flung open, and Ben and Jess burst into the kitchen.

"I'm starving!" Ben groaned dramatically, flinging his bag and coat to the floor, before his gaze alighted on the cooling cakes. "Ooh, can I have one of those?"

"They've got raisins in—" Gwen began, a warning, but Ben shrugged, already reaching for one.

"I don't mind raisins, actually."

Oh, don't you? she thought, smiling, and then nodded at the cakes. "Go on, then. You can both have one." She turned to Ava who had come back into the kitchen at the sound of her siblings. "You too, Ava, since you helped to make them."

"I flipped them," Ava announced proudly, and somewhat to Gwen's surprise, Jess smiled at her younger sister.

"Good job, Ava," she said, and for once she didn't sound surly or bored.

"Cup of tea, everyone?" Gwen asked as she went to fill the kettle, a smile spreading over her face like butter on toast. This was how she'd always imagined it—a full kitchen, a full heart. "How was school, you two?"

"It was okay," Jess said, and she sounded as if she meant it. Okay was a lot better than what it had been, Gwen knew, when Jess had come into the house like a whirling dervish, stomping through the kitchen and slamming the door upstairs, all with a face like thunder.

"I've joined the Minecraft Club," Ben announced. "It's pretty cool."

"Granny, these cakes are delicious," Ava pronounced solemnly. "I really do like raisins. I never knew I did, but I *do!*"

"It's always good to try new things, isn't it?" Gwen said in agreement. She plonked the kettle on the stove before turning to her daughter, who was still standing in the doorway. "Sarah? Cup of tea?"

Sarah was regarding the whole happy scene—the cooling cakes, the scattering of flour on the worktop, the heap of rucksacks and lunch bags piled on the floor and the children all sprawled around the table—with a slightly strange look on her face. Gwen could not interpret it at all. Then she turned to Gwen with a quick, bright smile that didn't quite reach her eyes.

"No, no, I really must be off. I've got to collect Mairi from her swimming lesson and Owen has a science project... there's always so much to do and it's such a busy time of year, isn't it?" She directed another one of her bright smiles to the children.

"See you lot later, all right? We'll have to do something together soon."

"All right, Aunt Sarah," they answered dutifully, and, Gwen thought, without much enthusiasm.

"What about that movie night?" Gwen pressed as she followed Sarah to the front door. "Get all the children together...?"

"Oh, I don't know," Sarah said as she buttoned her coat. It had started tipping it down, the golden autumn sunshine replaced by classic Welsh rain. "It's a nice thought, but..."

She let that sentence trail away and Gwen put her hands on her hips. "But what?" she asked, deciding her daughter needed to be challenged, and Sarah shrugged.

"We'll see," she replied, and then she was out the door, heading through the rain toward her car before she reversed down the lane.

Gwen watched her daughter drive away with a troubled frown. What exactly was bothering Sarah? Something was troubling her clearly, and Gwen knew she'd have to try to get to the bottom of it eventually.

She headed back to the children with a determined smile. It was so lovely to think of something other than her own health, or lack of it. To have children to care for, a busy life to lead, a kitchen full of baking and laughter. Maybe all they'd needed was a little time to get used to each other. The thought was incredibly encouraging, and it buoyed her heart.

"Right," she said briskly as she began to spoon tea into the pot. "Who wants sugar in their tea?" she asked, and smiled as everyone sang out, "Me!"

CHAPTER 20

ELLIE

"They've had a fab time," Emma assured Ellie as she stepped into the hallway of a smart brick house on Llandrigg's new estate on the opposite end of the village from Bluebell Inn. "Barely made a peep, to be honest. They've set up an entire Lego universe in the playroom. Come through."

Ellie followed Emma through a modern but comfortably messy kitchen, to a sunroom built out the back with squashy sofas and a truckload of Lego scattered across the floor. Her heart lightened to see Josh lying on his stomach on the floor, Zach next to him, heads bent together. Lego blocks were everywhere.

"You've had a good time, Josh?" she asked lightly, and her son grunted in response, too involved in his elaborate creation even to look up.

"They've been like that for hours," Emma said with a laugh. "Like two peas in a pod, they are."

"Yes, they really are." It filled Ellie with relief, to see it. She'd been worried about Josh, concerned about how quiet and withdrawn he sometimes seemed. She knew it took him a while to get used to things, but it was hard to know if he was happy or not. But here he was with a true kindred spirit. Now if only Jess could find a friend...

"Fancy a coffee?" Emma asked as she turned back to the kitchen. "We can leave them to it for a bit longer if you're not in a rush?"

"Oh..." Ellie knew she'd like nothing better than a coffee and a chat with her own kindred spirit, but she was worried about leaving Gwen alone with the others. Although, she acknowledged, Matthew was home as well, even if he seemed to be keeping to himself since he'd broken his arm, too tired or sore to make much of an effort about anything. Maybe an afternoon with his own children would be good for him.

"A quick one would be wonderful," she said, and Emma smiled and reached for the kettle.

Ellie slid onto a stool at the breakfast bar, a sigh escaping her without her even meaning it to.

Emma turned around, kettle in hand, one eyebrow arched. "Tough day?"

"No, not particularly." It hadn't been, not really. At least, not more than most days lately. Jess had slunk to school in a mood; Josh had clung to her. Ben, at least, seemed to be doing okay, and while Ava could be a bit clingy, she was getting better. All in all, progress was being made; this play date was surely the evidence of that.

After Ellie had dropped the kids off that morning, she'd headed back home; Gwen had disappeared upstairs and she realized she'd actually been looking forward to a bit of a chat with her mother-in-law—more progress! She'd ended up tidying the kitchen by herself before going to see what Matthew was up to. He'd been lying in the bedroom, scrolling on his phone, and when she'd tried to engage him in some conversation, he'd been distracted, as monosyllabic as Ben often was, and he'd told her his arm was aching as a way, Ellie suspected, to end the conversation.

She'd tried not to feel hurt, but she wondered why she seemed to be seeing even less of her husband when he *wasn't* busy. There he was, simply sitting around the house, and he seemed to have even less time for either her or the children. Ellie was doing her best not to get aggravated about it, but she feared she was failing, or at least starting to fail. They'd only been in Llandrigg for two weeks, and she knew she had to give the settling-in process more time for all of them—but what about her marriage? Did she need to be patient with that, as well?

"Do you want to talk about it?" Emma asked, and Ellie realized she'd been silent, staring into space, for at least a minute. The kettle had already started to boil.

"Oh, I don't know," she managed with a little laugh. "Moving—upheaving your whole life—well, it shows all the cracks, doesn't it? The cracks that were already there." Surely this wouldn't be happening with her and Matthew if there hadn't been something wrong at the start—a thought that was deeply unsettling.

Emma cocked her head, regarding her thoughtfully as she poured the water into the cafetière. "What cracks would those be?"

"Well, relationship ones, I guess." Ellie tried for another laugh, but this time she didn't quite manage it. She wasn't sure she wanted to talk to her new friend about the fault lines in her marriage; it didn't feel fair to either Emma or Matthew. And yet, she realized, she wanted—*needed*—to talk to someone about it, and the only other options were Gwen or Sarah. She definitely didn't know Sarah well enough yet, and as for Gwen... well, that relationship wasn't there yet, and Ellie wasn't sure Gwen would want to hear any implied criticism of her son.

"Husband?" Emma guessed shrewdly as she handed Ellie a cup of coffee. "Moving can be hard on a marriage."

"Can it? I don't think I realized." Ellie took a sip of her coffee. "Thanks for this."

"Well, it puts strain on it, doesn't it? He's stressed about a new job, you're stressed about your children making friends, *you* making friends..."

"*Yes*," Ellie said with feeling, so grateful Emma got it. "Yes. But Matthew—my husband—doesn't even have a job, at least not like that. We moved here for him to help my mother-in-law renovate the bed and breakfast business."

"Maybe that's part of the problem, then?" Emma suggested. "If he's used to feeling busy, at an office?"

"Maybe..." Ellie replied slowly.

Matthew had been unemployed for six months before they moved, and the same issues had been going on then. Was this not so much related to moving to Wales, as to Matthew losing his job, feeling useless? She recalled how he'd said he'd felt useful, tearing out those sinks, and she knew he'd needed that. But she hadn't expected him to keep this distance from her. They needed to talk about it, she decided. Properly. Although when they'd get a chance was another matter...

"Anyway, enough about me," Ellie said, conscious of how much she seemed to complain. "Tell me about what's going on with you. Have you thought any more about going back into event planning?"

"Well." Emma grimaced. "I'm not sure how many events are needed, around here. I'd have to go further afield, I think, to find some work."

"When Bluebell Inn opens again, maybe we could plan something," Ellie suggested. "Although, based on our progress so far, I don't know when that will be!"

Emma's face lit up. "That would be brilliant," she said, "if you're serious. I've always loved that old place. I hope you're able to keep its character, even with the renovations."

"Well..." Ellie thought of Matthew's plans for marble bathrooms and other high-end luxuries. "I hope so," she told Emma with a smile. She had a feeling Gwen hoped so, as well. Ellie glanced at the clock above the stove and realized it was later than she'd thought. "I should probably go," she told Emma reluctantly, for part of her wanted to stay in this cozy kitchen and keep chatting with a friend. "Next time, you'll have to tell me more about what's going on with *you*. I feel like I'm the one having a moan all the time."

"Moan away," Emma replied cheerfully. "I don't mind."

"I'll try to stop," Ellie replied as she slid off the stool. "For my sake as well as yours." She walked back into the sunroom, where Josh and Zach were still happily immersed in their massive Lego creation. "Come on, Josh," she said as she stooped down to touch him on the shoulder. "I'm afraid we need to go. It's getting late, and Granny will be wondering where we are." After a second's pause, she added quickly, "Daddy, too." She turned to Emma, who clearly hadn't missed that little exchange. "Maybe we could have Zach over sometime? Return the favor...?"

Emma smiled easily. "That would be brilliant."

Ellie hoped Gwen wouldn't mind an extra person adding to the general chaos. She still sometimes felt as if she had to tiptoe around her mother-in-law, although she wondered sometimes if that was more in her head than Gwen's. Things had started to feel as if they were getting better... until Gwen had become distracted, a bit distant. She really needed to ask her mother-in-law what was going on, for both their sakes.

"Thanks for having him!" she smiled at Emma as they left, and then she and Josh were walking back through Llandrigg in the evening sun which turned everything golden. Really, it was a beautiful place, Ellie thought as they passed the village green, with the church and terraced cottages, the rolling hills in the distance a stunning backdrop to the quaintness. Ellie stood still for a moment, simply drinking it all in, grateful for the beauty of the place, and grateful even that she *was* grateful, because she knew she wasn't often enough.

"Look at those clouds, Mom," Josh said, tugging on her sleeve, and Ellie noticed the billowing purple clouds that had gathered on the horizon. "Do you think it's going to rain?"

The blue sky was, Ellie saw, rapidly fading as the clouds scudded across the sky. Well, at least she'd enjoyed it while it had lasted, she thought as the first fat drops splattered on the sidewalk in front of them, and grabbing Josh's hand, she started to run.

They were laughing and wet by the time they made it back to Bluebell Inn, shucking off their soaked coats before coming into the kitchen, where everyone was gathered around the table, Toby sprawled underneath, drinking tea and eating, of all things, Welsh cakes.

"Sarah brought dinner," Gwen told Ellie with a smile, as it was her night to cook. "I've already popped it in the Aga."

"Oh... wow. That was kind of her."

And it *was*, although, in truth, Ellie didn't know how she felt about it. She'd barely seen Sarah since they'd arrived; admittedly, Sarah lived in the next village over and her children were at the comprehensive in Abergavenny, so there wasn't much chance to run into her, but still. It would have been nice to get to know her a bit more. She'd hoped to call her sister-in-law a friend, but she still felt like more of a stranger.

Ellie glanced down at her children, all seeming quite contented as they munched on their cakes. It seemed as if they liked raisins, after all. "Well, I don't suppose anyone's going to need to eat anything soon, anyway," she said with a smile. "These cakes look delicious."

"Me and Granny made them!" Ava piped up, looking proudly delighted. "Do you want one, Mummy?"

Mummy, not *Mommy*. Already, Ava was changing; they all were. It was inevitable, and a good thing, but it still gave her a funny little pang, to hear them sounding so British. So Welsh, even.

"I'd love one, Ava," she told her youngest, and she took one from the baking tray, nibbling it. Her children might now like raisins, but she still didn't, not that she was going to admit as much now, or ever. "Where's Dad?"

"In the sitting room," Gwen said. "He came in to say hello to everyone, but I think he's feeling a bit tired."

And a bit out of sorts, Ellie suspected.

"How's your day been?" she asked Gwen, and her mother-in-law gave her a surprisingly sweet and sudden smile.

"It's been rather nice, actually. Ava and I did some baking, as you can see—"

"The Welsh cakes!" Ava chimed in. "I flipped them, too."

"Yes, and everyone has decided they like them with raisins, after all."

Ellie knew there wasn't any sting in her mother-in-law's words, but she felt it all the same. She was the one who had said they wouldn't like them, admittedly and understandably because they never had before. But maybe she'd been too quick to assume, to judge. She should have given those cakes a chance, she thought wryly, and her children and mother-in-law, too.

"I'm glad," she said, and meant it.

Finished with their snack, the children drifted off, still seeming happy enough, and Ellie and Gwen were alone in the kitchen. Gwen had started tidying up, and Ellie began to load the dishwasher with cups, both of them working in companionable silence until Gwen noticed what she was doing.

"Actually, those have to be handwashed," Gwen said, biting her lip. "Sorry, I know it's a bit of a faff..." She ducked her head in obvious apology.

"No, no, *I'm* the one who is sorry." Hurriedly, Ellie took the cups out of the dishwasher; they were porcelain, with a gold rim. She should have realized they weren't dishwasher safe. "I'm still feeling my way around here," she confessed.

"I know you are." To Ellie's surprise, Gwen put a hand on her arm. "I know this can't be easy, Ellie. I'm sorry if I make things difficult. I probably do. In fact, I'm sure I do. I don't mean to, but I suppose I'm not used to sharing my space, and I'm afraid I put my foot in it more often than not. But I am pleased you're all here, truly. And I'm sorry. For... for all the times it seems as if I'm not."

"Oh, Gwen..." Ellie was incredibly touched by her mother-in-law's unexpected emotional outburst. "That's so very kind of you to say, but you don't make things difficult, honestly." As she said it, she realized she actually meant it; her mother-in-law hadn't done anything wrong; Ellie had just been so touchy all the time. "If anyone is making things difficult," Ellie confessed with a grimace, "I'm sure it's me. I just feel like I don't know how to *be* sometimes. Here, I mean." With Gwen, with Matthew, with her own children. She'd thought she'd known how much she'd be giving up in moving to Wales, but she hadn't realized she'd feel as if she'd lost *herself* along the way. "And that," she told Gwen, "has nothing to do with you."

"That's understandable," Gwen said quietly. "About not knowing how to be, I mean. It's such a big change for you. A lot to get used to, as well as helping the children to adjust, too, and with the added stress of Matthew breaking his arm..." She smiled, shaking her head slowly. "I don't know if I could do it, to be honest, Ellie. I... I admire you."

"Thank you." Ellie thought this was the most honest conversation, as well as the most encouraging, that she'd ever had with her mother-in-law. Maybe she'd misjudged Gwen all these years. She felt as if her mother-in-law understood far more than she'd ever given her credit for. "Growing pains, I guess," she said with a crooked smile. "For all of us, Matthew included." Ellie thought of how she'd wanted someone to talk to. Was it

Gwen, after all? "I'm trying to be patient with him," she confessed in a low voice, "but I'm afraid I don't feel very patient. He seems very... very sorry for himself right now." Belatedly, she realized she was talking about this woman's *son*. What if Gwen turned defensive? She might have ruined their fragile friendship before it had even truly begun.

"You're right, he is," Gwen replied matter-of-factly, and Ellie had to suppress a sudden laugh of surprise. "I gave him a talking-to about it, actually, and I was hoping he'd speak to you. He's finding this all hard, but it's coming across as self-pity, which, as you've rightly implied, is not a very attractive quality. But I should probably leave it there, as I don't want to interfere." Gwen gave a little sigh. "You *are* being patient, Ellie, and I hope Matthew works up the nerve to talk honestly with you. Give him a bit more time."

"Thank you," Ellie said quietly. She felt even more encouraged, and grateful for Gwen's involvement. She could wait a little while longer, she decided. Hopefully, Matthew would decide for himself when he was ready to talk. She gestured to the teacups by the sink. "Shall I wash these?"

"Yes," Gwen replied with a smile, "and I can dry."

They worked in companionable silence for a few moments; from upstairs, they heard a few thumps, followed by laughter. Gwen smiled at the sound, glancing at Ellie, who smiled back.

"It's nice to feel this house is properly lived in again," Gwen said. "It's been just me for so long, with only guests for company, and they're not the same as family."

"No. I don't suppose they are." Ellie paused, feeling the need to say something more, continue their newfound honesty and sharing. "I do hope we're not too much trouble, Gwen. This is an adjustment for you too, I know, in a different way, but a challenging one all the same. I don't know if I could have a family of six invading my space so thoroughly!"

"Yes, it is an adjustment," Gwen allowed, "but I'm so glad to have you here. Truly." She bit her lip, and Ellie saw how troubled she looked for a second, before she forced a smile to her lips.

"Is everything all right?" Ellie asked impulsively. She'd been meaning to figure out why Gwen had been distracted, but she'd never dared to ask so openly. Now, considering the strides they'd just made, she would. "Is there something worrying you?"

Gwen jerked a little, as if startled, and Ellie felt a tender concern for this woman who had given them so much.

"Gwen...?" she prompted, her voice gentle. "You can tell me, that is... if you want to." Although she had no idea what her mother-in-law might say.

Gwen took a steadying breath and then laid down the damp dish towel, folding it carefully over the railing of the Aga, her gaze lowered. She squared her shoulders as if she had to steel herself for whatever was next and Ellie waited, her heart lurching with trepidation as she wondered just what was going on.

"Actually," Gwen began carefully as she lifted her head and looked directly at Ellie, "everything isn't all right. I've been trying to find a way to tell everyone, but the truth is I've been too scared. I was going to speak to Matthew or Sarah, but I've never managed to find a moment. I should have, though. I should have made the time, but I didn't."

Ellie's heart felt as if it were suspended in her chest. Gwen sounded so very serious! What on earth could be going on? "What is it, Gwen?" she asked, bracing herself for whatever news her mother-in-law needed to impart.

"I need to tell you what's going on." Gwen nodded slowly, her expression resigned, a shadow of fear in her eyes that alarmed Ellie all the more. "I'm sorry I haven't before, and I'm afraid it's something quite serious."

CHAPTER 21

ELLIE

Something quite serious.

Gwen's sober words echoed through Ellie's mind as she stood and stared at her mother-in-law fearfully, a dripping dish-cloth in one hand. What could it possibly be?

"Of course," she finally managed to say when Gwen just continued to look at her with such sorrow. Ellie tossed the cloth into the sink, where it landed with a wet thud. "Anything, Gwen, of course. Should I... should I get Matt?"

"No, no, not just yet." Gwen gave a trembling little laugh, one hand pressed to her cheek. "I'll need to tell him and Sarah too, of course, but right now I think I can only manage one person."

And that one person was *her*? Ellie's stomach swooped at the thought of whatever Gwen was going to tell her, as well as the responsibility of being the one to hear it first and to respond. She and Gwen had made some personal strides in their rather fraught relationship this afternoon, but she didn't know if she was ready for this... whatever this was. But it seemed Gwen wanted to tell her, and that, she told herself, was a privilege.

"Of course," she said again. She gestured to the table. "Shall we... shall we sit down?"

Gwen nodded and they both sat at the big table in the center of the room. Outside, the rain had stopped and twilight was falling, the sky darkening to violet as the last of the watery sunlight streamed through the windows. Toby trotted in and, with an audible groan, lay himself down in front of the Aga. From upstairs, a few more thuds sounded, followed, thankfully, by more laughter, and then Ellie heard Matthew calling, "What's going on up there?"

She tensed, afraid he was annoyed by the noise, but then she heard his own answering laughter as he headed upstairs, and she relaxed, relieved by the little exchange, before turning back to Gwen and seeing how worried and sad she looked.

"What do you need to tell me, Gwen?" she asked gently.

Gwen sat very still, her hands folded on the table in front of her, her expression turning composed, or perhaps just resolute. What on earth was she going to say? Ellie couldn't even bear to think.

"I don't know where to begin," Gwen finally said after a moment, managing a shaky laugh. "So, I suppose I might as well just come out and say it. I... I have... *cancer*. Breast cancer. I found out last week."

"Oh, Gwen." Ellie's stomach swooped again as she gazed at her mother-in-law in sorrowful dismay. Based on everything Gwen had—and hadn't—said in the last few minutes, she realized she'd suspected something like this, but it still came as a terrible shock. Tentatively, she reached out to touch Gwen's hand, and to her surprise and gratification, Gwen gripped it tightly for a second before she released it, smiling almost in apology. "I'm so, so sorry," Ellie said quietly.

Gwen nodded, her expression now definitely resolute, her lips set in a line, her hands folded together once more. "I put off doing or thinking about it for too long, I know. I made the appointment, but then I didn't call them back... it just felt easier to pretend it wasn't happening, especially with so much else going on." She shook her head wearily. "Oh, it doesn't matter now, the whys and whats of it all." She shrugged as a sigh escaped her. "But there's no putting it off now. I start chemotherapy next week."

Ellie swallowed, trying to feel for the right words. "That's good, then," she said finally. "Starting treatment is always good."

"Yes, although the side effects of chemotherapy all sound rather dreadful, from what I've read." Gwen offered her a watery smile. "I'm certainly not looking forward to that. But, yes. It's a necessary step forward." She glanced down at her folded hands. "I know I should have told you before. And Matthew and Sarah."

"Don't worry about that," Ellie assured her. She felt a surge of sympathy for her mother-in-law, struggling with such news on her own. No wonder she'd seemed so distracted! "It doesn't matter now," she told her. "Have they said..." She paused, wondering how to ask a question about something so delicate, so dangerous. "Do you know what stage the cancer is? The prognosis...?" she finally managed, her voice hesitant, unsure if she should be asking that already.

Gwen shrugged again. "Early stage three, they said, so it could be better, but it also could be worse." She lifted her chin a notch. "As for a prognosis, I don't really know. The consultants can never make any promises, can they, but she sounded... somewhat optimistic?" She sighed. "At least, I think she did. But the truth is, I was in such a state of shock, I'm not sure I even took in all that she was saying."

"Oh, Gwen, I wish you'd told us," Ellie exclaimed, before adding quickly, "for your sake, I mean. Someone could have come with you, supported you through it, listened when you weren't able to..." She couldn't imagine going through it alone the way Gwen had.

"I know." Gwen smiled sadly. "But I've never liked any fuss, and somehow, with you moving here, and then Matt's broken arm and all the palaver about the house, I never found the right moment. I don't suppose I wanted to, really, and that's my fault, not yours."

"Well, I'm very glad you've told me now." There was no point taking Gwen to task for keeping this to herself, and the last thing Ellie wanted to do was make her mother-in-law feel any worse. "And, of course, you must tell Matt and Sarah when you're ready. I'm sure Sarah will want to go with you to your appointments." In fact, Ellie thought Sarah might insist on it, judging from what she knew of her sister-in-law. "But if there's any way I can help..." she added, although she couldn't imagine Gwen wanting her to accompany her. Still, she wanted to help her mother-in-law in whatever way she could.

"Yes, I suspect Sarah will." Gwen sighed, not sounding entirely pleased by the prospect. "The thing is," she said after a moment, "I don't want to be treated like a patient, or a child. I've managed this B&B on my own for years, and I can manage this. I don't need to be... to be *coddled* or treated like I've lost some of my marbles, simply because I've become a bit ill."

"There's no shame or weakness in wanting a bit of support through a tricky time," Ellie protested, but she knew what her mother-in-law meant. Sarah, she acknowledged, sometimes even made *her* feel like a child, and an unruly one at that. She hadn't realized Gwen might have the same response to her own daughter.

"I suppose I'm just not used to it," Gwen confessed with another sigh. "And I don't like the thought of being weak, help-less." She grimaced. "But I do recognize that I'll need help, if not now, then certainly later, if the side effects are what they say on the tin. It doesn't sound very nice at all."

"No," Ellie agreed, because there was nothing more she could say to that. She gazed at Gwen, who seemed so small somehow, her shoulders hunched, her face looking more care-worn than Ellie had ever seen it, and her heart squeezed hard with both love and concern. "Oh Gwen," she said impulsively, reaching for her hands once more, glad when Gwen took them. "I really am so sorry about this. And I don't know whether having us lot here makes it better or worse for you, but I'm glad we are, so we can help you. I do want to help you, truly. I just hope we're not too much trouble."

"Of course you're not," Gwen replied quickly, squeezing her hands, and Ellie couldn't keep from raising her eyebrows and giving her a wryly skeptical smile.

"Are you sure about that?" she teased gently. "Because I know we're terribly loud, and Ben alone is enough to give *me* a permanent headache, and Josh leaves his Lego everywhere, and Jess seems to be in a permanently bad mood—"

"It's fine," Gwen said, smiling as she patted Ellie's hands before she released them. "It's absolutely fine. They're settling in, and every day is easier, for all of us. And it really does feel wonderful, to have the house full again, the way it used to be. Grandchildren are different than guests."

"They're untidier, they eat more, and I doubt you've ever had any guests as loud as us," Ellie quipped, although she realized she was at least halfway serious.

Gwen gave a small laugh as she acknowledged the truth of it with a nod. "I suppose that's probably true."

Clumsily, wanting to hug her but unsure if her mother-in-law would welcome the contact, Ellie reached over and put her arms around her. "Thank you for telling me, anyway," she said. "I know that can't have been easy."

"Thank you for listening," Gwen replied, hugging her back, her voice choking just a little.

They hugged for another second before they both eased back, smiling self-consciously. Ellie was incredibly touched that of all the people Gwen could have told first, she'd chosen her. Maybe it had been more due to circumstance than anything else, but she was humbled, all the same. She wanted to make sure she did support Gwen as best as she could, and not just say she would. Already, though, she suspected her mother-in-law would chafe against being mollycoddled, as she'd said herself.

Before either of them could say any more, another thud, louder than before, sounded from upstairs, and this time it wasn't followed by laughter.

With a sigh, Ellie rose from the table. "I'd better go see to all that commotion," she noted, and Gwen nodded. "Do you want me to mention something to Matt?" she asked tentatively. "Or would you rather do it yourself?"

"Oh..." Gwen's voice wavered. "I'd better do it myself," she decided. "But thank you, Ellie. You really have been so kind."

Ellie smiled and nodded. She really did hope this was the new beginning they'd both needed, even if it had taken such terrible news to bring it about. She was glad Gwen's consultant was optimistic... maybe this really would be a new beginning, for everyone.

Upstairs, Josh was tearful, Ben mutinous, and Jess had blocked them all out by closing the door of her bedroom.

"Ben hit Josh, Mummy," Ava said with something like triumph.

A wave of weariness crashed over Ellie as she looked around the boys' bedroom, which was more of a mess than usual—a jumble of clothes, Lego, and Pokémon cards. Josh, although sniffling, didn't seem hurt, and Ben was scowling, seeming restless and bored.

"Where's Dad?" she asked, because she'd thought she'd heard Matthew coming upstairs to join the children while she'd been talking to Gwen.

"He went downstairs a while ago," Ben grumbled. "He's so boring now. He won't kick a ball around, even though it's his arm that's hurt, not his leg." He kicked the bureau's leg as if for emphasis, and Ellie's heart ached for him.

"I know it's hard, Ben," she said gently, "but Dad can't do any rough and tumble because he's got to keep his arm immobile."

"I know, but I'm *bored*."

"Then maybe you could do something helpful?" Ellie replied, her voice rising a little. "Why don't you go outside and collect the eggs from Granny's chickens? I don't think anyone's checked on them today. Josh can help you, and if there's any more scrapping, there won't be any dessert after dinner tonight, or tomorrow night." She folded her arms, giving her eldest son a gimlet stare. Too often, due to weariness, her parenting descended into nothing more than crisis management. She wanted to be proactive... in all sorts of ways. And it would be better for Ben and Josh to get outside, do something useful. Life didn't have to resemble an amusement park, after all. "Well, Ben?" she asked. "Josh? Are you going to hop to it?"

"Can I come?" Ava asked eagerly. "I like collecting eggs."

"Yes, you can." She gave Ben another quelling look. "Look after your sister, as well."

"Why do I—?"

"I mean it, Ben."

Once they'd trooped downstairs and outside, Ellie decided to go find her errant husband. Or not errant, she told herself as she came to stand in the doorway of their bedroom, but struggling, as Gwen had told her. She needed to remember that.

Matthew was sitting in an armchair by the window, his plastered arm resting gingerly on the armrest, his moody gaze on the distant hills, their peaks already lost in darkness.

"How are you doing?" Ellie asked quietly. She came into the room and closed the door behind her.

Matthew shrugged. "The same, I suppose."

"This is hard, I know."

He gave a restive sigh. "There's nothing all that hard about sitting around watching TV all day."

"For you, there is," Ellie returned gently. "You have always been a doer, Matt."

"Well, I'm not now, am I?" he replied, and she had to bite her tongue to keep from telling him not to feel so sorry for himself.

She knew this had all been challenging for her husband—being made redundant, almost losing their house, and now this latest setback—but she hadn't acted like it, Ellie knew. The truth was, she'd struggled with her own resentment at Matthew's setbacks, and that wasn't really fair.

"No, you're not," she agreed. "Not right now. But it won't last forever, and we can handle a few weeks off, can't we? Besides, you could still be involved with the architectural plans and things. Maybe we can see the silver lining, that this gives you time to get a proper business plan in place."

"Maybe..." Matthew replied, sounding both unconvinced and unenthused.

And just like that, in the space of a few seconds, Ellie's resolution to be patient and understanding went right out the window. "Matt, it's not the end of the world," she insisted. "And meanwhile there are four children who still need you. Ben misses playing football with you—"

"I'm still here, Ellie," he replied, an irritable edge to his voice. "I read Ava three stories before bed last night. I watched Ben play some alien-shooting game. I did a puzzle with Josh, and I tried to talk to Jess, but she wasn't having it. I know I can't do the active stuff, but I am *trying*, even if it's not enough for you."

Ellie suppressed a sigh. She didn't really need the laundry list of how her husband had shown he was a good father. She needed him present, emotionally as well as physically, in a way that she knew he wasn't, no matter how much he said he was.

But she wasn't sure how to explain that without getting his back up even more, and that was something she definitely didn't want right now.

"I know you're doing stuff," she said carefully. "And I appreciate it, truly. But sometimes it feels like you've checked out a bit... mentally, I mean. From us."

He rolled his eyes. "Wow, thanks."

"*Matthew*." Ellie couldn't hide the hurt from her voice. "We're on the same team, you know?" she reminded him quietly. "We're in this together. I want to help you. I want to make this work... for all of us."

"And all the while you're counting the days until you can reasonably suggest we move back to Connecticut," he finished with something of a sneer.

"What?" Ellie jerked back. "That's not true."

Not exactly, anyway. She knew there was a kernel of unfortunate truth to her husband's words, but no more, and she *was* trying... just as he'd said he was. So why were they still at odds with one another? Did their marriage only work when life was easy and untroubled? She never would have said so before, but that was when life *had* been easy and untroubled. This was hard... and they were making it even harder on themselves.

Matthew sighed and rubbed his face with his good arm. "I'm sorry, Ellie. I'm being a jerk, I know I am. My arm really hurts and I'm... I'm mad at myself, for getting into this situation in the first place. I shouldn't take it out on you, though. I know that."

"You can't help breaking your arm—" she began, but Matthew shook his head, his expression turning grimly obdurate.

"I don't mean that."

They were both silent, while Ellie tried to think of how to reply. Before she could, Matthew continued in a low voice, not looking at her.

"I mean... losing my job. Almost losing the house. Not being able to provide for you or the kids. Making us move. I've failed on a lot of fronts, as a father and a husband."

Ellie's heart ached to hear him being so honest. She'd known he'd struggled, but she hadn't realized quite how much. "These things happen, Matt," she said gently. "They weren't your fault. And we both chose to move, to help your mom. Because it felt right." And it certainly had been the right decision, considering Gwen's diagnosis. Not that she could tell her husband about that now; it was Gwen's to share, not hers.

He glanced at her, a painful honesty lighting his eyes. "Do you really believe any of that?" he asked.

"What..." She released the word in a shocked breath. His voice had been too matter-of-fact to be an accusation, and yet it had felt like that. "What do you mean?"

"It's just, you haven't always acted like it."

Slowly, Ellie lowered herself onto the edge of the bed, her mind reeling. All right, yes, she'd struggled not to feel resentful sometimes, it was true, but she hadn't thought that Matthew believed she blamed him for it all, because she didn't. Did she?

"You're not going to say anything?" Matthew asked with a twisted smile.

"I don't know what to say," Ellie admitted painfully. "It's been hard for me, too, and maybe I've felt that you haven't always realized that."

"I knew you blamed me—"

"I'm trying to be honest," she burst out. "Like you've been honest with me. I love you, Matthew, and I want to support you —in your job, in this move, emotionally, whatever it takes." She felt tears crowd her eyes and she blinked them back. "But it's been hard, especially when I haven't always felt like *you've* been supporting *me*."

"What—"

"I've had to watch my words, my attitude," Ellie continued

stubbornly, determined to get it all out now, since he had. At least, she hoped he had. If there was more, she wasn't sure she could take it. "Anything remotely negative is always taken as some sort of personal criticism. You haven't really appreciated how difficult I find trading suburban Connecticut for this tiny village in Wales, just dismissing my concerns about convenience and familiarity and, yes, having a darn Starbucks within thirty miles!" She let out a laugh that sounded more like a sob. "And, yes, I *know* we both agreed to this, and I *want* to give it a real, hundred percent try, but... it's hard. Really hard. It's been hard for you, and it's been hard for me. And maybe we just both need to realize that." A sigh escaped her, a gust of sorrow. "I know there are times when I could have acted better, been more understanding, but I guess I want you to acknowledge that it's a two-way street."

Matthew stared at her, his face expressionless, and Ellie tensed, anticipating another emotional shutdown. They hadn't talked this honestly since he'd first been made redundant, and she'd vacillated between being bracingly cheerful and not saying anything at all, because he hadn't seemed to want her to. She could mark the beginning of their alienation from each other from that point, but she'd pretended to herself that it was nothing more than a blip, if that. Judging by his stony expression now, however, maybe honesty was overrated.

"Matthew...?" she finally ventured, her tone hesitant, cautious, as she braced herself for another round of accusations and arguments.

Then his expression collapsed in on itself as he shook his head, tears gleaming in his eyes. She felt both relieved and sadder than ever, simply by how sorry he looked. "I'm sorry, Ellie," he said in a low voice. "I know it's been hard for you. Harder, maybe, than it's been for me."

"It's not a competition," she said gently.

"I know." He sighed, rubbing his good hand over his face.

"Although maybe I've tried to make it one. I know I've been feeling sorry for myself. Mum told me as much. It's not a good look on anyone, especially not your husband. I think my arm was the last straw. One thing after another, one failure after another..." He blew out a breath. "And now I can't even bear to look at the renovation plans, because I'm not sure what the point of it all is."

"Oh, Matthew." Ellie rose from the bed and went to put her arms around him. After a second's resistance, her husband accepted—and thankfully returned—her embrace, leaning into her and closing her eyes. "I'm glad you've told me all that," she said. "And I'm sorry we haven't talked more openly about this before now. But there is a point to the renovations, to being here. I know there is." She thought of what Gwen had just told her. "Especially now."

He pulled away a little to look at her. "Especially now?"

"You need to talk to your mom about that," Ellie told him. "But I'm glad we've talked. And I'm sorry I haven't been more understanding and patient."

"I know I've been the same."

"But now... this can be a fresh start—not just for our life in Wales, but for *us*." She smiled at him, feeling strangely shy, considering they'd been married for over fifteen years. "Can't it?"

Matthew smiled then, properly, in a way he hadn't in a long time, and pulled her toward him with his good arm, so she was tucked into his chest. "Yes," he said firmly. "It can."

He kissed the top of her head as Ellie closed her eyes with a rush of relief and gratitude.

"Now," he asked as he settled himself back in his chair, "what's this about my mum?"

CHAPTER 22

GWEN

Gwen perched on the edge of a plastic chair, every muscle tense even though she was doing her best to relax. Next to her, Sarah was sitting up straight, looking very officious and alert.

Since Gwen had told both Matthew and Sarah about her cancer diagnosis last week—a painful conversation for all parties —her daughter, bless her, had been doing her best to become Llandrigg's official cancer expert. She'd printed out several articles she'd found on the internet, and taken two books from the library, and pointed Gwen to countless blogs—everything from 'Cooking to Be Cancer-Free' to 'Daily Mindful Meditations' for cancer sufferers. Gwen was starting to feel as if she was nothing *but* the cancer, a blob of bad cells, which was exactly what she'd been worried about, but she knew she couldn't explain that to Sarah. Her daughter was only trying to help, in the way she knew best—by *doing*.

Sarah had always liked to be in control, Gwen knew, even when she'd been a little girl. She'd made schedules and organized her toys in soldier-like rows and run playdates like military meetings. Matthew, in his own way, liked to be just as active, but he was laidback when it came to making decisions.

Maybe too laidback, Gwen reflected, or at least uncommunica-
tive. She was glad Ellie had shared about the tension between
her and Matthew, but Gwen hoped that was being resolved.

When she'd told Matthew and Sarah about her cancer, Ellie
had sat next to Matthew and held his hand. Gwen had seen him
squeeze her fingers, and she'd been heartened by this show of
solidarity between them. Maybe things were already changing,
getting better.

As for Sarah... that was a little trickier. When David had
died, she'd wanted to arrange the funeral, give the eulogy, and
pick both the flowers and hymns. Gwen had let her do most of
it, because she knew that was how Sarah handled her grief and
she'd felt too wrung out to fight her or do those things herself,
but she wasn't sure she could deal with that level of interference
this time around. This was her life—her cancer, even—and she
wanted to be the one making the decisions. She hadn't quite
been able to articulate that to Sarah yet, though.

"I think you should be seen soon," Sarah said tetchily. "That
lady over there came in after us and she's just been called in.
Perhaps I should have a word with the nurse—?" She half-rose
from her seat and Gwen stayed her with her hand.

"Sarah, there's no need. They'll call me when they're ready,
and to be perfectly honest, I'm happy to wait. It will all come
soon enough." She gave her daughter a wan smile that Sarah
didn't return. "Please don't fuss."

"I'm not fussing," Sarah replied as she sat down with a
harrumph. "I just want to know what's going on."

Gwen suppressed a sigh. "I know." Just as Ellie had
predicted, Sarah had insisted on coming with Gwen to her
chemo appointments, even though Matthew and Ellie had
offered, as well.

Sarah fidgeted for a few moments, and then rose to go talk
to the nurse anyway. Gwen knew she simply couldn't help
herself. She had to *do* something, to be active and involved, if

not in control. Cancer, unfortunately, was not all that controllable, by anyone.

"Gwen Davies?" A nurse in scrubs stood at the door that led to the consulting rooms, scanning the room with a faint smile.

Sarah stopped midway to the desk and Gwen rose from her seat.

"That's me."

Her legs felt a little wobbly as she walked toward the nurse with Sarah by her side. She wasn't scared exactly, but she certainly felt nervous. Although she'd been given a leaflet about what to expect from the treatment, every sterile-sounding fact she'd read in the last week flew out of her head in that moment. She felt like a little child, and she knew then that she was actually glad Sarah was here. She needed her daughter's commanding presence to carry her along.

The next half-hour passed surprisingly quickly, with the nurse and then the consultant explaining everything to her and then checking her vitals. She was hooked up to an IV and the drip was started while she made herself as comfortable as she could in a reclining chair.

"It looks just like water," she remarked as she gazed at the droplets being squeezed down the tube and into her body. "Hard to believe it's something that does so much." Something that could cure her, but also hurt her. The very nature of chemotherapy, she supposed.

"Yes, and causes so many side effects," Sarah said, which was no more than Gwen had been thinking, but she didn't really need her daughter to point it out to her. Sarah looked anxious as she turned to give Gwen a direct look. "Do you think you're ready for those, Mum?"

"I don't think anyone can be ready, not exactly."

She'd been told she'd most likely feel tired and nauseous,

and also that she'd probably lose her hair eventually, although maybe not until a second round. Gwen had made a joke that she didn't have all that much to lose anymore; she wore her hair in a short bob, and it had become thinner and more brittle with age. The nurse had smiled, but Sarah had, quite uncharacteristically, looked close to tears. This was hard for her daughter, Gwen realized afresh, and, unfortunately, she didn't know how she could make it any better.

Clumsily, because of the IV in her hand, she reached over and patted Sarah's hand. "It's going to be okay, Sarah," she said gently. Even if she knew she couldn't actually make that promise, she felt her daughter needed to hear it.

"I know," Sarah replied, so quickly the words sounded rote. "Breast cancer has an incredibly high five-year survival rate now."

Five years. Once again, Gwen thought that really didn't sound so long.

She managed a small smile. "That's good to hear."

"Is it?" Sarah replied, her lips trembling before she pressed them together. "Sorry. I want to be more positive. I really do. I'm trying—"

"You don't need to be positive for me," Gwen told her. She thought she could actually do without her daughter's determined positivity, not that she would say as much. "It's okay to be scared, Sarah," she said instead. "I'm scared."

"I'm not," her daughter answered quickly. "I'm not the one with cancer, in any case."

Gwen's lips twitched. "True."

Sarah looked at her unhappily. "I didn't mean it... *unkindly*, Mum. I only meant that this is about you, not me. Don't worry about how I'm feeling. Let's focus on getting you better."

Gwen smiled and gestured to the IV. "That's what we're doing."

"Yes." Sarah nodded and tried to smile, and Gwen wished

she was better at comforting her daughter. Clearly Sarah needed it, but Gwen suspected that, to Sarah, accepting any sort of comfort or sympathy smacked of weakness, as well as not being in control.

Sure enough, a few minutes later, she went to talk to the nurse and ask her to adjust the IV, even though Gwen was comfortable enough.

A few minutes after that, she started fussing with the magazines, and urged Gwen to drink some water, and then asked if she wanted a snack.

"Thanks, love, but I think I just want a bit of a rest," Gwen answered, and closed her eyes.

She knew her daughter meant well, and she loved her dearly, but right then, she felt it was going to be a long few weeks.

CHAPTER 23

JESS

Having a friend, Jess discovered, made school just about bearable.

She hadn't even fully realized just how utterly miserable she'd been before until she got off the bus the morning Granny was going to her first chemotherapy appointment and Sophie waved to her from across the school courtyard.

"Hey, Jess!"

Jess waved back, and Sophie fell into step beside her as they walked through the double doors. It was the first time since school started that Jess hadn't had to walk in by herself, dreading every moment of that endless journey.

She'd figured out, since that first day last week when Sophie had found her in the music room, that her new—and only—friend wasn't considered cool, but then neither was she. It seemed a very long time ago when she and Chloe had almost been part of the in crowd of seventh grade, if only on the fringes. Then eighth grade had come around and they'd found themselves definitely not one of the cool girls, but not total geeks, either. Now, however, she was out in the stratosphere of year nine, too irrelevant even to be considered a geek, but at least she wasn't alone.

After she and Sophie had met in the music room, they'd seen each other a few times across the cafeteria, and although they hadn't spoken, they'd given each other small, cautious smiles. Then, one day last week, they'd both shown up to the same lunchtime music club. Jess hadn't been planning to go, but the teacher who had found her hiding out in the music room had told her she either had to go to a club or go outside for the lunch break, and she couldn't stand the thought of wandering around the schoolyard alone yet again.

When she'd seen Sophie sitting at one of the tables in the classroom for the club, they'd both grinned—and their friendship had felt like it had been cemented.

"How's your granny?" Sophie asked now as they headed inside, and Jess was touched she'd remembered; she'd only mentioned it once, after all, in part because she didn't want to think about it too much. She might still feel like she didn't know her grandmother all that well, but she didn't like the thought of her having *cancer*. Her mom had said she thought Granny would be okay, but Jess didn't know whether to believe her.

"She seemed okay this morning. She's going for her first chemotherapy today, although I don't think she'll have side effects right away. Still, she said it was pretty treatable, so that's good."

Sophie nodded sympathetically. "My granddad had cancer last year. It was hard, but he got better. I hope she'll be okay."

"Thanks." Jess wasn't sure if Granny would be okay or not, no matter what she'd said about it being treatable; her mom hadn't given her many details, and both her parents had seemed distracted when they'd talked to her about it, as they'd so often been since they'd moved to Llandrigg. They were always smiling at her in a way that didn't reach their eyes, not that Jess was trying all that hard to smile back.

As glad as she was for Sophie's friendship, and as much of a difference as it did make, she still missed Connecticut—and Chloe. She missed her house, and her bedroom that she hadn't had to share with Ava, and everything about her old life— caramel lattes with her mom on Saturday morning, getting French fries on the way back from ice-skating, curling up on the sofa in the family room while her mom made dinner in the adjoining kitchen. Sometimes she'd even snuggle with Ava, watching some stupid show like *Super Why*, which Ava always loved.

Just thinking about it all now, as she put her stuff away in her locker, made a pressure build in her chest. Yes, having a friend made school more bearable, and she genuinely liked Sophie. Life wasn't unendurable anymore, but... she still missed the way she'd used to be. She missed the way her whole family had used to be.

They'd been different, back in Connecticut, as a family, Jess thought. They'd been closer.

And as for Chloe... well, it hurt too much to think about Chloe.

Would she *ever* feel like this was home?

"Hey, look!" Sophie nudged Jess's shoulder and pointed to a poster outside the music block.

"Lunchtime Talent Show," Jess read, and then glanced at Sophie. "It's not till the end of October. Do you want to go or something?"

"It's for auditions," Sophie explained, her eyes alight. "Why don't we try out?"

"Try out?" Jess couldn't help but sound alarmed. She liked singing with Sophie in the music room, but in *public*? Since starting at the school, she'd been trying to keep a low profile. Auditioning for a talent show seemed very risky, opening herself up to scrutiny, teasing, public humiliation. *No thanks.* "I don't know..." she said hesitantly.

"You have a great voice, and I can play the piano," Sophie insisted, hands on her hips. "I wouldn't suggest it if I didn't think we had a chance. I'm not *that* deluded!" She grinned and then nodded at the poster. "Why not, Jess?"

Why not? Silently, Jess looked over at a tight clique of girls in their year, including the one who had teased Sophie when they'd been coming out of the music room last week. They all had shiny hair and loud laughs, the newest phones and lots of makeup.

Sophie followed her gaze. "I don't care about them," she stated, even as she flushed. "Do you?"

Did she? Jess didn't even know the girls' names. Why should she care about what they thought? And yet, what she did know was that girls like that would make fun of both her and Sophie just for trying out. It probably wouldn't even matter if they were good or not. They were still fair game to them.

She glanced again at the poster, deep reluctance warring with the tiniest flicker of interest... and, she knew, she didn't want to disappoint her new friend.

"I'll think about it," she promised.

Jess was still thinking about it when she got off the bus with Ben that afternoon. As usual, her brother raced ahead while she trudged toward Bluebell Lane alone, trying not to feel a little down. Chloe hadn't messaged her in over a week, and yet she'd posted two new photos on Instagram this morning—both of them with Emily.

Only a few short months ago, Chloe never would have posted anything on Instagram without consulting Jess. They would have gone through every photo, agonized over the caption and hashtags, checked for any likes or comments together. Now Chloe was posting pictures with Emily, and she wasn't even *telling* Jess about it. Maybe she shouldn't even be surprised, considering she wasn't even on the same continent anymore, and at least she had a friend now, too, but... it still hurt.

"Ben? Jess?" her mother called from the kitchen as Jess let herself into the house. "How was school?"

She asked that every single day, and every single day Jess gave the same answer. *Fine.* What else could she say? It wasn't *great*, the way her mom wanted it to be, and if she told her about Sophie, her mom would get all dewy-eyed and ridiculous and think everything was solved, when it wasn't. She might be friends with Sophie, but she still really missed Chloe. Her mom, Jess thought, did not want to understand that.

With a pang, Jess remembered what had happened just before she'd left for the bus—some girls had seen her and Sophie looking at the audition poster again, and they'd teased them about it.

"Oooh, are you two going to try out?" one of them had asked with patently fake excitement, and then she and her friends had burst into raucous laughter as they'd walked away. Sophie had claimed she didn't care, but Jess knew she did.

She didn't want to, but she felt it all the same—that unpleasant, squirming sensation, like snakes were in her belly or pins needling her skin. She'd tried to hold her head up, but she'd ended up slinking away, and that had made her feel even worse, especially because she was afraid Sophie had noticed.

"Jess?" her mom poked her head into the hallway with a smile. "How was school?"

Jess didn't even think about changing her answer, or all the things she never told her mom, because she knew her mom would just try to find a way to make it seem better, when it *wasn't.* "Fine."

Her mother's smile turned playful, her tone a tiny bit petulant. "You always say that these days. I suppose it's better than what you said before, but—"

"But *what?*" Jess cut her off, not wanting to get into it.

There was no point explaining to her mother how hard she was finding everything, even with a friend. She would just tell her to be patient and keep trying, all the while looking like Jess had disappointed her for even saying anything. Her mom didn't get it at *all*. "It's not like you want to hear anything else," she muttered under her breath. "I'm going upstairs."

"Don't you want to know how Granny is?" her mom called as Jess hurried up the stairs.

Guilt flashed through her for forgetting, and even though she knew it didn't make sense, she was angry with her mom for mentioning it. She *knew* she should have asked about Granny.

She turned around, her shoulders slumped. "How is she?"

Her mother managed a small smile, although she still looked worried, a deep frown carved between her eyebrows that definitely hadn't been there before they'd moved to Wales, or at least before her dad had lost his job. "She's tired, but okay. Resting in her room now."

"Okay," Jess said, glad at least her grandmother seemed okay, and she headed upstairs. She heard her mother's sigh—a sound of frustration and disappointment—as she rounded the corner, and she paused by her grandmother's door. "Granny?" she asked cautiously as she peeked around the corner.

Her grandmother's eyes fluttered open and she smiled. "Jess." She sounded pleased to see her, but Jess was alarmed at how tired and, well, *frail* she looked. Did one round of chemo do that to you?

Jess inched into the room. "How are you?" she asked.

"Not too bad. Just a little tired." She eased up against the pillows, a little color coming into her cheeks. "The more important question is, how are you? Is school getting any better?"

Jess hadn't realized her granny had even noticed that school was bad, but then she supposed she had been slamming a lot of doors. "It's okay," she said. "Getting a little better, I guess."

"That's good to hear. You know, I never had to move

schools, but I imagine it's quite hard. Sometimes I wished I had the chance to move, because you can get a bit stuck in a rut, can't you? Staying in the same place?"

Jess had never thought that before, but now she wondered. Would Chloe have become friends with Emily if she'd stayed in Connecticut? She'd always assumed not, but what if Chloe had dumped her because she wasn't cool enough? She'd always been more interested in the in crowd than Jess had been.

Jess saw that her grandmother's eyes had fluttered closed and she tiptoed out of her room as quietly as she could. Up in her own room, she looked at Chloe's Instagram again. She hadn't commented on either of the photos, but lots of other people had, with smiley faces and hearts and fire emojis. Maybe her grandmother was right, Jess thought, but she still wished she could have stayed in Connecticut.

With a sigh, she flung herself on her bed and opened Snapchat.

Hey what's up? she wrote, with a photo of herself looking silly—eyes crossed and tongue sticking out, like she was happy.

Back in Connecticut, Chloe would have replied instantly. But now, as Jess lay on the bed and waited, she could see that her message wasn't even opened. She told herself it was because Chloe was still at school, but she knew Chloe checked her phone during any breaks. Jess waited a whole hour, all the way through Chloe's lunch break, when she almost definitely would have checked her phone, and the message remained unread.

It still hadn't been read by the time Jess got ready for bed that night, feeling thoroughly miserable, because by that time Chloe would have been home from school, and Jess could see that she'd been online. She just hadn't bothered to read Jess's message.

She slouched downstairs to put her phone on charge, stopping when she saw her mom sipping a cup of tea at the kitchen table.

"I've got into the very British habit of having a cup of tea before bed," her mother told her. "Do you want one? We have peppermint."

Jess hesitated, because she didn't really like any kind of tea, but she felt so lonely and mixed up inside, and she couldn't remember when she'd last talked to her mom properly. They'd used to have some pretty fun times together; her mom could get in a silly mood sometimes, and Jess recalled them collapsing into giggles over some reality TV show they'd watched together. She missed those days.

"Okay," she said, and her mom's beaming smile was all the assurance she needed that she'd made the right choice.

It took her mom only a few minutes to make the tea, and then they were seated at the table together, and Jess wasn't sure what to say, and her mother didn't seem to know either, because they were both silent.

"I don't know if I should ask you about school," her mom finally admitted wryly. "Because I know you don't like me asking about it. But when I do ask, it's because I care, that's all."

Jess fidgeted with the handle of her cup, her hair sliding into her face. "I know."

"But maybe we could talk about something else," her mom suggested. "Would you like to do something fun this weekend?"

Jess looked up cautiously. Her mom had seemed too busy and hassled to think about *fun*. "Like what?" she asked.

"We could go swimming at the pool in Abergavenny," her mom suggested. "Or even drive into Cardiff and see the sights. I don't know what they are, but there's got to be something."

"There's a science museum my friend told me about," Jess ventured. "Techniquest. It sounds kind of cool."

"Your friend told you?" her mom said, brightening at this news. "Great. Well, maybe we could go there on Saturday."

"Okay." Jess knew her mom was trying, and she wanted to try too, and Techniquest did sound cool... but why hadn't Chloe read her message, never mind replied to it? It was like a slap in the face, and Chloe *knew* that.

Maybe she should forget about Chloe, she thought with sudden, rebellious defiance. If she was having such a fantastic time with Emily, well, Jess could have a great time with Sophie. She didn't have to sit around moping and missing her.

"Mom," she asked, "can I send one more message on my phone?" She knew her mom was strict about not using the phone once it was on charge for the night. "To my friend?" she added, and her mother's lips twitched.

"Trying to soften me up?" she teased. "I'm glad you've made a friend, Jess, and yes, you can message her—just this one time."

With a quick grin, Jess reached for her phone to message Sophie.

Re the audition—let's do it!!

CHAPTER 24

GWEN

"Go on, go on, or you'll miss your reservation!"

Gwen gave Matthew and Ellie a wan smile as she did her best to make her voice cheerful but firm. It was the Friday after she'd started the chemotherapy, and it also happened to be Matthew and Ellie's sixteenth wedding anniversary. She'd booked them a reservation for dinner at a Michelin-starred inn on the outskirts of the village, and insisted she could manage the children at home.

"Let me do this," she'd told Ellie when she had, predictably, resisted, concerned for Gwen's health. "I'm not an invalid. Not yet, anyway. My consultant assured me I have a few more weeks before I'm anything more than a little tired, so I want to enjoy feeling mostly all right while I can. And it will be good to have some time with the children. I do enjoy it." She gave Ellie a no-nonsense look. "I haven't spent enough time with them, and I want to, especially while I'm still mostly well." Even if she did feel tired right down to her bones, a physical exhaustion she'd never felt before, in all her days, like she was walking through a fog. But tiredness was just that, and she could work with it. Get over it. Mostly.

Reluctantly, looking anxious, Ellie had agreed to the plan, and now she and Matthew were dressed up to the nines—Ellie in a little black dress and heels, Matthew sporting a coat and tie —and heading out for dinner.

"*Mommy!*" Ava cried from behind Gwen, clearly gearing up to cry, and Gwen waved them off even more firmly, staying Ava with one hand on her shoulder.

"Go... just go. We'll be fine." She turned to smile down at the little girl. "Won't we, Ava?"

"Mommy..." Ava's voice wobbled.

Finally, with one more kiss and hug for Ava, they went, and as the car headed down the lane, Gwen closed the door and turned to the four children looking at her with varying degrees of uncertainty, boredom, and disinterest. She really hadn't spent enough time with them, she thought, although she'd made a few strides. Now she gave them all a cheerful smile.

"Right... how about pizza for tea?"

"Do we even *have* pizza?" Jess asked dubiously, arms folded, expression doubtful. She'd seemed a bit more cheerful, or, more accurately, less sullen, in the last week, but her moods still swung like a roundabout, and Gwen was never quite sure what mood was going to greet her at the end of the school day.

"Even better, we have pizza dough," Gwen told her with the same resolute cheer. She'd dragged herself out of bed to make it that morning, even though she'd been exhausted, every movement making her whole body ache. Still, she'd been determined to do this for her grandchildren, and she still was.

Ava wrinkled her nose. "What do we do with pizza *dough*?"

"Make pizza, of course!" Gwen replied. "And the best part is, you can decide the toppings yourself. Artisan pizza. Or maybe the right word is bespoke."

Both words flew over the children's heads and Ava frowned. "I only like cheese."

"Then cheese you will have," Gwen assured her. "Come on, everybody, into the kitchen. We'll get everything out."

It didn't take too much effort to get the children all organized in the kitchen, pounding and rolling the pizza dough with a bit more enthusiasm than they'd first exhibited while Gwen got out the cheese and tomato sauce and various toppings—black olives and red peppers for Jess, who seemed slightly more enthused. Josh said, hesitantly, that he'd try pepperoni, if it wasn't too much trouble.

"Of course it isn't, darling," Gwen assured him. "I bought some salami to cut up just for that purpose, and it's not too spicy, so I think you might like it."

As she bustled about the kitchen, she almost felt like her old self—tired, yes, but industrious and cheerful, humming under her breath as she guided Ava's chubby little hands on the rolling pin, and offered Ben the choice of pepperoni, olives, peppers, or mushrooms.

"Mushrooms, *yuck*," he said with gruesome theatricality, and she smiled.

This was the sort of thing she'd envisioned when she'd asked Matthew if he and his family wanted to live with her at Bluebell Inn—happy times with the grandchildren, memories in the making, a cheerful, busy kitchen.

It lasted for twenty minutes, like the calm before the storm, although Gwen didn't realize it at the time. She simply enjoyed the activity, Ava's giggles and Jess's quick smile, Josh and Ben actually seeming to get along as they decorated their pizzas with toppings, Ben having the idea of making funny faces—a red pepper for a mouth, olives for eyes.

Then Josh knocked the bowl of tomato sauce onto the floor, splattering Jess's new sparkly white top with drops of red, and before Gwen could react, Jess had let out a cry of dismay and shoved her brother hard in the shoulder. Josh shoved her back, and somehow Ben got involved with the shoving as well, a pizza slid to the floor with a splat and then Ava started to cry.

"*My pizza!*"

"Wait... *wait!*" Gwen called out desperately, flinging her hands up, trying to slow down the disaster that was already being unleashed—first in slow motion, and then seemingly faster and faster. It was already too late—Jess had stormed off, and Ava, standing in the middle of the kitchen, had begun to bawl properly. Josh was clearly struggling not to cry, as well, and Ben had managed to step in the spilled tomato sauce and was tracking red footprints around the kitchen. Poor old Toby, alarmed by all the noise, had slunk out to the hall.

"*Enough!*" Gwen commanded, loud enough for all three to fall silent, surprised at her suddenly stern tone, one she hardly ever took. "Ben, take off your shoes before you track any more sauce about, and then please go set the table. Ava, wash your hands. Josh, help me clean up this sauce. And don't worry—there's more in the fridge of everything. Ava, we'll make you another pizza."

She took a steadying breath and let it out slowly, gratified when they all did as she asked.

A few minutes later, everything was calm again, and the three children were finishing decorating their pizzas. Jess had already finished hers, so Gwen popped it in the oven along with the others, set the kids to playing an ancient game of Cluedo she'd found in the cupboard, and then went upstairs to find her eldest granddaughter.

Jess was in the room she shared with Ava, hunched on her bed, still in her stained top.

"If you take that off, I can put it to soak," Gwen said gently. "I think the stains will come out with a bit of white vinegar."

Jess sniffed and shook her head. "It doesn't matter."

Carefully, Gwen perched on the edge of the bed. "I think it does."

Jess plucked at the stained top, her head bent so Gwen couldn't see her face. "Chloe gave it to me," she half-mumbled.

"Chloe? Is that someone from America?"

"Yeah, my best friend. *Ex*-best friend," Jess clarified rather vehemently and plucked at the top again.

Ah. In a flash, Gwen realized this wasn't so much about the tomato sauce or even the top, as it was about the friend. "What happened to make Chloe your *ex*-best friend?"

Jess shrugged. "It doesn't matter."

"You keep telling me that things don't matter, Jess," Gwen told her gently, "but I don't believe you. They seem to matter very much indeed."

Jess didn't reply and Gwen let the silence stretch on. Sometimes, she knew, there was nothing you could say to make it better.

"Chloe has *forgotten* me," Jess burst out, her voice trembling with emotion. "She doesn't even open my Snapchats, and she keeps posting all these photos with her new BFF... someone we didn't even like, one of the *in* girls. I hate it!"

Gwen had only understood about half of what Jess had said; she had never heard of Snapchat, and she didn't know what a BFF was, but she certainly got the gist of what she was feeling, and understood it all too well.

"That sounds hard," she said after a moment, her tone quiet but heartfelt. "Very hard." Jess looked up at her, tears trembling on her lashes. "In fact," Gwen added, "I'd say it... it stinks."

A small, incredulous smile quirked Jess's mouth. "That doesn't sound like something you'd normally say, Granny."

"Well, it is," Gwen replied robustly. "Sometimes life just— stinks. It's rubbish. Like this cancer. Like your friend Chloe forgetting you. Like your dad breaking his arm." And maybe even like them moving to Wales, from Jess's point of view, unfortunately. "There's no getting around it, there's no groping for some silver lining. It just *is*, and you have to live with it."

"Yeah," Jess answered feelingly. "You're right. Mom always tries to make me feel better, but I don't *want* to hear about all the friends I'm going to make here, or how great this place is, or how beautiful the village is, or how lucky we are to live in this old house." She gave Gwen a guilty yet defiant look. "Sorry, but it's true."

"I understand completely," Gwen replied, unfazed, if a little shaken by the litany of things Jess didn't like. She still understood how her granddaughter felt. "Even if you live in the nicest place in the world—and I am partial to Llandrigg as well as Bluebell Inn, I have to say—it doesn't take away the pain of missing where you were." She paused, reflecting. "Or even *who* you were, in that place."

"Do you... do you feel like a different person?" Jess asked hesitantly. "Because of the cancer?"

Gwen considered the perceptive question for a moment. "Sometimes," she admitted. "At the moment, it's more of being afraid that I'm going to change, and what that might look like. Feel like, too. I haven't yet, I don't think much anyway, but I know I will. I'll have to, and there's nothing I'll be able to do about it. That scares me." She didn't think she'd been as honest with anyone else about how she felt about her diagnosis, Gwen realized. It was surprising, and yet also sweet, that it was Jess who had inspired her confidences.

"But you'll still be the same on the inside," Jess told her loyally, and Gwen smiled.

"Yes... I certainly hope so." She wasn't entirely sure she would be, but she appreciated her granddaughter's words. "But we weren't talking about me, we were talking about you. And Chloe. Why do you feel she's forgotten you?"

Jess heaved a big sigh. "I don't even care that much about Chloe. I mean, I do, I really do, but I understand why she'd get a new best friend. It's not like I'm *there*. She has to hang out with someone at school and stuff. I do get that, even if I wish she'd answer my messages once in a while. It's just... here... I feel so... lonely." The smile she gave Gwen was heart-breaking, and it wobbled.

"Oh, Jess, I'm sorry." Gwen paused to pat her granddaughter's hand. "Is there anyone at school you can be friends with?" she asked. "I imagine it must be hard being new. Are there any possibilities, though? Any kindred spirits?"

Jess nodded, although she still looked dispirited. "Yeah, there's one girl... Sophie... she's really nice, and I like her, and I think we could be really good friends eventually, but... she's not Chloe, and she doesn't really know me yet. Or, really, she knows me as the biggest loser in the whole school, and I guess I don't like that." Jess kicked at the bedframe with her foot. "That isn't the real me. At least, it wasn't, not before I moved here, and everyone decided I was."

"Well, I for one don't think you're the biggest loser in the school," Gwen told her. "Not by a mile! But being new is, for now, part of who you are, and that's all right." She hesitated, feeling her way through the words, the ideas. "We're all complicated people—there are different parts to us, some bits we like and some we don't so much. Some we can change, or will change with time, like being new. And as time goes on, maybe Sophie will get to know the other parts of you, and being new won't be a bit that matters so much."

"Maybe," Jess said, but she didn't sound convinced, or particularly enthused by the whole idea, and Gwen couldn't blame her. She was only thirteen, after all. Waiting for anything felt endless, especially when the possibility of change was so vague.

"Small comfort now, I know," Gwen said with a commiserating smile. "The waiting is hard. It always is. I certainly find it so."

Jess ducked her head. "I'm sorry I shoved Josh."

"And I'm sorry he spilled sauce on your top."

"I know he didn't mean to."

Gwen decided this was a good moment to head back downstairs; she could hear some sounds—clatters and thuds—all of which could potentially be alarming. "Why don't you change and bring down your top? I'll give it a soak and we'll see if we can get that stain out. I think we might be able to."

"Okay." Jess gave her a shy smile. "Thanks, Granny."

"It's no trouble." Gwen contented herself with another pat of Jess's hand before she headed downstairs. That had been, she reflected, the first proper conversation she'd had with her granddaughter, and she was very glad for it.

CHAPTER 25

ELLIE

"They'll be fine, you know."

Matthew gave Ellie a smiling look as she drove along Llandrigg's high street to the inn on the far side of the village. He had scrubbed up nicely, broken arm and all, and she hoped she had, as well. It had been ages since they'd been out alone together, ages since they'd had a chance to talk properly, besides that conversation the other day, which had felt both painful and potentially fraught, and had caused them to be cautious with one another since, even strangely shy. Still, Ellie told herself, it had been progress, and she hoped more progress might be made tonight.

"I'm more worried about your mother than the kids," she told him as she turned onto a narrow country lane on the outskirts of Llandrigg. "She's so tired from the chemo, and you know how they can be a handful. Ava had already turned on the waterworks before we were out the door..."

"And she can turn them off again, just as quickly. Besides, my mum is made of strong stuff, stronger than you think. She'll be okay. I think she'd like some time alone with her grandchildren."

"I suppose so."

Gwen had said as much, and Ellie believed her, but she was still worried. After their surprising and touching heart-to-heart, she was trying not to take her mother-in-law for granted, or read the wrong motives into her actions or words. Gwen might *say* she could watch all four children for an entire evening, because she was worried about Matthew and Ellie's relationship, but did she mean it? Could she do it—and how much would it cost her? The last thing Ellie wanted was for Gwen's health to be set back.

"Let's just concentrate on having a nice time," Matthew suggested. "If something goes truly pear-shaped, Mum will call. She has both our numbers. I can't remember the last time we've been out."

"It must have been back in Connecticut, before..." Ellie trailed off, not wanting to mention his redundancy. They'd talked about that enough, surely.

"Yeah, when we had more money." He sighed and looked out the window, at the row of quaint, terraced cottages sliding by.

Ellie bit her lip, caught between guilt at mentioning it, and a slight annoyance at her husband's reaction. Were they already falling back into those tired patterns of sniping at each other for no good reason? She hoped not. She'd really wanted to make an effort tonight to get back on track.

"It was very nice of your mother to make us this reservation and pay for the meal," Ellie remarked with determined diplomacy. "You're right. We should do our best to enjoy it. I'm glad we can have some time together." She turned to smile at him, and to her relief, he smiled back.

They'd been in Llandrigg for nearly a month now, but it still felt like early days on so many fronts. Ellie knew she had to be patient—in making friends, in her children settling in, in her and Matthew finding their way, but she wanted to see evidence of gains. Tonight, she hoped, would give her that kind of proof. And, she acknowledged fairly, there *had* been some gains already; Jess had, for the most part, seemed a bit less sullen, and Ben was enjoying the Minecraft and football clubs. Josh had made a friend, and Ava seemed happy in her school. And Ellie had made a good friend in Emma, as well, plus she felt she was getting along better with Gwen. As for her and Matthew...

Well, that's what this evening was all about.

The inn was lovely, tucked at the end of a narrow country lane, its cobbled courtyard wreathed with fairy lights. Inside, it was all aged oak and open fires, with a delicious smell of food, wine, and woodsmoke scenting the air. Ellie felt her cares falling right away, properly glad now that they'd come out, that Gwen had made it happen. She would have to thank her when they returned.

It had been so long since she and Matthew had had any proper alone time, time to chat and laugh and not just discuss the mundane practical matters of family life—or worse, sit in silence and tension. She was longing to reconnect, to feel close to her husband once again.

"What are you going to order?" she asked as she perused the select and delicious-sounding menu. They were sitting at a cozy table tucked into an alcove by the fire, candlelight flickering between them. "Should we order appetizers, too?"

"Why not? It's not every day you have a sixteenth anniversary, is it?" He gave her a crooked smile, but from the shadow in his eyes, Ellie could tell he had something on his mind, and she felt her stomach cramp with nerves. She wanted to have a heart-to-heart, absolutely, but a happy one. Still, she told herself, if Matthew had something to say, she wanted to hear it, and this lovely inn, with the crackling fire and the clink of crystal, was as good a place as any to do so.

They ordered their meals and a bottle of wine, and as Ellie

sat back and watched the flames spark and flicker in the fire-place, she felt herself truly start to relax.

"This really is nice," she remarked. "It feels so peaceful. I don't think I've had a moment to simply sit and *be* for a long while."

"It feels like that's all I've had, since I broke my arm." Matthew grimaced as he toyed with the stem of his wine glass and looked around the room. "Not that I'm feeling sorry for myself," he added, and Ellie smiled and took a sip of her wine.

"No, of course not," she agreed, gently teasing him, and then she waited.

He definitely had something on his mind, and maybe it would be better if he just got it out in the open.

"What is it, Matt?" she asked after a few minutes had passed and her husband hadn't said anything more, simply gazed around the room, at the other diners chatting and laughing, drinking and eating, not sitting in silence the way they were.

He glanced back at her warily. "What is what?"

"Something is on your mind, I can tell." She gave him what she hoped was a playful smile. "Why don't you let me in on the secret?"

"No secret." He smiled wryly in return before letting out a sigh. "But you're right, I do have something on my mind, and I have for a while."

"Okay." Ellie waited, trying to look alert and interested and not as nervous as she felt. His somber expression was making her feel like this was going to be some kind of bad news, and they'd surely had enough of that lately. "What's up?"

Matthew paused for a moment before he answered. "I don't think the renovation is going to work," he said finally. "At all, I mean."

Ellie stared at him for a moment. "Because of your arm? Three more weeks and—"

He shook his head. "Not just my arm. I'm not qualified to do it all myself, or even much of it... certainly not as much as I wanted to. I think you knew that all along, though." He gestured to his broken arm. "And it's true this doesn't help, since I can't get started on things for weeks, anyway. But the truth is, I think Mum dreamed up the whole idea of a renovation just to try to keep me busy. Give me a reason to come over and to make me feel *needed*. I don't think it's something she really wants, and I don't want to make more of a hash of it than I already have."

Ellie was silent for a moment, absorbing everything he'd said... and hadn't said. They'd already talked about how being made redundant had been a blow to her husband's self-confidence, even his sense of self, but she didn't think she'd actually understood how much, until she gazed at him now, looking so defeated.

"I don't know about that, Matt," she said slowly. "Some of the rooms were pretty shabby. And you have a lot of good ideas—"

"Yes, but she doesn't even *like* those ideas," he replied. "She doesn't want the en suite bathrooms, marble and nice fittings and all the rest. That's not the feel of the place, anyway, and never has been. I should have consulted with her before, I realize that now. It's her business, after all. But I don't want to do it just so I can be kept busy, like some toddler being given a set of building blocks." He pressed his lips together as he gazed into his wine glass. "I don't need or want to be patronized."

"I don't think anyone means to patronize you," Ellie replied carefully. "And the work still needs to be done, especially now the rooms are in such a state—"

Matthew looked up, grimacing. "I can put things back easily enough, once my arm is healed. But I think I'll tell Mum I'm not going to go ahead with all my plans. I can try to get a proper job... maybe something in Cardiff."

He sounded so dispirited, that Ellie's heart ached for him—

and for them. And a job in Cardiff? Where had *that* come from? The vision they'd all had when they'd moved to Wales was a family business, working together, sharing life. A slower pace, peace and quiet, that charmed existence that had seemed so promising. Even with the hardships and challenges they'd experienced so far, Ellie didn't want to let go of that dream. She didn't want to live a lesser version of their Connecticut life here in Wales, with Matthew commuting every day, busy and hassled, their lives lived apart...

"How long would it take to drive in and out of Cardiff?" she wondered out loud.

"It's an hour each way, give or take, depending on traffic."

An hour! Ellie could not keep from looking appalled. That was twice the commuting time he'd had back in Connecticut. Surely they hadn't moved halfway across the world for *that*.

"I thought I'd talk to Mum tomorrow," he continued doggedly. "Maybe we could rent a place, like you wanted. Give Mum some space, some peace and quiet."

"Matt," Ellie said gently, "considering her current condition, I don't think it's space your mom needs now—"

"We'd still be close by," he argued, "and she could get some more rest, without the kids banging around all the time. We could stay in the village, check in on her every day. More than once a day, if needed."

Ellie hesitated. The thought of having their own space was still very tempting, just as it had been a month ago, but she knew instinctively that Gwen would be incredibly hurt if they all moved out right after they'd arrived, and she had come to enjoy her mother-in-law's company. The children, too, had all taken a genuine liking to their no-longer-faraway granny. Ellie also knew that Matthew's vision of the bed and breakfast as some upscale boutique wasn't shared by Gwen, and most likely hadn't been very feasible to begin with. But there was a lot more going on for her husband than that. What to tackle first?

"I think I agree with you," she replied slowly, "that the vision you had for the place isn't really workable."

His lips tightened and he raised his eyebrows. "So..."

"So maybe we need a *new* vision. One we can figure out together." Ellie leaned forward, determined now, and starting to get excited as well, although for *what*, she wasn't yet quite sure. But she felt it—the start of something. Something possible and *good*. "I don't think you really want to get a job in Cardiff, do you, Matt?" she asked. "Back in the rat race that you hated, working for a big, faceless corporation?" He opened his mouth to protest, but Ellie hurried on before he could say anything. "Matt, I know the redundancy really knocked you for six. You said as much. And I also know I wasn't as supportive as I could be—"

"That has nothing to do with this, Ellie—"

"Still, it needs to be said—"

"We talked about this before. We were both hurt. I get it." The words were clipped, almost dismissive.

"Then why are we still arguing?" she demanded, exasperated. "Look, the B&B was meant to be a family project, a way to bring us all together. Instead, it's become another way for you to try to prove yourself."

Ire flashed in his eyes. "I'm not—"

"But it doesn't have to *be* that way," Ellie insisted, leaning over to touch his hand, a gesture of reassurance. "Matt, you don't have to prove anything to me, and I... I don't have to prove anything to you. That's not what marriage is about. I think we both approached this whole thing the wrong way round—we should have been doing it together from the beginning, and instead I feel as if it's driven us further apart. I don't want it to be that way."

He let out a little sigh as he squeezed her hand. "I don't either, Ellie, but what's the solution? We can't move back to Connecticut, at least not easily."

"I don't want to move back to Connecticut."

Matthew looked surprised, and Ellie realized *she* was surprised, as well, because she actually meant it. After a month of longing for just that thing, in one way or another, she realized, to her amazement, that she didn't want it anymore. Yes, the transition to Llandrigg had been hard, and still was, but good things had happened as a result. She was becoming closer to Gwen, and she felt needed, and they were all, slowly but surely, making new friends. She didn't want to go back and pick up the tattered remnants of her old life; she wanted to make their life *here*, embroider something new and good and whole. Together.

"What if... what if we did it all *really* differently, Matt?" she asked slowly. The beginnings of an idea were forming in Ellie's head, unfurling into bloom like a flower. "What if... instead of glamour and elegance, which are great in their own way, we tried for something more friendly and homegrown? Something more... *us*? And more Gwen, too, I think." Her voice rose in excitement. "What if we *changed* our vision?" The idea was taking shape in her mind, if in a vague way—something more holistic, more welcoming and family-friendly, embracing everything Gwen had wanted Bluebell Inn to stand for.

Matthew cocked his head, looking curious but cautious. "Changed our vision?" he asked. "How, exactly?"

Ellie had a moment to think of a response as the waitress came with their appetizers. Matthew toyed with his salmon en croute while she tried to put her thoughts in some semblance of order. She'd been speaking off the cuff, letting the idea bloom inside her without really considering the particulars she knew her husband would both need and want, but now she felt her way through the concept.

"Yes, changed it to something more homegrown. More... relaxed. Family friendly, because, well, we're a family."

He frowned, but she thought she saw a spark of interest

light in his eyes. At least she hoped she did. "What do you even mean by that?"

"I'm not entirely sure," Ellie admitted with a small smile, "but your mom has always loved the *homely* welcome of Bluebell Inn, the lovable feel of it, that it's the kind of place where you don't have to worry about muddy boots in the hallway, or things like that. That sense of... of comfort isn't something we want to lose."

"I wasn't intending on losing it," Matthew replied. "Just trying to make things a bit nicer, in line with other bed and breakfasts I've seen. Standards are high, Ellie. Markets are so competitive these days. If people go away for a break, they want it to be top notch."

"That's true." Ellie tried to keep her tone gentle, even though she wished he wouldn't make this feel like an argument. She wanted to move past that, past the perceived criticisms, the unspoken tensions. She thought they were, but then something would happen or was said that made her feel as if they hadn't moved past any of it at all, or at least not as much as she would have liked. "I'm not saying there was anything wrong with your original vision for the B&B," she told him. "In fact, it's probably the most marketable plan out there. You're right in that Bluebell Inn was not up to the standard of most places. It needed some TLC, for sure..."

"But?" He raised his eyebrows. "Because there is obviously a but."

"But, like you said, it's not your *mother's* vision," Ellie continued. "So, what if we developed her vision rather than... than ours?" She'd almost said "yours" but had thought better of it at the last moment. Matthew, she feared, wasn't fooled.

"Ellie, I'm not sure my mum even *has* a vision. Like I said, I think she dreamed up this whole scheme simply to make me feel better. I sometimes wonder if she would have been happy trundling along as she was, shabby though everything had become. She still had some regulars come every year, and she just about managed to make a living from it."

That possibility must hurt him as much as his perceived failure, Ellie thought. She knew he didn't want to be pitied. He didn't even really want to be helped.

"I don't think that's true," she told him quietly. "Your mom needs your help, now more than ever. And the bed and breakfast absolutely needs some renovation."

"Considering I made a hole in the ceiling," he returned ruefully, "it certainly does now, but, like I said, I can put everything back—"

Ellie took a deep breath. "What I'm really saying is, why don't we expand on the homeliness? We could pitch a stay at Bluebell House as a sort of catered-for family vacation... encourage children to get involved, helping in the veg patch or with collecting eggs... meals could be around one big table, everyone getting to know one another, family style." As she spoke, she found herself warming to the idea, her voice rising in enthusiasm. "There could even be games and things offered at night—or a community barbecue on the weekend... there are all sorts of things we could do. To give people the vacation they want—time with family, memories being made, not just plush towels and infinity showers."

She sat back, smiling, realizing just how much she liked the idea—child-friendly family vacations where someone else was doing the cooking and cleaning, but you felt as if you were at home, only better. It sounded like heaven to her, but her husband did not look entirely convinced.

"People book a holiday to get away and relax," he said after a moment. "Not feel like they're still at home."

"But Bluebell Inn is never going to compete with luxury hotels or health spas in that regard," Ellie argued, trying not to feel stung that he seemed so unconvinced by her idea. She knew he needed time to let go of one dream before believing in another. "Not even with a renovation. It's just not big enough, really, and it doesn't have the grounds. So isn't it better—wiser—to offer something completely different? Something the luxury hotels *can't* offer?"

"I don't know..." Matthew prodded his starter a bit morosely. "I suppose. It is something different, as you've said, and it might be what a certain demographic wants. You could talk to Mum about it."

But Ellie didn't want to talk to Gwen about it on her own. "Why don't *we* talk to her?" she suggested.

He shrugged. "It's not my idea."

"*Matt!*" Ellie couldn't keep the exasperation, as well as the hurt, from her voice. "We're a team, aren't we? We work together. One unit. That's what this is meant to be about, that's where I was going with this whole idea, that it's something we build together." He stared at her unhappily and Ellie gazed back with a ferocity born of love. "Don't shut me out, please," she said softly. "Let's do this together."

Matthew broke their locked gazes first. "I'm not shutting you out," he finally responded. "At least I'm not trying to."

"It feels like it, sometimes," Ellie replied quietly.

"I just don't have this vision that you seem to," he told her, clearly trying to sound reasonable and, to Ellie, failing. "At least not yet. It's not some big rejection of you or your idea, Ellie, just as what you said wasn't a rejection of mine. It's just... I didn't think of this. You did. And so it makes more sense for you to talk to her than for me to."

He began eating with determined relish, leaving Ellie no choice but to drop the subject and begin her own starter, mushrooms in garlic sauce that she had absolutely no interest in any longer. Her appetite had vanished. She'd really been hoping Matthew would have gotten as fired up about her idea as she was, that they could embark on this new chapter, hand in hand, *together*, but once again it didn't seem like it was going to happen that way. What else could she do?

After a few rather tense moments, Matthew started talking about the kids—the football club Ben wanted to join and Josh's science project—and, with effort, Ellie kept up her side of the conversation, injecting as much enthusiasm as she could into her voice as they discussed whether they might go away for the October half-term, or if Jess would want to try ice-skating in Cardiff. She wished their conversation had played out differently, but she was practical enough to understand why it hadn't.

Losing his job had been a serious setback for her husband, and she needed to appreciate that, and be more patient. She just wished they could both get over it and at least start to move on— no matter what the future looked like.

CHAPTER 26

JESS

"Are you ready for this afternoon?"

Jess looked into Sophie's expectant face and tried not to show how nervous she was, how reluctant, even though she'd agreed to audition a while back. She'd been thinking about it ever since Sophie had first mentioned it, and now that the day had actually arrived, all she felt was dread. How on earth could she stand in front of the music teacher, and who knew how many students, and *sing*?

"I don't know, Sophie..." she began, and Sophie's face fell.

"Oh, come on, you're not going to back out now, are you? We've been practicing for weeks."

"I know, and you're brilliant," Jess replied quickly. "Really, you are. It's just, I've never sung in public before."

"You have an amazing voice," Sophie insisted staunchly. "And if you don't audition, you'll never know whether you would have been picked or not. Besides, it will only be in front of the music teacher, Mrs. Farris, and she's really nice."

Mrs. Farris—and anyone else who was planning to audition or drifted in to watch during the lunch hour. Jess doubted it would just be the teacher; there would be at least a handful of students, as well, watching and probably giggling behind their hands.

"I don't know," she said again, as she closed her locker and slung her backpack over one shoulder. "I want to, but... can I think about it a little more?"

"But we've signed up." Sophie was doing her best not to look disappointed and, Jess feared, annoyed. She was backing out at the last minute; if she were Sophie, she'd be annoyed, too. "She'll be expecting us," she insisted. "Why not at least give it a go?"

Without meaning to, Jess glanced over her shoulder at the popular girls gathered in their tight, exclusive clique down the corridor.

Sophie followed her gaze, her mouth tightening.

"Is that why you don't want to audition?" she demanded in a low voice. "Do you really care what they think?"

Sort of, Jess thought, but didn't want to say so. Sophie, it seemed, was determined not to let the in crowd derail her dreams. Jess wanted to have that same determination and confidence, but she'd been at this school for less than a month. She wasn't sure she did, not yet anyway. "I'm just not sure I'm good enough," she said again.

"To audition? That's the whole point, to find out if you are." Sophie shook her head, her hands planted on her hips. "Come on, Jess. Don't chicken out now just because of *them*." She jerked her head toward the group of girls. "Do you really want to live your life in fear of people like that?"

It sounded like something her mom or dad would say. And Jess knew she didn't—of course she didn't—but neither did she want to be made a fool of, especially when she was so new here. She might torpedo her chance of making any more friends, and as much as she liked Sophie, she wouldn't mind some other friends, too. She sighed and said nothing, hitching her backpack further up on her shoulder.

"Look," Sophie began, tilting her chin up a notch, "I know I'll never be cool, and I'm not even going to try. I don't want to be. I just want to be myself and do my own thing, and you should, as well. My mum says those girls aren't even happy."

"How would she know?"

Sophie shrugged. "She's a psychologist, so maybe she has some answers, I don't know. But why do they have to put other people down all the time? People who are secure in themselves don't need to do that kind of stuff."

Which sounded like something Sophie's mom would say, Jess thought. Easy for an adult to believe, but not so much someone her age having to face them down every day in the corridor, deal with their laughter and their sneers.

"Come on, Jess," Sophie said, her voice lifting with determined enthusiasm. "Let's do this. What do you say?"

Jess glanced at the girls again; not one of them was paying her any attention and if they ever did, she knew it would only be to tease or mock, their lips curling as they rolled their eyes. She didn't even want to be friends with girls like that—the Emilys of Abergavenny—and she definitely didn't want to live under their shadow.

"Okay," she said as her stomach swirled with nerves and her heart leapt. "I'll do it."

All morning, Jess felt as if she'd swallowed a swarm of butterflies as she watched the clock tick steadily toward lunch. She struggled to pay attention to any of her lessons, her mind racing as she thought of the audition, opening her mouth and singing, actually *singing*, in front of who knew how many people.

When the bell rang for the final lesson before lunch, Sophie met her in the music block, her face flushed with excitement.

She didn't seem nervous at all, while Jess was jelly-legged with fear.

"Ready?" Sophie asked, and Jess barely managed to nod.

She had never, ever done anything like this before. She and Chloe had always been happy to stay in the background; the only time she'd been on a stage was in the third-grade class play, and then she'd been a *tree*, for heaven's sake. She hadn't had a single spoken line. She was afraid if she opened her mouth now, she might croak instead of sing. Her heart was pounding like a drum and her palms were slick with sweat.

Just as she'd feared, the audition room was full of people— two other teachers she didn't recognize, and all the other students who were planning to audition, plus friends who had come to support them, and a few other hangers-on besides, who just wanted to see the acts, and probably laugh at them.

"I can't sing in front of all these people!" Jess hissed to Sophie, who shrugged her words aside, although admittedly she was looking a little more nervous than she had before.

"It'll be fine."

It *wouldn't* be fine, Jess was sure of it. She'd make a complete fool of herself, and she'd never live the embarrassment down. It had been hard enough starting a new school, but with a big embarrassing episode to her credit, as well? She couldn't bear to think of it, how people might tease her in the hall, start singing when she walked into a classroom... it would be *awful*.

"And next we have Sophie and Jess," Mrs. Farris looked up from the sign-up sheet she was holding. "Ready, girls?"

Sophie started forward confidently while Jess hung back.

"Come on," Sophie whispered, and a ripple of sound ran through the crowd, of amusement or derision, Jess didn't know. Already it was starting—the teasing, the mockery. Her stomach cramped.

"Sophie..."

"*Jess.*" Sophie turned around to give her a fierce,

commanding look, dark eyebrows drawn together. Jess read the look in her eyes as if she'd said the words out loud—*it's too late to back out. It will be worse if you do.*

Except, it wouldn't *feel* worse. It wouldn't feel as bad as walking onto that stage with trembling legs and a hollow feeling in her stomach. And yet she was doing it—walking forward one dread-filled step at a time, until Sophie was seated at the keyboard, and Jess was standing in front of the microphone, trying hard to keep her legs from shaking visibly.

"When you're ready," Mrs. Farris told them with a smile, and Sophie played the opening bars of the pop song they'd been practicing for the last few weeks.

Jess opened her mouth to sing—and nothing came out. Not a sound, not a breath. It was as if she was the Little Mermaid, and her voice had been stolen. This was going to be every bit as bad as she'd feared.

Sophie threw her a panicked look and then played the opening bars again. Jess saw at least two dozen kids all staring at her in varying degrees of boredom, indifference, pity, or glee—and then she saw Mrs. Farris give her a sympathetic, encouraging smile, a little nod. She could do this. She *had* to.

She took a quick breath, opened her mouth again, and then began to sing. The first note was wobbly, and she saw how everyone noticed, but then the second was better, and then she remembered her voice and the rhythm and by the time the chorus came round, she was belting it out and, with a tremor of delight, she saw that several kids were nodding along, swaying to the music, enjoying it. She was doing it, she was actually *doing it*!

As the last note faded away, Mrs. Farris applauded, along with a few others.

"Well done, girls, very well done, indeed! I'll have the list of successful acts up on the noticeboard by the end of the day."

"You were amazing, Jess!" Sophie exclaimed as they left the room, and Jess let out a shuddery breath.

"I'm just glad it's over," she admitted. And yet... she had enjoyed herself, in the end. It was surprising, how much.

"But if we make the list," Sophie reminded her with a grin, "we'll have to do it again, and in front of the whole school!"

Jess didn't know if she could bear to think about that, but... she suddenly realized she *did* actually hope they were chosen. She wanted a chance to do it again, and even better this time, without the nervousness, that first wobbly note.

The rest of the afternoon seemed to creep by as Jess waited for the final bell to ring, so she and Sophie could check out the noticeboard in the music block. Once again, Jess found she couldn't concentrate on any of her lessons, but for an entirely different reason. She wasn't nervous about singing; she was nervous about *not* being able to.

Finally—*finally*—the bell rang, and she raced out of the classroom, meeting Sophie in the corridor. They exchanged nervous smiles as they walked toward the music block, faltering a bit before they strode forward, to the bulletin board.

"There it is!" Sophie exclaimed as they both caught sight of the printed list of successful acts that had been pinned up that afternoon.

"I'm afraid to look," Jess admitted with a nervous laugh, half-covering her eyes, but Sophie strode forward, quickly scanning the names.

A few endless seconds passed while Jess waited, peeking between her fingers.

"We're on it!" Sophie finally exclaimed jubilantly, and Jess's jaw nearly dropped in surprise as she took her hand away from her eyes. Despite her newfound hopes, she hadn't actually been expecting it.

"We... we are?"

"*Yes!*" Sophie turned to her, her face flushed with excitement, her eyes bright. "We're going to be performing in the autumn concert to the whole school!"

The whole school... Again, Jess felt that sinking feeling, that flutter of nerves, but resolutely she pushed it away and smiled back at Sophie, determined to enjoy this.

"Yes," she replied, tilting her chin up a notch. "We are!"

CHAPTER 27

GWEN

Sunlight filtered through the gap in the curtains as Gwen lay in bed and listened to the thumps and thuds that meant her four grandchildren were up and getting ready for school. Normally, she would have been up as well, usually for an hour already, at least, having made coffee and collected the eggs, fed the chickens and unloaded the dishwasher, enjoyed a few moments' quiet before happy chaos descended on the house.

This morning, however, she felt as if she could barely lift her head from the pillow. Her limbs felt leaden, and her empty stomach churned. It was little more than a week since she'd started chemotherapy, and the effects of it were certainly beginning to be felt.

"Mom... Josh took the last of the Weetos!"

"Mom... where's my school jumper?"

"Ow, Mom, don't brush my hair so hard!"

Gwen listened to the familiar chorus of questions and complaints and felt a surge of sympathy for Ellie, who was undoubtedly racing from one near-crisis to the next. Matthew would be helping too, as best as he could with his arm still in a cast, but Gwen knew well enough that when children wanted something done, they tended to ask their mum.

Usually, she tried to help in the mornings, although she'd got the feeling that Ellie was trying to keep the children out of her way, to give her some peace and quiet. Still, she did her best to find hairbrushes or missing shoes, make sure lunch boxes and PE kits were remembered. Often, though, she ended up feeling as in the way as Ellie seemed to fear the children were, not knowing where things were or how they were done.

This morning, she wouldn't be in the way. Although she'd intended to get up half an hour ago when she'd first woken, she hadn't stirred. Hadn't felt *able* to stir. Why did her head feel so heavy, her stomach so empty? She closed her eyes, telling herself it would just be for a moment.

She woke to Ellie's soft voice at the door. "Gwen... Gwen?"

Gwen blinked the world into foggy focus. Her stomach still churned, and her head felt as if it were full of cotton wool. "I'm here," she called, her voice little more than a croak. Goodness, what was *wrong* with her? She needed to get a grip...

"Sorry to disturb you." Ellie peeked her head around the doorway, looking uncertain. "I wanted to let you sleep, but your chemo starts in an hour, and I thought you might want some time to get ready."

"An hour?" Startled, Gwen eased herself into a sitting position, conscious of her mussed hair, her sleepy, and no doubt rather gormless, look. "Is it really that late? I only meant to close my eyes for a few minutes..."

"You needed the rest." Ellie smiled sympathetically. "Can I get you something? A cup of tea? Some toast?"

Gwen's stomach revolted at the thought of any food, but she hoped a cup of tea might help shake her out of this stupor. "Thank you, Ellie. A cup of tea would be lovely. I'll come down to the kitchen as soon as I've dressed."

"All right." Ellie slipped out of the room, and Gwen forced

herself out of bed, even though she struggled not to pull the duvet back up over her head and let herself sink back into sleep.

When she made it downstairs, Ellie had a pot of tea ready, and some buttery toast as well.

"Just in case," she told her. "I'll eat it if you don't."

"I'll try some," Gwen promised. "Thank you. That's very kind."

She perched on the edge of a chair, feeling about a million years old, as Ellie poured her a cup of tea.

"Are the effects of the chemo kicking in?" she asked quietly, and Gwen grimaced.

"I suppose so. I don't think I've ever felt this tired before."

"Shall I drive you to the hospital this morning? I'm free, and I thought it might be nice to have a chat."

Have a chat? Gwen barely felt capable of stringing syllables together, but she managed a weak smile. "That's very kind of you, Ellie..." She paused, because Sarah had been driving her every morning, but she didn't think she could face her daughter's well-meaning brand of officiousness today.

Sarah would no doubt tell her what she needed to eat, do, or even think in order to beat the effects of the chemo along with the cancer. She would also be nervous and edgy, as she had been every day, snapping at nurses and fussing with the IV, worried that Gwen wasn't coping as well as she should be. Gwen didn't think she could manage her daughter on top of her symptoms, not today.

"That would be nice," she told Ellie. "Thank you."

She reached for her phone and sent a quick text to Sarah, whom she knew would be getting ready to pick her up. *Ellie's taking me to the hospital today. You can have a rest!*

Would Sarah be hurt by what she might see as a brush-off? Gwen hoped not. In any case, she felt too tired to worry about it. It had been hard enough simply to get out of bed.

. . .

A short while later, they were in the car, and Ellie was keeping up a cheerful patter while Gwen tried not to slump against the window. Goodness, she was so very tired. Her eyelids felt as if they had weights attached to them, and kept drifting shut.

"Matt and I had some thoughts about the bed and breakfast renovation," Ellie ventured a bit hesitantly as she turned into the hospital parking lot. "I wanted to share them with you, but we don't have to talk about them now if you're not up for it. I just wanted to let you know we'd had a discussion."

Thoughts about the bed and breakfast? Gwen's stomach curdled with dread. The last thing she wanted was to hear about her son's plans for marble en suites or a fitness gym in the barn. Or maybe he wanted to go in a different direction—yurts in the garden, a yoga studio... Gwen didn't think she could take any of it now. She could barely think at all.

"I'm sorry, Ellie," she said with a little grimace. "I'm feeling so tired today. Do you mind if we have chat about it a bit later?"

"Of course not," Ellie said quickly. She smiled, but Gwen could see both the disappointment and the worry in her eyes. "I didn't mean to pressure you. Whenever it's convenient, Gwen, of course. There's absolutely no rush at all. I just wanted to put your mind at rest, really, that we haven't forgotten about it."

"Thank you," Gwen murmured, grateful for her daughter-in-law's understanding. She didn't think Sarah would have felt the same, as guilty as that thought made her.

CHAPTER 28

ELLIE

Ellie sat next to Gwen, who was dozing in her reclining chair, the IV dripping the chemotherapy drugs into her arm. The room was quiet, with four patients all in chairs like Gwen's, all looking as tired and worn out, some also dozing.

Ellie glanced down at the magazine she'd been skimming through and put it aside. She couldn't concentrate on anything, not with Gwen looking so poorly next to her. Somehow, seeing her hooked up to the IV, her face drained of color, her eyes closed, made it all feel so much more real, so much *worse*. She'd been an idiot to want to talk about the bed and breakfast plans today, as if Gwen would be interested in hearing anything about those. There were far more important things for her mother-in-law to concern herself with, like getting better.

"Don't look so worried," Gwen said with a small, wry smile as her eyes flickered open. "It's the chemo that's making me feel this way, not the cancer. And that must mean it's doing its job. At least that's what I tell myself, anyway."

"It certainly is," Ellie replied bracingly. She felt a flash of guilt for Gwen having to worry about how *she* felt. She wasn't the one who was ill.

"I know things have been hard for you," Gwen continued quietly. "In so many ways. And I doubt I've made things easier."

"Oh, you *have* made things easier, Gwen," Ellie said quickly. "And you don't need to think about that right now. Just concentrate on yourself, and getting better."

"But I want to think about it. I think about myself far too often, and frankly I'd rather not. A distraction is far preferable." She straightened a little in her chair. "Do you think the children are starting to adjust to living here?"

"I think so. I hope so, anyway." Another flash of guilt streaked through Ellie. Sometimes she felt as if she didn't even know what was going on in her children's lives, especially with Ben and Jess. She'd had a nice chat with Jess recently, but it had been the first one in ages. She needed to make more of an effort to connect; the problem was, she was never sure whether to commiserate with their worries and sorrows, or try to bolster and encourage them about the future. "Ava seems to have plugged herself right in," she told Gwen, "and Josh has made a lovely friend. Ben is enjoying his clubs." She smiled wryly. "As for Jess, your guess is as good as mine."

"It's harder for them, since they're that little bit older," Gwen replied. "And I know Jess is missing her best friend, who seems to have gone awfully quiet on her. Chloe, isn't it?"

"Has Jess fallen out with Chloe?" Ellie gazed at her mother-in-law, startled that Gwen had some intel she didn't. "I didn't realize that." And maybe she should have.

"I think she feels Chloe has forgotten her, since she's moved so far away."

"I can understand why she might worry about that, although she hasn't said as much to me." Ellie sighed dispiritedly. "I wish Jess would confide in me more."

"Sometimes your mother is the hardest person to talk to," Gwen replied with a small, sad smile. "Matthew hasn't wanted to talk to me about the bed and breakfast plans very much. I know he's disappointed, and worse than that, I think he feels defeated. I wish I could help him more... but you said you both had some new plans?"

"Yes, but we don't have to talk about them now." And they weren't exactly Matthew's plans, either, Ellie thought. She had hoped he'd get more on board in time, but a few days on, he hadn't. This was still her idea, and hers alone.

"No, no," Gwen replied, "tell me, I'd like to hear." She gave another wan smile. "Distraction, remember?"

"Well..." Haltingly, Ellie began to explain her dreams of having the bed and breakfast be something more homegrown and family-friendly. "I thought it would play to the place's strengths," she said, her voice becoming more earnest as she told Gwen about it, "as well as yours. Letting people chip in... old-fashioned game nights and big breakfasts all together around the table, like one, big, happy family... but maybe it's crazy?" Her voice held a hopeful lilt; she couldn't tell anything from her mother-in-law's face, although Gwen had been listening intently the whole while, a slight furrow between her brows. "If you don't like the idea," Ellie added quickly, "that's absolutely fine. It's your business, after all, not mine, and I really don't mean to interfere—"

"Ellie." Gwen put a gentle, restraining hand on hers as she smiled. "Enough with the apologies and backtracking. They're not needed, I promise, and we've tripped over ourselves too much as it is, trying to get along when I think it was easier than either of us ever realized."

"You... think so?" Ellie asked uncertainly.

"It feels that way to me. Maybe having cancer is making me more honest, but I'm sorry that we haven't got on better over the years. I know we haven't not got on, but I feel as if there's always been this *tension* between us, unspoken but felt." Gwen scanned her face. "Am I wrong?"

"No," Ellie admitted in little more than a whisper. She felt both guilty and gratified that her mother-in-law was talking like this. They were finally addressing the elephant in the room, the one they'd skirted around for ages, but she wished she'd had the courage to talk about it more honestly before now. "I don't think you're wrong, Gwen."

"I think I was taken aback when Matthew started dating you," Gwen admitted. "Because I didn't want him to stay in America. I don't think I blamed you—at least I didn't *mean* to blame you—but I think I carried some resentment all the same. I'm sorry for that."

"You don't need to be sorry, Gwen," Ellie said. She felt tears thickening in her throat and she had to blink rapidly to keep them back.

"I think I do. I should have been more welcoming. More accommodating. Not just now, when you've all moved here, but before. A long time ago."

"I should have been more understanding," Ellie replied. "And more accepting. I let myself get annoyed, and I felt resentful, as well. I'm sorry, too."

"Good." With her non-IV hand, Gwen reached over and squeezed Ellie's hand. "I'm glad we've got that sorted at last. I don't know why we didn't before, except maybe we couldn't. These last few weeks have changed me, and I think maybe they've changed you, as well."

Ellie nodded slowly. It was true; she felt changed. She didn't think they could have had this conversation before now, even if she wished they could have.

"Now," Gwen said a bit more briskly, "about your idea for the B&B. The truth is, I *love* it. It's exactly what I want for any bed and breakfast I run—and David would have wanted it, too. I think we were going for that, in our own, smaller way, before, but I love your ideas about game nights and children helping in the garden—it would be wonderful!" Her face lit up for a moment before she paused, a slight crease appearing between her brows again. "But what does Matthew think? Really? Because it's not at all what he'd been planning, is it?"

"No," Ellie agreed, trying to rally with a smile. "It's not. And I'm not sure what he thinks, to be honest, but he was willing for me to pitch it to you, at any rate, so that's a good sign, I guess."

"Ah," Gwen said, and there was a wealth of understanding in her voice. Ellie's smile wobbled. "Be patient, Ellie. This is hard for him. He's always been proud." She let out a little sigh. "Just like Sarah. I don't know where they get it from." She gave her the ghost of smile. "Must have been from David."

Ellie let out a little laugh. "Yes," she agreed, smiling. "It must have been."

"I'm proud of you," Gwen told her, "for thinking of it in the first place. Matthew will get on board in time, I'm sure of it, but in the meantime, be proud of your own idea. I'm certainly grateful for it."

"Thank you," Ellie replied, startled and gratified by Gwen's words. She hadn't even considered being proud of her own idea, but as Gwen had spoken, she'd realized she was—and it was a nice—as well as needed—feeling.

CHAPTER 29

GWEN

Gwen was still feeling tired as she and Ellie headed back to Bluebell Inn, once the chemotherapy had finished. It had been nice to have a chat, and she was so very glad they were finally making real progress with their relationship. She couldn't think why she hadn't truly grasped the nettle before, but maybe, as she'd said to Ellie, she hadn't been able to. One of the unexpected blessings of having cancer, she supposed. You stopped avoiding uncomfortable heart-to-hearts.

She was also heartened by Ellie's ideas for the bed and breakfast—a far cry from Matthew's talk of en suite bathrooms and gyms, and a huge relief, exactly the kind of idea she could really get behind.

As Ellie turned into Bluebell Lane, Gwen's heart sank a little, for Sarah's battered Rover was already parked by the house. She hadn't told Gwen she was coming over, and she hoped her daughter hadn't been offended by her decision to go with Ellie. She didn't think she could handle a hurt-filled confrontation right now.

"Sarah?" she said as she came into the kitchen. Her daughter, she saw, had been busy—there was a foil-covered casserole resting on top of the Aga, the sink had been scrubbed, and the kettle was boiled.

"I'm making tea," Sarah announced in a brisk, brittle voice. "I thought you could do with a cuppa after your chemo."

Actually, Gwen's stomach was churning from the treatment, but she gave her daughter a warm smile all the same. "That sounds lovely, Sarah. Thank you." She glanced at Ellie, who was standing in the doorway, looking uncertain. "Ellie? Would you like one?"

"Actually, I have a few things to do before I pick up Ava and Josh," Ellie replied, backing out into the hall. "But thank you. Nice to see you, Sarah." She gave her sister-in-law a quick smile and wave before disappearing upstairs.

Gwen didn't really blame her. She knew how formidable Sarah could seem, could *be*. She was a little intimidated herself by the way she was whirling around the kitchen, moving from Aga to sink and back again with dizzying speed. With a sigh, Gwen lowered herself into a chair at the table as Sarah continued to around the kitchen.

"You seem tired," Sarah remarked, and Gwen let out a little laugh.

"I'm sure I do. That is a side effect of the treatment."

"I mean more tired than usual." Sarah almost sounded accusing, although of what, or whom, Gwen didn't know.

"I believe the effect is cumulative," she answered after a moment. "That's what the consultant told me, anyway, so it will get worse before it gets better."

"Yes, I suppose that makes sense." Sarah brought the teapot to the table and poured them both cups. "I was surprised you had Ellie take you today," she remarked diffidently as she passed Gwen her cup.

Gwen tried not to sigh. She'd been expecting this, but, in truth, she wasn't sure how to handle it. "Surprised?"

"It's only, I've been taking you every day."

"Yes, which is why I thought you could use a break."

Sarah pursed her lips as she stared down at her tea. "Was that really the reason, Mum?" she asked, her voice vibrating with hurt in a way that made Gwen feel a rush of both love and guilt. She knew how important it was for Sarah to feel as if she were helping, just as she knew she couldn't keep managing her daughter and doing her best to keep her happy, not when she felt so tired and ill.

"It was part of it, Sarah," she said as she wrapped her hands around her cup of tea, grateful for its warmth. She always felt so cold after her treatments.

Sarah gave a little nod before she raised her chin. "So what was the other part?" she asked.

Gwen hesitated before answering mostly honestly, "I wanted to spend some time with Ellie."

"You spend loads of time with Ellie. She lives with you, for heaven's sake!"

Gwen felt as if they were both heading toward a cliff, and there was nothing she could do about it but hold her breath, close her eyes, and go over.

"Ellie wanted to talk to me about some ideas for the bed and breakfast," she said after a moment, knowing she was still hedging. "That was part of it, too."

"What ideas?"

"Just about how to market it, really," Gwen replied. "Nothing concrete yet."

Sarah was silent for a moment. She took a sip of tea, and then put down her cup.

"You've never asked *me* about plans for the bed and breakfast," she said finally, and Gwen did her best not to goggle at her. She hadn't expected this response from her daughter, not in a million years.

"Ask you...?" she repeated faintly. "But... but, Sarah, in all the years you've lived near Llandrigg, you've never seemed interested." She'd always been too busy with her own family and life to care much about the bed and breakfast. At least, that was how it had always seemed to Gwen; whenever Sarah remarked upon it, it was to say how much time and energy it seemed to take, and wouldn't Gwen prefer to retire and enjoy life a little bit more?

"I wasn't interested," Sarah replied with a bitter edge to her voice, "because it was obvious you were keen for Matt to take up the reins, not me."

"What..." Gwen shook her head slowly, her mind reeling from this unexpected turn in the conversation. "Sarah, if I'd ever thought for a moment that you and Nathan wanted to help with the bed and breakfast..."

"Oh, we couldn't have done," Sarah answered impatiently. "I know that. I'm not saying differently, not really. It's just..." She drew a quick breath. "I feel as if you're cutting me out. As if you don't want me to help... with anything."

Here they were, right at the precipice of everything unsaid between them, the source of all the tension. Why, Gwen wondered, were the relationships with the people you loved the most the hardest?

"I'm very grateful for your help," Gwen told her after a moment.

"But?" Sarah returned, still sounding bitter. "Because I am definitely sensing a 'but'."

"Oh, Sarah." Gwen let out a gusty sigh, knowing she had to be honest with her daughter, just as she had been with Ellie. "I love you dearly, but the truth is... sometimes it's been hard work, having you taking me to chemo."

Hurt made Sarah's face crumple before her expression hardened. "*Hard work?*" she repeated tightly. "*I've* been hard work, helping *you* out? Driving you to the hospital, bringing you meals, tidying up... *that's* hard work for you?"

"I'm sorry, I didn't mean it exactly like that." Gwen wished she could take the words back. Hurting her daughter wouldn't help anyone, and yet she knew she had to at least try to explain before Sarah was irreparably offended.

"How did you mean it, then? Because I'm not sure what else you could mean. Either you appreciate and want my help, or you don't, and it very much seems like you don't." Sarah's voice broke on the last word and, seeming annoyed with herself, she brushed at her eyes. "I'm so sorry for being such a nuisance."

"You're not a nuisance," Gwen exclaimed. "That's not what I mean at all. It's just... I know this is hard for you, darling. I know how you like to feel in control, in charge. You want to *do* things. I understand that, truly—"

"You're saying it as if it's a bad thing, to be like that," Sarah replied with a sniff.

"Not bad," Gwen said quickly. "Not at all. Just... sometimes a bit... tiring. For other people." She bit her lip, hating that she might be hurting her daughter with her words, and yet knowing she had to be honest. She couldn't keep handling both Sarah and her chemo treatment. She knew she couldn't. "Sometimes," she explained carefully, "I feel as I have to manage you along with everything else."

"*Manage* me?" Sarah drew herself up, her eyes flashing. "I promise you, Mum, you don't need to *manage* me. I've just been trying to help you. The last thing I'd ever want to do is make things harder or worse for you." Her voice vibrated with both hurt and anger. "But if my help is so difficult for you, and if I'm the real reason you're so tired, then I suppose I shouldn't offer it any longer. I've got my own troubles, anyway—"

"You do?" Gwen had wondered what might be going on in her daughter's life; she never liked to admit any weakness, and Gwen never felt she could press her. "Tell me about them. I want to know—"

"Do you really?" Sarah retorted. "Because I wouldn't want to *tire you out* with my problems."

"Oh, Sarah." Gwen's eyes filled with tears. "I do want to know. And I'm sorry for the way I sounded. I didn't mean it like that, honestly—"

"And as you have *Ellie* to take you to chemo and do all the rest," Sarah finished as she rose from the table, her body taut with wounded affront, "clearly I'm not needed or wanted here." She dumped her teacup in the sink with a clatter, and turned toward the door.

"Sarah, please," Gwen said again, truly distraught now. "I really didn't mean to hurt you." Her head was pounding, her stomach churning, and she longed to lie upstairs in her darkened bedroom for several hours. A big set-to with Sarah was the last thing she needed, and she couldn't bear it if her daughter stormed out now, with things between them so damaged.

"You haven't hurt me," Sarah replied stiffly as she gathered her coat and bag. "I just didn't realize how difficult I was making things for you. But don't worry. I won't trouble you any further, I promise."

Gwen rose from the table, one hand outstretched. "*Please*, Sarah—"

"Bye, Mum," Sarah said, her voice turning thick with tears, and before Gwen could say another word, her daughter was out the door, closing it behind her with a firm click that was halfway to a slam.

Gwen slumped back in her chair and dropped her head into her hands. All the fragile optimism she'd felt, chatting with Ellie, had drained right out of her. How could she have hurt Sarah so badly? Honesty was clearly overrated, especially with those you loved. She'd only made things worse—and what could she do now to make things better?

Really, she thought with a sigh, she couldn't have possibly handled that conversation any worse. She never should have told Sarah she was hard work. What a hurtful thing to say. And yet she *was* hard work, and Gwen had been too tired to temper her honest words with the gentleness she knew was needed.

She heard Ellie return with Ava and Josh; with a murmured word, Ellie directed the children to the sitting room, no doubt worried Sarah was still raging in the kitchen. Gwen sighed at the thought. She would ring Sarah tonight, she decided, and try to explain, or perhaps simply apologize, again—not that her daughter would accept it. Yet she still had to try.

"Granny?"

Gwen looked up to see Josh standing in the doorway, smiling shyly. He was the quietest of Ellie and Matthew's four children and, Gwen suspected, sometimes overlooked, happy as he was to do a puzzle or play Lego by himself. She'd been much the same as a child.

She summoned a smile for him, tired though she was. "Yes, darling?"

"Are you..." Josh hesitated, winding one skinny leg around the other like a stork. He looked uncertain and very young. "Are you okay?"

"Am I okay?" Gwen's eyes filled with tears as she registered the question full of loving concern, and out of the mouth of an eight-year-old. "Oh, Josh... yes. Yes, I'm okay. I will be, at any rate." She held out her arms, and after a second's pause, Josh came forward, putting his arms around her before he slipped onto a chair at the table.

"We saw Aunt Sarah leaving. She looked cross."

Gwen nodded. "She was cross, I'm afraid. I need to apologize to her."

"Were you cross?"

"No. Just tired." She smiled sadly at him. "I should have handled our conversation better, I'm afraid, and I didn't."

"That's what Mom says when she shouts at us sometimes," Josh said with an endearing little grin. "That she's tired."

"Yes. Mums are often tired, and they have good reason to be." She gave him a sympathetic smile and his face suddenly brightened.

"Do you want to do a puzzle?"

"A puzzle?" Gwen looked at him, surprised. He'd never asked her to do anything with him before. "All right."

Josh hopped off his stool and, a few moments later, he returned with a box.

"Three hundred pieces," Gwen remarked as she took in the box with the picture of the solar system on the front, most of the pieces looking to be nothing but black sky. "This looks rather challenging."

"The hard ones are best," Josh replied as he opened the box, and Gwen smiled. Perhaps she needed to have a little more of that kind of can-do attitude.

Josh was clearly an experienced puzzle-completer, for he was soon sorting pieces into edges, corners, and interior, and instructing Gwen to do the same.

They worked in companionable silence for a few moments, sunlight slanting through the window, and slowly Gwen felt her insides unclench as a still sort of peace settled over the room. She'd explain to Sarah and apologize. It would be okay. She'd make sure of it, whatever it took.

"Now it's easier to do the edges," Josh explained, once they'd sorted all the pieces. "Look, see?" Neatly, he slotted two pieces together, and Gwen smiled.

"You've got a very good system here, Josh."

Perhaps that was her problem, she reflected as she slotted a few pieces together, feeling a surprising satisfaction at being able to do it. Her life was a jumble, like the pieces in the box before they'd been sorted. It all felt so overwhelming. But if she simply took one challenge at a time—the bed and breakfast, her diagnosis, her daughter—then they would be more manageable. She'd find their place; she'd fit them in.

Impulsively, she reached over and gave Josh's thin shoulder a quick squeeze. "Thank you for including me in this. I've really enjoyed it, Josh."

"Josh?" Ellie's voice sounded a bit strained as she came into the kitchen. "There you are. Didn't I tell you not to bother Granny?"

"It's fine," Gwen assured her. "Actually, it's been rather nice. We've been doing a puzzle."

"Oh, but, Josh—"

"I *wanted* to," Gwen said quickly. "Honestly, Ellie, it's been lovely. Just what I needed." She gave Josh a warm smile, and he beamed back.

"Well..." Ellie still looked somewhat unconvinced, her gaze darting around the kitchen as if she expected Sarah to be hiding in a cupboard.

"Sarah went home," Gwen said.

"Yes, I saw her leaving in her car." Ellie hesitated, and Gwen suspected she both did and didn't want to ask what had happened.

"I'm afraid things got a bit out of hand," Gwen admitted on a sigh.

"Granny's tired," Josh supplied. "And when she's tired, she gets cross. Just like you, Mom."

"Oh, really?" Ellie looked amused, and she and Gwen shared a laughing look before she ruffled her son's hair. "Come on, you. You've got Lego club tonight. Did you remember?"

"Oh, yeah!" Josh brightened as he clambered off his chair. "It's a new club at the village hall," he explained to Gwen. "And Lego is my favorite!"

"Not puzzles?" Gwen teased and Josh paused, a frown on his face as he considered the matter seriously.

"Puzzles are second," he told her, and Gwen nodded in understanding.

As he and Ellie went off to get ready for his club, she realized she felt better already, thanks to her grandson.

And she resolved to ring Sarah tonight. She would find a way to mend the rift that had opened up between her and her daughter, no matter what it took.

CHAPTER 30

ELLIE

A headache was starting to band Ellie's temples as she walked briskly to the village hall with Josh skipping by her side. They were already five minutes late, thanks to Ava having a tantrum about being left at home, although Gwen had managed to distract her with the promise of a baking session with Granny, even though Ellie feared her mother-in-law wasn't really up for it, after her chemo; Matthew had gone out for the afternoon, Ellie didn't know where.

She'd had a text from Sarah, fired off in anger, it would seem, for it simply said that Ellie could handle all of Gwen's chemo appointments from now on, and good luck to her. Ellie didn't know what that meant for Gwen and Sarah's relationship, but it couldn't be anything good. It wasn't anything good for her fledgling relationship with Sarah, either, and meanwhile she would have to take on a lot more than ever before, in addition to working on the bed and breakfast plans and managing her family. She wanted to help Gwen, of course she did, and she would, but her head throbbed just thinking about it all.

Her mother-in-law had *cancer*, she reminded herself sternly. Of course she was going to do whatever she could to help and support her. But why did it have to feel so *hard*? It didn't help that Matthew was still being fairly monosyllabic; or that Jess was seriously sporting some teenaged attitude, seeming to fly in a rage when Ellie so much as suggested she check if she had any homework—not even do it, just *check*, and yet somehow such a mild request seemed to infuriate her daughter. She'd thought things had been getting better, but just when she started to hope, it was all several steps back and things seemed to be getting worse, instead.

Sudden tears stung Ellie's eyes and she blinked them away impatiently. All right, so life was a tiny bit challenging right now. *And* she was homesick. She wanted her circle of friends and a caramel macchiato from Starbucks—there *was* one on the way to Cardiff, she'd learned, so that, at least wasn't impossible —and the New England sunshine streaming down. Never mind. This too would pass... she hoped. She had meant what she'd said to Matthew, about not wanting to move back to Connecticut. You couldn't go back, no matter how much you might want to. Ahead was the only option.

Her gloomy, grumpy mood stubbornly remained, however, as she dropped Josh off at the village hall and headed home again. Gwen had got Ava involved in a big baking project, which was wonderful, but the kitchen was now a mess and Ellie had to both tidy up and sort out dinner, and Matthew was still out.

Ben and Jess had got into a heated argument about some-thing to do with some noticeboard on the way home, and Ben was now flinging his stuff all around the kitchen—his blazer was dusted in flour before Ellie managed to open her mouth—and Jess had stomped upstairs, slamming her door so hard it felt as if the whole house rattled. Ellie's headache got that much worse.

"I'm sorry, I'll tidy up," Gwen said, wiping her hands on her apron. She looked knackered, and Ellie felt guilty for her sour mood, which her mother-in-law must have clocked.

"No, no it's fine, I'll do it. Ava will help. Can you switch the kettle on, love?" She smiled at her daughter, who hopped off her stool, eager as ever to help. "Go have a sit down in the living room, Gwen. I'll bring you a cup of tea."

Gwen went off gratefully, and Ellie set about tidying the kitchen before she decided what she was going to do with a kilo of mince that was on its sell-by date.

"Ben, don't get out those crisps," she instructed, spying her son hunting through a cupboard from the corner of her eye. "Dinner will be in just a little while."

"Mummy, you said *crisps*, not *chips*," Ava piped up. "You're sounding British!"

"So I am," Ellie agreed with a tired smile.

The kettle clicked off, and she brought Gwen her tea, and fried the mince up with a jar of tomato sauce.

"Where's Daddy?" Ava asked, sounding bored, and Ellie tried to answer pleasantly.

"I don't know. He went out somewhere. Maybe he had an errand." Although since he couldn't drive with a broken arm, Ellie didn't know what he'd been doing in Llandrigg. "*Ben!*" She picked up the open packet of crisps, her voice full of exasperation. "I told you...!"

But her son was nowhere to be seen.

Jess slunk into the kitchen just as Ellie was laying the table.

"Ew, bolognaise," she said in a tone of disgust.

"I thought you liked bolognaise?" Ellie tried to keep her voice light.

"No, of course I don't." This, despite Jess having asked for seconds of it only last week.

"Well, I'm afraid it's all there is tonight," Ellie said as cheerfully as she could, and Jess grimaced.

"I won't eat it. I'm not hungry, anyway."

Ellie suppressed a sigh. "Jess, you need to eat."

"I told you, I'm not hungry!" Her daughter's eyes flared

with sudden rage, and Ellie feared, a sheen of tears. What was really going on here?

"Jess, sweetheart, is everything okay?" she asked in a gentler tone, which had the effect of making her daughter even more furious.

"Why are you even asking that? Why would you think it wasn't?"

"Because you seem—"

"What?" Jess flung at her like an accusation. "What do I *seem*, Mom? Go on, tell me."

Ellie stared at her in helpless bafflement. "Like you don't like bolognaise," she said at last, on a sigh. "Oh...!" She hurried to the stove where the supposedly simmering sauce was now smoking. "None of us is going to like bolognaise tonight," she muttered as she took the pan off the Aga. She hadn't yet got the hang of cooking on it, and she feared she never would.

Jess huffed theatrically, as if the burned bolognaise was somehow proof of her own dislike, or perhaps just her mother's obvious inadequacies, and something in Ellie snapped.

"That's enough, Jess," Ellie said shortly, and her daughter let out an aggrieved cry.

"I didn't *do* anything."

"You've been moaning and whinging since you came in the kitchen," Ellie retorted, knowing she should stop, yet somehow unable to. "And I've had quite enough, thank you very much."

"*You've* had enough!" Jess repeated in a voice that was half-snarl, half-sob. "*I've* had enough! I hate it here! I hate Wales! And I hate *you!*" With another sound, that was definitely a sob, she stormed out of the kitchen.

Ellie heaved a sigh as she started scraping the burned bits of the bolognaise into the bin. She shouldn't have lost her temper like that, she knew, but sometimes it was so hard, one thing after another, all of it feeling so relentless, so endless.

The front door opened, and Matthew's voice floated through to the kitchen.

"I'm home!"

Ellie closed her eyes briefly and prayed for patience. Her eyes were still closed when he came into the kitchen.

"Hey." He sounded concerned, and wearily Ellie opened her eyes. "You okay?"

"Sort of... not really," Ellie managed, although she was glad for the tender expression on her husband's face.

"Will this make you feel better?" he asked, and to her surprise, he revealed the grande caramel macchiato he'd been hiding behind his back.

Ellie let out a wobbly laugh of surprise. "Where on earth did you get that?"

"At the Starbucks on the way to Cardiff. Better drink it quick, before it's cold."

She shook her head in amazement, taking a sip and then sighing in appreciation. "I've missed this," she admitted. "But what were you doing on the way to Cardiff? How did you even get there?"

"There's a big DIY place on the way there," he told her. "I thought I'd walk around and get some ideas... about how to make this place more like you said. An old mate of mine, Gareth, drove me. I didn't realize he was still in Llandrigg, but we ran into each other the other day."

Ellie lowered her cup, amazed at all this news. "Really?"

"It makes sense, doesn't it?" he told her with a crooked smile. "I know I didn't respond as well as I should have, because it was so different to my idea... which was clearly absurd." He let out a little laugh that made Ellie's heart both ache and lift. "But over the last few days, when I've managed to let go of my pride and really think about it, it seemed like not just a good idea, Ellie, but a great idea... something we can both get behind."

"Oh, Matt." Ellie's voice trembled, and she put down her coffee to step closer to him.

He wrapped his good arm around her, his lips brushing her hair. "Sorry it took me so long," he whispered, and she hugged him tightly, trying to be careful of his cast.

"It doesn't matter."

He gave her another squeeze. "Now drink your coffee before it gets cold!"

CHAPTER 31

JESS

Jess slammed her door and then hurled herself onto her bed, burying her hot face in her pillow. Her mom was *so* unfair. And everyone here was so mean. She hated *everything,* she hated it all more than ever.

The sobs shook her frame as her tears soaked her pillow. It had all started that morning, when she'd come into school. Sophie had been waiting for her at the door, the look on her face both mutinous and miserable.

"What is it?" Jess had asked immediately, for she'd known right away that something was wrong. Really wrong.

"Never mind." Sophie had shrugged, looking away, and that was when Jess had become aware of all the stares and whispers. She'd glanced around and seen how people smirked or looked away. She'd felt herself start to flush, a prickly sensation creeping all over her body, and hadn't even known what had happened yet.

"It's the music board," Sophie had muttered under her breath. "Don't look."

Even though she'd known she shouldn't, Jess had headed down the corridor toward the music block, and the noticeboard where she and Sophie had seen their names on the concert list. She'd frozen as she'd stood in front of it. Someone—someone *horrible*—had printed out headshots of the two of them, taken from their Instagram accounts no doubt, and scrawled "Nerds" in thick red marker over their faces. As she'd stared at the pictures, Jess had felt herself go hot and then cold, while a tide of titters and whispers had grown in volume behind her.

"It doesn't matter," Sophie had said, but Jess hadn't been able to answer. Singing in the concert and her friendship with Sophie had felt like the only two good things about her life in Llandrigg, and now they'd both been ruined. "Jess..." Sophie had put a hand on her arm, but Jess had shrugged it off.

For a reason she hadn't been able to understand, she'd felt furious with Sophie rather than whoever had played the cruel prank on them. She'd walked away from the board and Sophie without a word, and had headed to her locker, keeping her head down, freezing out the world... including her only friend.

By break, the photos had been taken down, but the damage had been done. The whole thing had been made worse by the head teacher's well-meaning words at assembly, reminding everyone about the school's zero tolerance toward bullying. *As if.*

Jess had done her best to ignore all the smirking and sidelong looks, but it had taken everything she had.

Sophie had tried to talk to her at lunch, but Jess had avoided her. She'd still been angry, and as she couldn't explain why even to herself, she'd pretended not to see Sophie in the lunchroom and then she'd ducked into an empty classroom. It had been her worst day of school yet, where she'd felt physically sick with the sheer misery of it all.

And now her mother was angry at her, and her brother, who knew about the prank, had teased her about it on the bus, saying she was "a total nerd, and everyone knows it," and Jess really didn't think she could take anymore.

Her phone pinged and Jess lifted her head from the pillow. It was a Snapchat from Chloe, making her usual cross-eyed funny face, tongue sticking out, with *I miss you!!!!* as the message. The tiniest of smiles tugged at Jess's mouth. Chloe hadn't messaged her in ages.

I miss you too, she typed and took a selfie of her tear-streaked face. She couldn't pretend she was having a good time. She didn't even want to.

Chloe sent another photo, this one with her mouth wide open in alarm, and a dozen sad-face emojis.

Everyone here is horrible, Jess texted, feeling only the tiniest flicker of guilt for including Sophie in that blanket statement. *I hate it so, so much.* That much was definitely true.

I hate it here too! Chloe messaged back.

What about Emily? Jess couldn't keep from texting back, bitterness curdling in her stomach. *Your new BFF,* she added, but then deleted it before she sent it.

Chloe sent another raft of sad-face emojis. *She's so fake. I want my BFF back.*

A wave of homesickness crashed over Jess, pulling her under. *I do too,* she texted, and a breathy sob escaped her. *So much. If I could come back there, I'd leave right now. I'm totally serious.*

Why don't you? Chloe texted back. *My mom says you could stay with us for as long as you wanted. You could come back to school!*

Jess's heart turned over at the thought of it. To be back in Connecticut with Chloe... back where everything was familiar, where she belonged... why not? *Why not?*

Are you serious? she texted, her fingers flying, her heart racing.

Chloe sent a bunch of thumbs ups and hearts. *YES!!!*

For a second, hope buoyed inside her; to go back to Connecticut! To live with Chloe! It felt like the best dream ever. Then Jess sank back against her pillows, dispirited. Her parents would never agree to it. Her *mother* wouldn't.

My parents wouldn't let me, she texted, everything in her sinking.

What if you were already here? Chloe texted. *What could they really do then?*

Jess caught her breath.

Do you mean, like, run away?

You could leave a note. You can book a ticket online! All you need is your passport and a credit card.

Jess let herself think of it. She knew where her parents kept all their passports—in a strongbox under their bed. And she thought she knew how to book a plane ticket online; she'd seen her parents do it loads of times. She could even use her mother's credit card; she kept it in her handbag in the sitting room. There was a bus to Abergavenny from the same place as the school bus, and from there she could take a train to London, and then there had to be a way to get from London to Heathrow.

Another message pinged from Chloe.

When you're thirteen you can travel by yourself. You don't even need a letter from your parents. I checked online.

Jess drew another sharp breath. *Seriously?*

Yep.

She held her phone in her hand, her mind spinning. Could she actually do this? Her parents would *freak*. But by the time they realized she was gone, she'd be too far away for them to bring her back. And once she was at Chloe's, and they saw that she was safe and happy…

She wouldn't even have to go to school tomorrow. She wouldn't have to face all the sneers and smirks and stares *ever again*.

Or Sophie…

Remembering the look of hurt on her friend's face when

she'd walked away from her made Jess's stomach cramp. She'd been such a bad friend.

Well? Chloe texted, and recklessly Jess texted back.

Let me see if I can get a ticket.

Chloe sent a series of hearts, rainbows, and hooray emojis while Jess reached for her laptop, her heart starting to thud.

CHAPTER 32

GWEN

Gwen could hear the loud clanking and clattering of pots in the kitchen, and suspected Ellie was annoyed, or perhaps just tired.

She was certainly tired herself—slumped in this chair, her head lolling back, she was barely able to keep her eyes open. Ellie had brought her a cup of tea that was cooling on the table next to her; Gwen didn't feel she had the energy to so much as take a sip. Doing the puzzle with Josh and baking with Ava, pleasant as both activities had been, seemed to have exhausted her. She had so little energy these days, she knew she needed to conserve it, but even so, she couldn't regret spending time with her grandchildren. It was so very precious.

A noise had Gwen opening her eyes; she hadn't even realized she'd closed them until she saw Jess sidling into the room, looking guilty, or perhaps just uncertain.

"Jess?"

"Are you all right, Granny?"

"Yes, just tired." Gwen managed a smile. "What are you up to?"

Jess shrugged, her gaze sliding away. "Oh, nothing."

"Nothing?" Gwen straightened, wincing at the pain in her

joints. Goodness, but she felt old. "What kind of nothing?" she asked lightly, because it was clear, even in her rather befuddled state, that something was going on with her granddaughter. She was twisting a strand of hair around one finger as she nibbled her lip nervously.

"Mom and Dad are talking in the kitchen and I don't want to disturb them," she said after a moment, and Gwen smiled sympathetically.

"They've got a lot on their plate. I don't think I'm helping matters very much."

Jess just shrugged, and Gwen tried again.

"How are things with Chloe?"

For a second, something flickered across Jess's face; it looked like an odd mix of guilt and excitement. "She's pretty good," Jess answered. "We're messaging again, actually."

"That's good." Gwen smiled. "Friends go through ups and downs, don't they?"

"Yeah, I guess so."

A wave of fatigue crashed over Gwen, threatening to pull her under. She leaned her head back against the chair. "Perhaps Chloe can visit here one day," she suggested. "That would be fun, wouldn't it? You could show her all the sights."

Jess gulped. "Yeah... maybe. Or... or I could go see her."

Gwen's eyes fluttered closed as Jess darted across the room. When she opened them again, her granddaughter had gone, but Gwen had the unsettling sensation of having missed something important, although she had no idea what it was.

Gwen didn't know how long it was that she drifted into a doze; at some point, Josh came in to tell her it was time for supper, and Gwen stirred enough to say she wasn't that hungry, and she'd eat later. She heard the comforting sound of chatter and the clink of dishes from the kitchen, the occasional burst of laughter. The dark cloud that had been hovering over the house seemed to have moved on, or at least she hoped it had. When she woke up, things would be better. She'd remember to ring Sarah...

When she stirred again, it was already dark, the sitting room full of shadows, and someone was sitting across from her. For a disorientating second, Gwen thought it was David; even though he'd been gone for twenty years, she could remember the way he sat, his head braced by his hand and cocked to the right. An incredulous smile started to spread across her face when she heard her son's voice.

"Mum?" Matthew asked and straightened, dropping his hand. "Are you awake?"

"Goodness, do you know, for a moment I thought you were your father." Gwen let out a little laugh, and then she laughed again when she saw the alarmed expression on her son's face. "Don't worry, Matthew, I'm not losing the plot yet. It was just the way you were sitting, with your head in your hand—just the way your dad used to sit." Gwen let out a long, sorrowful sigh.

She didn't indulge in grief too often, but in her vulnerable state, she missed her husband more than ever. If he'd been here, he would have taken her to her chemo treatments, he would have sat with her and done the crossword with her; he would have brought her weak tea with just a splash of milk, the way she liked it. He would have charmed the nurses and told silly jokes and kept her smiling—and when she wanted quiet, he would have known instinctively to keep his mouth shut.

She missed him so much, more now than she had in years.

"Mum, are you okay?" Matthew asked.

"Yes, just feeling a bit sentimental, I suppose." Self-consciously, Gwen dabbed at her eyes. "It does happen once in a while, you know. Is everything okay? Ellie seemed a bit bothered earlier. I think she has too many demands on her, and I know I'm one of them."

"You're not, Mum, and I know Ellie's busy. We're sorting things out."

"Are you?" Gwen asked, unable to keep from sounding skeptical.

Matthew gave her the ghost of a smile. "Yes, actually, we are. We've been chatting through the plans for the B&B. She told you about those?"

"Yes, and I thought they sounded wonderful."

"Well, so do I," Matthew told her firmly. "It took me a little while to warm to it, but I have and now I'm completely on board." He paused. "With everything. I know I haven't made things easy for Ellie lately, and I'm still laid up with this arm, but I am trying now. Properly. Thanks to you."

"Oh, Matthew..." Gwen smiled at him gratefully, finding herself near tears. Goodness, but cancer, or maybe the chemo, was making her emotional! "I'm so very glad to hear that."

"I know you are. Thanks, Mum, for helping to sort me out. I needed a talking-to, I know I did."

"You just needed time," Gwen murmured, her eyes fluttering closed as if they had weights attached to them. She simply couldn't keep them open any longer. She felt so dreadfully tired...

"Mum? Mum?" Matthew leaned forward and touched her arm, and then he laid a cool hand across her forehead. "Mum," he exclaimed, his voice full of alarm, "you're burning up!"

CHAPTER 33

ELLIE

"She's picked up an infection," the consultant explained as Ellie and Matthew sat in a little room off the oncology ward later that evening, having rushed Gwen to the hospital. "Which can happen quite easily at this stage, because the white blood cell count is so low. It should respond well to antibiotics, and she can be home and resuming treatment in a couple of days."

"I didn't even realize she was so poorly..." Ellie couldn't keep the guilt from curdling her stomach as she thought of how grumpy and hassled she'd been, while Gwen was so ill. "She must have picked it up from one of the kids."

The consultant smiled in understanding as he spread his hands wide. "It happens. You caught it quickly, before it's become too serious, so well done."

But she hadn't caught *anything*, Ellie acknowledged. Matthew was the one who had noticed, and only when Gwen had practically passed out! Ellie had been feeling annoyed and overwhelmed by her children's moods, Sarah's sudden aggression, her husband's absence, and Gwen's need. She'd sent Gwen off to the sitting room and basically forgotten her, especially when

Matthew had come in and told her he was on board with her idea for Bluebell Inn, which was wonderful, but right now she felt horribly guilty for not seeing just how ill her mother-in-law was.

Matthew put an arm around her shoulders and Ellie leaned into his solid warmth. "It's going to be all right, Ellie," he said quietly. "And, in any case, you shouldn't blame yourself. You're not Atlas. You don't have to carry the world on your shoulders, you know."

Except she sort of did, Ellie thought glumly, because who else was going to do it? She knew Matthew wanted to help, and he would, but... when it came down to it, all her responsibilities still weighed heavily.

Gwen was sleeping peacefully, so they left the hospital, with Ellie promising to come by in the morning. "I hope it hasn't all kicked off at home," she remarked wearily as she climbed into the car. They'd left Jess in charge, which usually meant an argument broke out between her and Ben.

"Hopefully not," Matthew said as Ellie started the car. They drove through the parking lot and out into the rainy autumn night, the world dark and wet all around them. "Autumn in Wales," he remarked wryly as raindrops spattered the windshield.

"It does make the grass very green," Ellie replied with an answering smile.

Matthew did a double take. "Does that mean you're getting used to live in Llandrigg?"

"Getting there," Ellie replied. Her moods still seemed to swing high and low, but she was starting to feel as if an even keel was at least a possibility. "I'm glad you're on board with the idea for the B&B."

"Me too." His tone was heartfelt. "I've already got some plans I hope you'll like—I was thinking we could put a door between two of the bedrooms and make a family suite, and maybe turn the study into a games room. We could get table football, a bunch of board games—"

"Oh, Matt," Ellie exclaimed, "that's just the kind of thing I was thinking of—or wishing I could think of, really. It's the spirit of it exactly."

He gave her a quick grin, his eyes sparkling in a way Ellie couldn't remember them doing in a long time. "I just wish I could get rid of this cast on my arm so I could really get going," he said with a sigh, and then a smile. "But I know I need to be patient."

Just as she did. They were both learning, Ellie thought. Learning and growing. And Matthew seemed to feel that way too, for as they headed toward Llandrigg, he reached for her hand and held it in his. Ellie smiled and squeezed his fingers, and they drove the rest of the way in a silence that felt sweet.

Amazingly, the children were all settled when they came into the house—Ava and Josh in bed, and Ben and Jess doing homework at the kitchen table.

"Thank you for managing everything so well, sweetheart," Ellie said softly as she paused in the doorway of the kitchen. Jess was at the table, books spread in front of her, along with her laptop, her head bent over them. "I don't know what we would have done without you here to hold down the fort."

"It's okay." Jess ducked her head, and with a flicker of guilt, Ellie remembered their cross words from earlier.

"I'm sorry for losing my temper before dinner," she said. "I shouldn't have gotten so angry."

"It's fine." Jess's gaze was focused on her laptop, and so, with a sigh, Ellie decided to leave it. She'd had her quota of heartfelt moments for the day, it seemed, and she was grateful for them. She could look forward to a few more tomorrow.

She was feeling optimistic as she went to bed, and she held

onto that feeling as she got up the next morning. The children seemed in good spirits; Jess in particular was practically buzzing with energy as she bumped a big duffel bag down the stairs.

"Goodness, what is that for?" Ellie exclaimed with a laugh.

"Sophie and I are going to try on different outfits for the autumn concert," Jess explained as she put the bag by the door. "So, I brought lots of stuff."

It cheered Ellie to think that her daughter had made a good friend and was even singing in the concert—and that she'd wanted to tell her mother about it. "Sophie," she repeated thoughtfully. "Should we invite her over for dinner sometime?"

Jess shrugged, glancing away. "I dunno. Maybe."

Or maybe not quite yet, Ellie thought as she took in her daughter's slightly guarded expression. But the children *were* settling here, she realized with a sense of grateful relief. Like with so many other things, she just needed to be patient.

"I can't wait to see you both in the concert," she said, and Jess mumbled something in reply before grabbing her coat and slinging the duffel bag over her shoulder.

Ellie held onto her thankful heart and optimistic mood all day; Gwen was alert and cheerful when she and Matthew arrived at the hospital, and the consultant said she was responding well to the course of antibiotics. When she went to pick up Josh and Ava from school, Josh had another playdate set up with Zach, this time at their house, and Emma invited her over for a coffee later in the week, to which Ellie agreed enthusiastically.

"Remember what I said about maybe doing some PR for Bluebell Inn?" Ellie asked her, and Emma nodded, her eyes alight with interest. "Well, we've got some new ideas about how we're going to renovate and advertise... I'd love your thoughts on it all."

"I'd love to give them," Emma told her warmly. "You can tell me all about it when you come over."

"I will," Ellie promised, laughing a little as Ava tugged on her hand. She was in raptures because she'd been invited to a birthday party.

"A princess *and* unicorn party, Mummy!"

Ellie pulled her daughter in for a quick hug, almost as thrilled as she was by the invitation. "That sounds wonderful, darling. Just your sort of party."

As they headed back to Bluebell Lane, Ellie decided to wait by the bus stop for Ben and Jess. She should have done that more often, she thought, checking in with them a bit more actively. Well, she'd start today. She'd ask Jess how she got on with the outfits, maybe suggest she try a few on and show the family. They could make a fashion show of it, get Ava involved...

She really needed to make more of an effort with her oldest, spend more time listening and less lecturing. She was looking forward to a fresh start for everyone.

But when the school bus pulled up to the stop, only Ben got out with a bunch of other kids Ellie didn't recognize. She frowned as he sloped toward her, clearly alone.

"Ben, where's your sister?"

Ben shrugged, seemingly unconcerned. "She didn't get on the bus."

"What?" Ellie stared at him in shock. "What do you mean, she didn't get on the bus? She had to have—"

Ben shrugged again. "Dunno. I didn't see her at school all day, either, but then I wasn't really looking out for her."

"What..." Ellie's stomach hollowed out and she reached for her phone, swiping it quickly to call Jess, but it went right to voicemail. "Does she have a rehearsal this afternoon?" she asked anxiously. "Or maybe she went to Sophie's house..." She hadn't made any mention of going anywhere but school, and Ellie didn't even know where Sophie lived or what her last name was. How could she not have made sure she knew those things? "Ben, did she tell you anything?" Ellie demanded. "This morning, maybe?"

Ben shook his head. "Nope."

Ellie ground her teeth as she tried Jess's phone again. It went to voicemail once more, and Ellie left a harried message. "Jess, it's Mom. Just want to know where you are, as you didn't get off the bus." Which Jess knew, obviously. "Please ring or text me as soon as you can and let me know how you are. Love you."

"Mom, is Jess going to be okay?" Josh asked, sounding anxious, and Ellie tried to give him a reassuring smile.

Ava tugged on her sleeve. "I need to have a wee."

"All right, let's go home. Hopefully Jess will be in touch soon." Perhaps she was overreacting. There had to be an innocent, obvious explanation to Jess's absence. Of course there was. She was with Sophie; maybe they'd stayed in town. She'd text any minute...

Yet as Ellie headed back to Bluebell Lane with her tribe in tow, she couldn't keep worry from throbbing her temples. Where was her daughter?

Anxiety knotted Ellie's stomach as they arrived back at the house. Ben threw his backpack into the corner and started rummaging in the cupboards for a snack, seemingly unconcerned by his sister's no-show.

"Did Jess say anything to you?" Ellie asked again as she started picking up the clutter of coats, backpacks, and lunch boxes that always ended up in a heap in the hall. "Anything at all about her plans?"

"I told you she didn't." Ben spoke through a spoonful of Nutella straight from the jar. Ellie held onto her patience.

"Are you sure, Ben? And what do you mean, you didn't see her at school today? Do you normally see her at school? At lunch or in the halls or somewhere?" Ben was year seven while

Jess was year nine; Ellie couldn't imagine their paths crossed all too frequently, or willingly, for that matter, but they must occasionally.

Ben shrugged. "I dunno. I didn't see her today, anyway."

"But where do you think she would have gone?" Ellie persisted. "She would normally text me, if she was off somewhere. She wouldn't just go somewhere on her own." Although Jess hadn't been "off somewhere" since they'd moved to Llandrigg. Ellie supposed she should be happy that her daughter might finally have somewhere to go, and someone to go there with, but she still wanted—*needed* —answers.

Ben dipped a spoon into the Nutella jar again, and Ellie snatched it out of his hands.

"That's enough of that. You can have it on toast, but not straight from the jar. It's disgusting." She screwed the lid on and put it back in the cupboard. "Are you sure you don't know anything?"

"Well..." He screwed up his face in what looked to Ellie like a parody of concentration. "I know she was upset."

"Upset?" The anxiety Ellie had feeling tightened every muscle. That was why Jess had been in such a foul mood last night? She should have realized, or at least suspected. "Why?"

Ben shrugged, his gaze sliding away. "Something on the music board."

"What?" Ellie stared at him in confusion.

He turned back to the cupboards, on the hunt for more food.

"Ben, seriously. Stop looking for snacks and tell me what you know. It's important. What about the music board?"

With a heavy sigh, Ben turned around. "Some jokesters put up photos of her and Sophie on the noticeboard and she was really upset about it. It was only up there for, like, an hour or so..." Another shrug.

"Photos? Of her and Sophie? That's the friend she's singing with?"

"Yeah."

Ellie frowned, trying to understand what had happened. "What kind of photos?"

"Just pictures of their faces, probably taken from Instagram. But they'd written 'Nerds' in red marker, and everyone was laughing about it."

"Oh, no..." Ellie stared at him in dismay. How could people —children—be so cruel? Jess had only been at the school for a month. To be teased like that, so publicly, would have been awful for her. Why hadn't Jess told her? Why hadn't she asked more questions, tried to find out what was really bothering her daughter? And what did it have to do with her not being on the bus this afternoon? Ellie was afraid to think.

Then she remembered the heavy duffel bag Jess had bumped down the stairs, claiming it was full of outfits for her and Sophie to try on. But if she hadn't even gone to school... Ellie's mind raced. What if it had been full of clothes for Jess herself? What if her daughter was running away? Panic iced Ellie's insides. She needed to ring Matthew.

"Mom..." Josh tugged on her sleeve. "Jess is going to be okay, isn't she?"

Ellie gave him a distracted smile as she listened to Matthew's phone ring. He had stayed at the hospital with Gwen, but he might have turned off his phone in the room. *Please pick up, Matt...*

"Mom?" Josh said again. "Is she?"

"Yes, she'll be fine, Josh," Ellie replied. "We just need to find her." The phone switched to voicemail.

An hour crept by with painstaking slowness, each minute seeming endless in its uncertainty. Ellie could not keep herself from texting or calling Jess every five minutes, even though it continued to switch to voicemail, as did Matthew's phone. Why was no one picking up? Should she call the police, or was that an overreaction? It wasn't even two hours since Jess should have come off the bus. The police would probably ask her to wait for a little while. But what if they didn't? Panic made her feel paralyzed. Jess was only thirteen.

Another half-hour passed while Ellie made dinner and left more texts and voicemails for Matthew and Jess. Then, finally, Matthew rang her.

"I'm just leaving the hospital now. Do you need anything from the shops?" He sounded so relaxed that Ellie didn't know whether to scream or laugh at herself.

"Did you not see all my missed calls?" she demanded.

"No, my phone was switched off... Ellie? Has something happened?"

"Jess didn't get off the school bus, and she hasn't come home. She might not have been at school all day." Her voice hitched, rising in anxiety. "I don't know where she is. And Ben says she'd been bullied at school."

"*Bullied—*"

"I'm worried she might have run away," Ellie confessed, her voice trembling now. "She had a big duffel bag with her this morning. She said it was for some outfits for her and her friend, but I just don't know..."

"I'll be home in fifteen minutes," Matthew promised her. "I'm just getting into the Uber. We'll figure it out then. She'll be okay."

"Should I call the police?"

He hesitated, and in that second's silence, Ellie felt the terrible weight of his fear as well as her own.

"I suppose you should," he replied heavily. "I'll be back as soon as I can, Ellie, I promise."

It felt utterly surreal, to dial 999 and wait for the dispatcher to pick up. Ellie felt numb as she explained the situation. "My daughter was meant to come home from school, but she hasn't shown up and I'm worried she might have run away."

In a voice that was so calm it felt unfeeling, at least to Ellie, the dispatcher went through the routine questions. Had she called or texted Jess? Yes, of course she had. Had there been any calls from school regarding her absence? No, but perhaps Jess had made some arrangement without her knowing. She suspected her daughter could forge her signature; she'd seen it enough times. Her brother hadn't seen her in school. Was she unhappy? Depressed?

Tears stung Ellie's eyes as she answered the last one in a whisper. "I think she was unhappy," she whispered. "And maybe even depressed." She'd known that, really, but she'd insisted to herself—and to Jess—that things would get better. Why hadn't she really listened?

"Nine times out of ten, a teenager shows up after causing a bit of worry," the dispatcher told her, but the words were far from comforting. What about the tenth time? Where could Jess possibly *be*? "We'll send two police officers over to your house. Just in case."

Ellie had only just ended the call when Matthew burst through the front door. "Is she home?" he asked, the words torn from him, and Ellie shook her head miserably.

Ava, Josh, and Ben, all three of them now sensing the severity of the situation, clustered around nervously, Ava tugging on Ellie's sleeve, Josh leaning into her, and Ben scowling.

Matthew raked a hand through his hair. "Where could she be?" he wondered out loud, just as Ellie had.

Where would Jess possibly go? How would she get there? What if, Ellie wondered with a clutch of fear, her little girl was wandering the streets of a city somewhere—Abergavenny or Cardiff, or even London, adrift and alone as darkness fell? The thought was utterly terrifying. Jess didn't have any real street sense. She was a suburban, and now a village, kid. She'd never even taken a train on her own, or a bus, without Ben. She'd never gone on her own anywhere before, so where would she go now, in a country that was still so unfamiliar to her?

A sudden thought slammed into Ellie, leaving her breathless. "Matthew," she said, "do you think... do you think Jess would try to go..." Home.

Before she'd said it, Matthew's eyes had widened in understanding.

"Back to America?" he ventured.

As Ellie and Matthew stared at each in growing fear, the lights of a police car washed the room in blue.

CHAPTER 34

GWEN

"Mum?"

Gwen's eyes fluttered open, and groggily she tried straighten in her hospital bed at the sight of Sarah, looking uncharacteristically and rather endearingly uncertain.

"Sarah," she said, her voice warm as she blinked the sleep from her eyes. "I'm so glad you've come. I was meaning to ring you last night, but unfortunately events overtook me." Gwen smiled wryly, but her daughter didn't return it. Sarah looked completely miserable as she perched on the chair next to Gwen's bed.

"I should have been the one to ring. And I should have come earlier. Matt texted me last night..."

"It's all right, Sarah," Gwen told her gently. "I know you've been angry with me, and you're right to be. I never should have said what I did yesterday. I'm so sorry. Please believe me, that I never meant to hurt you."

"It's not that." Sarah's eyes filled with tears and surprised by this uncharacteristic display of emotion, Gwen reached for her hand. "I mean, it is, I suppose, in a way, but I'm not angry. I was just... *hurt.*" She confessed the emotion in a shuddering breath; Gwen knew how hard it had to be for her.

"I'm so sorry I hurt you," Gwen said quietly. "I shouldn't have—"

"But that's the thing, Mum," Sarah interjected. "You *should* have. The last thing I want to be is hard work to you. I really was trying to help, even if I wasn't. I'm glad you've told me, even if I wasn't at the time."

"You're not hard work—" Gwen protested, and Sarah let out a wobbly laugh.

"I obviously am." She managed a rueful smile as she freed her hand from Gwen's to wipe her eyes. "And you know what? I *know* I am. Deep down, anyway. I know I fuss, and nag, and try to boss everybody around, and I even know it annoys you. But I just feel like I have to *do* something. Because if I don't..." She trailed off, biting her lip and shaking her head.

Gwen smiled tenderly at her daughter. "I know," she said softly. "Sarah, darling, I know."

"And the truth is... I wanted to seem in control of your treatment because everything else in my life is going a bit pear-shaped. I couldn't handle anything more going wrong and that was selfish of me, I know."

The problems Sarah had referenced yesterday, Gwen realized. "Sarah, what's been going on?" she asked with a frown. "Will you tell me now?"

Sarah sighed unhappily. "Yes, I suppose, although, I didn't want to say before. I didn't want to admit anything was going wrong at all. But the truth is, Owen is having trouble in school, and Mairi has fallen out with her friends. Or rather, they've fallen out with her. She's miserable, poor thing. And Nathan..." Sarah paused. "Nathan's got a new boss who doesn't like the way he does things. He's in constant fear of losing his job, and we can't manage without it, so there's that stress, as well."

"Oh, love..." Gwen had suspected something was going on

with her daughter, but she hadn't realized there had been so much. She was glad Sarah was willing to tell her now.

"I didn't want to burden you with any of it," Sarah continued, "and the truth is, I didn't want anyone to know I wasn't coping perfectly well. You seemed so busy with the bed and breakfast, and with Matt and Ellie..." She let out another shuddery breath. "And frankly, I was jealous." She ducked her head. "I hate admitting that, but it's true. I've been here all along and you've never asked me to help with the B&B."

Gwen opened her mouth and Sarah held up a hand to stop her shocked protest.

"I know, I know. I never acted as if I wanted to help. I never even acted as if I was interested in it, and I was always so busy. And maybe I didn't want to help, Mum, I can be honest about that, but I suppose, in a rather childish way, I wanted to be *asked*, which makes me very contrary, I realize. And ridiculous."

Sarah gave a watery smile and Gwen's heart expanded with love. How, at her age, could she not have realized her daughter's hard, prickly shell hid such a soft vulnerability beneath? Just as everyone's did.

"Sarah, I'm so glad you've said all this," Gwen told her, reaching for her hand again. "You have no idea how much. I should have realized... but blind fool that I am, I didn't. I thought you were getting on perfectly well by yourself, and you didn't want or need my interference. Sometimes I felt a bit... left out, I suppose, having no idea that you might feel the same. But the important thing is, I know now, and that makes a huge difference." She squeezed her daughter's hand, wanting to imbue her with all her love and affection. "Darling, I want you to be involved. I'd love your input. Your house is so beautiful... I could surely use your decorating skills!"

Sarah made a face. "And what about Ellie?"

"What about her?"

"I don't feel as if we really get on. And, admittedly, I haven't made that much effort. I should have, but..." She blew out a breath. "She didn't seem to want to, with me. I sent her a text yesterday that probably terrified her, but I was so angry and—well, hurt. But she hasn't seemed particularly interested in getting to know me, or asking for my advice—"

"And that," Gwen guessed shrewdly, "is what you really wanted?"

"Well..." Sarah let out an abashed laugh. "Yes, I suppose it was."

Gwen smiled in sympathy. "I think Ellie's finding her way, but she still feels a bit lost and adrift," she said quietly. "She's just made an enormous move, and it takes time to adjust. I know she'd appreciate your friendship, Sarah... your *genuine* friendship, and not just you showing her how well you know Llandrigg, or all the activities you're involved in."

Sarah let out a surprised laugh as she pretended to clutch her chest. "Ouch. You certainly are telling me like it is, aren't you?"

"Out of love," Gwen assured her with a smile. "For your sake as well as everyone else's."

"So, if I take you to chemo again," Sarah teased, "I can't fuss with your pillows?"

"Or bother the nurses," Gwen returned with a smile. "No, absolutely not. But you can do the crossword with me. Or just sit with me in the quiet, which is what I'd like most of all."

Sarah's expression grew serious and a bit teary. "I'd love to do that, Mum."

Gwen smiled, even as she went a bit teary herself. How was it, she wondered, that it took so much heartache and even tragedy for her family to find their way to each other again? Matthew and Ellie, her and Sarah... she was hopeful that bridges were being mended or even built... and they were stronger than ever before. She longed for that to be true. She was determined to do whatever she could to make it happen.

"Thank you, Sarah," Gwen told her daughter. "I love you, you know."

"And I love you." Sarah let out a laugh as she slapped her knees. "Right, that's enough mushiness from me! How about a cup of tea?"

Gwen laughed, relieved as she sank back against the pillows. She'd really been worried that she might have fallen out with Sarah in a terrible way. "A cup of tea," she told her daughter, "would be wonderful."

CHAPTER 35

JESS

Heathrow Airport was absolutely enormous. And it was heaving with people, everyone seeming as if they were in a very important rush, and they knew exactly where they were going.

Jess clutched her duffel bag to her chest and tried not to look as panicked and frankly terrified as she felt. Her plane left in three hours; it had taken ages to get to the airport, with so many changes, so many busy bus and train stations to navigate, and no one seeming to care about her at all. She felt very small, and very young, and she hadn't even got on the plane yet.

That morning, she'd texted Sophie, asking her to tell her form tutor that she was at home with a stomach ache. Admittedly, a parent was meant to ring, but Jess hoped that Sophie being a model student would give her some credibility.

It did, because Sophie had told her the form tutor accepted her word, although Sophie herself wasn't too happy about it.

Where are you? she'd texted. And then, making Jess feel guilty, *Are we still friends?*

She shouldn't have ignored Sophie yesterday, she knew. It had been a rotten thing to do, and yet she'd just been feeling so miserable.

Yes, of course we are, she texted back. *Sorry about yesterday. I was just really upset.*

Where are you? Sophie had texted again.

Just need a day off, Jess had replied, and then she'd switched her phone off. It was better, she decided, if people couldn't get in touch with her. She didn't think she could handle any text messages from anyone just now, and she wouldn't have any idea how to respond to them.

The bus to the train station in Abergavenny hadn't been so bad, but the train from Abergavenny to London Paddington had been endless, with two changes, in Newport and Bristol Temple Meads. It had been hard enough navigating the stations, finding the platforms; she'd wondered how on earth she was going to manage the airport.

Jess still couldn't quite believe she'd actually done it. She'd bought a ticket to New York JFK on her mother's credit card—which had been hundreds and hundreds of pounds!—and the train ticket to London, as well. She'd packed her clothes and managed the bus and train, and she'd even worked up the courage to ask the porter in Paddington how to get to Heathrow.

He'd been kindly rather than suspicious, and directed her to the Heathrow Express train, which Jess hadn't bought a ticket for. As she no longer had her mother's credit card, she'd had to empty her own meagre bank account to buy the alarmingly expensive ticket, but at least it had been easily done, and by four o'clock in the afternoon—just when she should have been getting on the school bus to go back home—she'd arrived at Heathrow.

Checking in had been easy enough, on a computer, and she could take her duffel bag as carry-on so she didn't even have to talk to anyone who might be suspicious of a teenaged girl traveling alone. Going through security had been a bit alarming; she'd forgotten to take off her shoes, and she'd held up the line, to several people's muttered irritation, but the attendants had been kindly enough, smiling at her.

"First time traveling on your own, love?" one of them had asked, and Jess had nodded.

"Yeah, going to visit my grandparents," she'd said, the lie tripping off her lips, and the security attendant had smiled.

Once she'd got through security, she could hardly believe she'd managed it all. She was actually here, at Heathrow, and soon enough she could get on a plane. All she needed to do was find her gate and wait to board the plane.

Board the plane... could she really do it? Did she even want to, anymore? When Jess had arrived at Heathrow, she'd Snapchatted Chloe with a picture of her in the airport, but it had taken Chloe over an hour to reply. And when she had, it hadn't exactly been encouraging—a couple of exclamation points, that was it. And then Chloe had posted a picture on Instagram of her and Emily giving each other makeovers after school.

Jess's stomach had cramped when she'd seen that photo. What happened to Emily being so fake? Had Chloe even told her mother that Jess was coming? And how was she supposed to get from JFK to Chloe's house in Connecticut? It had to be over a hundred miles away, and she didn't think there were any buses or trains. She didn't know if there were, anyway, and she didn't like the idea of traveling through New York City alone, and at night. She couldn't even begin to imagine doing it.

It had been relatively easy to get this far, but Jess was starting to have some serious doubts about the rest of the trip, especially if Chloe—and her parents—weren't happy to see her. Why wasn't Chloe helping her? Texting her with ideas, options? Maybe Chloe had changed her mind, or never expected her to actually come. Jess knew full well how you could text something and not remotely mean it, even if you were feeling it in the moment.

But she'd gone and done it. She couldn't go back now. She wasn't even sure how she would, because she didn't have any more money or her mom's card. She was stuck here, at this busy airport, unless she made herself get on that plane.

What would her mom and dad be thinking right now? It was after five, and they would know she was missing. Ben would have told them she hadn't gotten on the bus. They had to be worried... but *how* worried? Maybe they were glad to have a break from her surliness. But no, Jess thought, that wasn't true. They'd be frantic, absolutely frantic, and it was all her fault. Her stomach churned at the thought.

Jess pictured the table in Granny's kitchen laden with food, the room warm and cozy as darkness fell. She pictured Ava asking her to color with her after dinner—Jess almost always said no—and Josh doing one of his epic puzzles. Even Ben wasn't so bad, although he could be annoying. This morning, as they'd got on the bus, he'd said sorry for teasing her yesterday, that he hadn't meant it, and the people who had posted the photos were stupid.

And Granny... what if she made Granny more ill, by worrying her, just when she'd really started to get to know her, to *like* her? And with Granny in hospital, it really hadn't been a good time to leave... not that there was a good time. And Jess had been afraid if she didn't do it right away, when Chloe had asked her, she never would have... or Chloe might have changed her mind.

Jess's eyes stung. She already missed her family, more than she ever had before... but how could she go back? She'd already bought the ticket. She'd checked onto the flight. And the problems at school wouldn't go away. She still dreaded going in tomorrow, and every day after that. She still hated it all, and yet... if Sophie could do it, maybe she could, too? She could try, at least... except it was too late. She was *here*.

She took a deep breath and tried not to cry.

What she needed to do, she decided, was find her gate. She'd sit down and catch her breath. She'd already decided she wouldn't text her mom until she was on the plane, so she couldn't be stopped, but now she felt an unbearable ache to let her parents know where she was, to make sure they weren't worried. Just to *hear* their voices...

Weighed down with her duffel bag, she lumbered toward her gate and collapsed heavily into a plastic chair. When Jess slid her phone out of her pocket, it lit up like a firework. Eight missed calls, six new text messages, and four new voicemails. So, her parents *were* worried, and for some reason that made Jess feel the happiest she'd been all day.

"We are now going to begin boarding Flight 765 to New York JFK," a voice intoned on a loudspeaker, and Jess tensed. "Could those in boarding section D please come to the gate."

Jess checked her boarding pass—she was in section C. The moment of truth was almost upon her.

She glanced down at her phone, scrolling through the texts from her mom. *Jess, where are you? I'm worried... Ben says you weren't at school... Whatever is wrong, we can work on it together... Please ring and let me know you're safe... I love you, Jess. So much.*

Tears stung Jess's eyes and then one slipped down her cheek.

"Would those in boarding section C please now come to the gate."

Jess watched as everyone headed in an impatient herd toward the gate. Airline attendants were checking passports and ushering people into the corridor that led to the plane. It was now or never.

Quickly, Jess checked her Snapchats—nothing from Chloe. Another look at Instagram; Chloe and Emily were having an unheard-of midweek sleepover, because they were studying for a test together. Chloe had left her last message unread. Did she not realize Jess was on her way to see her, live with her? She didn't even care. If Jess showed up, Chloe would probably be shocked—and so would Chloe's mom.

What was she doing?

For the first time, Jess saw clearly—so clearly—that going back to Connecticut was not the answer. It never had been. She was running away from her problems, which she knew her parents—and her granny—would tell her was not a good idea. She could almost hear her granny saying something like, *"You can try to run away from your problems, Jess, but the trouble is, they usually come with you."*

It sounded like something her grandmother would say, anyway. Jess missed her, and her parents. And even her brothers and sister. She missed everything about Bluebell Inn, and Llandrigg, and the life in Wales she'd thought she hated. Right then, she wanted it all back.

"Would boarding section B now come to the gate..."

Recklessly, Jess swiped her phone. The call was picked up after half a ring.

"Jess?"

Jess took a deep breath, her voice wobbling as she spoke. "Mom?"

CHAPTER 36

ELLIE

"Oh, Jess, *Jess.*" Ellie's voice came out in a sob of relief as she sagged against the kitchen cupboards. "Where are you, darling? Wherever you are, we'll come and get you. Are you safe? Are you well? You're not hurt?"

"Yes, I'm okay." Her daughter sounded so sad and so small, Ellie wanted to pull her into the tightest hug right then and there. "I'm... I'm at Heathrow Airport."

"*Heathrow*...!" Ellie's mind spun. So Jess had been trying to go back to Connecticut. "How..." she began, only to have Jess explain in a small voice.

"I wanted to go home."

Home.

Ellie closed her eyes. She had a dozen questions about how Jess had managed to get all the way to Heathrow, never mind through security and customs and all the rest, if indeed she'd gotten that far, but those could wait for later. "Which terminal, Jess?" she asked. "We'll come right away to collect you." It was a three-hour drive without traffic, and it was already six o'clock at night. But none of it mattered. All Ellie wanted was her daughter safe at home.

Home. This was home now, but clearly for Jess it hadn't been. She should have realized how much her daughter had been struggling.

"Umm... terminal five."

"All right. Sit tight, sweetheart. Maybe find a café where you can be comfortable. We'll be there as soon as we can. And call me if you need anything, or if you just want to talk. For any reason at all. *Any reason.*"

Her voice throbbed with emotion and Jess let out a small sound, something between a laugh and a sob. "Okay."

"I love you, Jess. So much. Dad and I both do. And I'm coming to get you."

"Okay." Jess sniffed. "Thanks, Mom."

Ellie disconnected the call with a shuddery breath of pure emotion. Relief made her knees feel like jelly, her whole body weak. "She's okay," she told everyone gathered around— Matthew, Ava, Ben, and Josh all breathed out a collective sigh of relief. "She's at Heathrow."

"Heathrow...!" Matthew looked surprised, even though it was a possibility they had considered. Ellie didn't think either of them had actually believed Jess would go so far, but at least she hadn't got on the plane. "I suppose I'd better ring the police and tell them she's okay."

The officers had only left a few minutes ago, after taking Jess's details. Ellie had struggled not to break down as she'd explained the situation. *I think she's had trouble settling here,* she'd said, and it had felt like a confession, an admission of her own failure as a mother. Why hadn't she realized just how unhappy her daughter was? Why hadn't she done something about it?

"I'll drive to Heathrow," she told Matthew. "Jess and I argued last night. Well, the truth is, I lost my temper. I can't help but feel it contributed to her running away."

"That was not your fault," Matthew told her firmly. "We'll

get through this, Ellie," he promised her as he put his good arm around her. "Together."

She nodded, her cheek pressed against his shirt, as she tried to hold back tears. It felt as if everything had fallen apart, and yet here they were, building it back up again. Together, just as Matthew had said. Perhaps you needed difficult situations to happen in order to realize what was important. What mattered the most. She was certainly realizing what mattered now—*her family*.

The three-hour drive to Heathrow along dark, rainy stretches of motorway felt endless, but it gave Ellie time to think. To plan how different things were going to be, moving forward. She'd listen more, and worry less. She'd get Jess and the other children involved in the plans for the B&B; they all had something to offer, and they all needed to feel they belonged. She'd make sure they spent more time together as a family, the six of them, but also with Gwen, and maybe even Sarah and Nathan and their kids, too.

She hadn't, Ellie realized, really given their life in Llandrigg a chance. She'd convinced herself she had, simply by moving there in the first place, but the truth was she'd been dragging her feet all along. Matthew had seen that, and Gwen had too. Maybe Jess had seen it, which had given her the liberty to act the same.

But it was all going to be different now, Ellie thought as she pulled into the short-term parking at terminal five. Starting right now.

She texted Jess as she hurried into the terminal, the brightly lit, big open space making her wince after the darkness of the car.

She strode toward the coffee bar where Jess had said she was waiting, by the international arrivals, scanning the faces of weary and jet-lagged travelers who sat hunched over their lattes, their suitcases by their feet.

"*Mom!*"

Ellie jerked around and then let out an exclamation of pure relief as Jess hurried toward her, dragging her duffel bag behind her.

"Oh, Jess. *Jess.*" She pulled her daughter into her arms, hugging her tightly.

"I'm *so* sorry, Mom." Jess's shoulders shook as she pressed her face into Ellie's shoulder. "I've made such a mess of everything."

"You haven't, Jess. I'm so sorry I didn't realize you were going through such a hard time. Ben mentioned something—"

"The noticeboard?" Jess confirmed with a ragged sigh. "Yeah. But it didn't have to be such a big deal. I know that, but..."

"This has been hard on you, Jess. Perhaps on you most of all, since you're older than the others. I'm sorry I haven't been more understanding. I should have been, especially considering how I was struggling, too!" She let out a sad laugh as she shook her head. When she'd been feeling lonely and adrift, why hadn't she realized her daughter would be too, but even more so?

"I'm sorry I've been so difficult," Jess whispered. "Especially with Granny being so sick." She drew back, her face pale and pinched with anxiety. "Is she okay...?"

"She's doing much better on the antibiotics, and she should be home in a few days." Ellie hugged her again. "I'm so glad to see you."

"I bought a plane ticket, Mom," Jess confessed. "On your credit card. I'm sorry. I'll pay you back..."

"That doesn't matter," Ellie replied firmly. They could sort out the repercussions and consequences later. Much later. "Let's just get you home."

. . .

Exhausted by the day, Jess curled up in the passenger seat and was asleep by the time Ellie pulled onto the M4. She glanced across at her daughter, looking so young and vulnerable, and her heart ached with love. She realized afresh how, in the midst of all the busyness as well as her own difficult adjustment to life in Llandrigg, she had forgotten to look beneath the sulks and scowls of her children. They'd been having a hard time, too. Of course they had.

But now, she hoped and prayed, they'd be able to pull together rather than apart. Become stronger than ever, supporting each other, learning and loving and growing together.

By the time Ellie pulled into Bluebell Lane at nearly one o'clock in the morning, she was gritty-eyed with fatigue. Matthew met her at the door, pulling her into his arms for a quick hug before he went to help a very sleepy Jess into the house.

"It's going to be okay," he told her once Jess was settled in bed, and they were getting ready to go to sleep. "I know this has been hard, Ellie, hard on all of us in different ways. We've all made mistakes, me especially. I'll be the first to admit that, but we will get through this, stronger than ever. I'll make sure of it."

Ellie smiled at him, utterly weary, yet also unbelievably thankful that they'd come this far—together. "I know," she replied.

"Did I tell you the new idea I had for the B&B?" Matthew said, his eyes alight with enthusiasm as he climbed into bed.

Ellie let out a tired laugh. "You mean besides the family rooms and board games? No, I don't think you did."

"Well, along the lines you were talking about, I was thinking about making an obstacle course for kids in the back of the garden. Using some old tires and beams and things like that. It's about my speed when it comes to carpentry, and Ben and Josh could help, too. I think they'd like it."

Ellie climbed into bed and snuggled into Matthew's arms, her cheek resting against his chest. "I think," she said as she let out a yawn and fatigue crashed over her, "that sounds brilliant."

As she drifted off to sleep, she felt her body relax in a way it hadn't maybe in all the time she'd been in Llandrigg—a softening from the inside out, the tension that had clenched her stomach and knotted between her shoulder blades since she'd arrived, finally, thankfully gone.

Maybe, she thought sleepily, that was because she was finally where she needed to be—home.

EPILOGUE

NINE MONTHS LATER

It was a beautiful day in early June, everything sparkling with sunlight and dew, the world reborn. Bluebell Family Bed and Breakfast was having a rebirth as well, and this summer afternoon was its opening celebration.

A bright blue ribbon was stretched between the gateposts and a new sign, hand-painted by a local artist and mum from the village school, stood proudly by the gate. The house was freshly whitewashed, the shutters at every window painted the exact violet-blue shade of the bluebells that clustered in the shady corners of the garden.

"Where should I put this, Granny?" Jess asked as she came outside with a pitcher of fresh American-style lemonade. It had been her idea to incorporate some of their American heritage into the B&B, including fluffy pancakes and maple syrup for breakfast, and an American flag flying by the Welsh one in the front garden.

"On the table there, by the gazebo, I think," Gwen said. She felt both excited and nervous for the day—what if no one showed up? What if too many did, and they ran out of the gorgeous pistachio macaroons Sarah had baked for the occasion, another soon-to-be Bluebell specialty?

Back in October, after she'd got out of hospital following her infection, and Jess had come home safely, and Matthew had finally got the cast off his arm, they'd all had a big family consultation around the kitchen table—complete with tea and Welsh cakes. Sarah and Nathan had come too, along with Owen and Mairi, and everyone had listened to Ellie and Matthew talk about their ideas for the better-than-ever B&B, before opening it up for questions, concerns, and ideas.

There had been all three—of course—with Sarah, somewhat predictably, concerned that it wasn't viable economically. Gwen knew Nathan's job was still in doubt and money was foremost on her daughter's mind.

"There's only one way to find out," Matthew had told his sister, "but I have done some market research and there just isn't this kind of venue right now—there are family camping and even glamping sites, but not a proper B&B."

Sarah had been grudgingly convinced, and offered to do the bookkeeping; Owen and Mairi, showing more enthusiasm than Gwen had seen from them in a long while, had asked if they could help Matthew with the obstacle course, along with Ben and Josh. Jess and her friend Sophie were in charge of the games room, and Ava was helping Gwen in the garden. Ellie, and her friend Emma, were managing the publicity and event planning. Everybody had a job, Gwen had thought, and everybody was working together.

Of course, there had been the expected—and some unexpected—jolts and bumps along the way. They'd had to put in more fire doors, and the obstacle course needed a health and safety inspection. The website Ellie had designed had crashed, and the advertising had been far more expensive than anyone had expected. Knocking through a wall to make a family suite had nearly caused the ceiling to come down again, and for the first week the website went live, there hadn't been a single booking. Ellie had been white-faced with panic, but Gwen had told her the word would spread—and it had. They were now fully booked for the next month.

She could hardly believe they'd accomplished so much, in such a short amount of time. Together.

They had all come together to work to create something new and unique, and it had taken not just the whole family, but the whole village. Each bedroom had a handmade cover quilted by a local craftswoman, and a hand-thrown pottery jug of flowers, also made locally. The honey, butter, milk, and jam had all been made locally, or by Gwen herself, who had finished her last course of chemotherapy two months ago. At her scan next month, she'd find out if she was in remission, but she felt well, and that was a huge blessing. It had been a long, hard nine months in many ways, but Gwen was thankful to be where she was—standing on her own two feet, with her loving family all around her.

"Everything's ready, I think, Mum," Matthew said as he joined her by the gazebo, where she was arranging the plates of macaroons. "I think it's going to be great."

Over the last few months, Matthew had really got into the spirit of the place; he'd made the obstacle course with Ben and Josh, Owen and Mairi, as well as an epic treehouse that spanned the three oaks clustered at the bottom of the garden, a rope swing that swung out over the little valley, and a new chicken coop that Ava had named "The Egg Hotel." With his help, they'd turned the B&B's garden into a children's wild paradise, and Gwen couldn't wait to see their guests exploring and enjoying it.

As for today, everyone in the village was coming to celebrate their success and officially open the B&B. Gwen could hardly believe how many people had shown an interest. She knew

Ellie had got to know quite a few people in Llandrigg over the winter, and while Gwen suspected her daughter-in-law didn't *quite* feel like a local just yet, Gwen knew she would one day, and most likely one day soon. She'd silently rejoiced to see a new friendship spring up between Sarah and Ellie, as Sarah and Nathan had both become more involved in the B&B, too. It really was a family affair.

Gwen's gaze traveled over the garden, to Jess, who was heading back inside to fetch another pitcher of American-style lemonade. Jess had also blossomed over the winter, although Gwen knew school had continued to possess some challenges. While her granddaughter was never going to be one of those cliquey "in girls" she'd once talked about, she'd settled into a solid friendship with Sophie, as well as her cousin Mairi, who had been, surprisingly, at something of a similar loose end.

All in all, Jess was happy in school, as were her other three grandchildren. They all still had their good and bad days, their fair share of both ups and downs, but that was life, wasn't it? You had to take the good with the bad, the hard with the easy. The important thing was, they were all thankful, and they were a team.

"What if no one comes?" Gwen asked Matthew, knowing she shouldn't worry but doing it anyway.

With a laugh, he pointed to the lane. "I don't think that's going to be a problem, Mum."

With a disbelieving laugh, Gwen caught sight of the crowds already streaming up the lane from the village. It looked as if practically everyone in Llandrigg was showing up for their opening, and maybe from a few other villages, besides.

"Goodness," she exclaimed. "I suppose not."

Nerves continued to flutter in her stomach as she watched the crowd arrive. They were already fully booked for June and July—a prospect that was both terrifying and thrilling. She didn't think she'd been fully booked in all her years of running the bed and breakfast.

"Ready, Mum?" Matthew asked. "I think you should be the one to officially begin the festivities."

"I think we should all do it—"

"We'll stand beside you," Matthew replied, "but this is your bed and breakfast, Mum. Yours and Dad's."

Tears misted Gwen's eyes. "He'd be so proud, you know," she whispered. "Of you."

"Of all of us," Matthew agreed.

"Yes, of all of you. All of us." She nodded and brushed at her eyes.

As Matthew stepped back, Gwen surveyed the garden. Ava was running through the area they'd cultivated into a meadow of wildflowers, chasing a butterfly. Josh and his best friend Zach were hunting for snails in a muddy patch made just for that purpose. Ben was kicking a football with Owen, and Jess was giggling and whispering with Sophie and Mairi. Gwen's heart expanded with thankfulness at it all.

She saw Ellie walking toward her, smiling, and her heart expanded all the more. She'd found the most unexpected and wonderful friend in her daughter-in-law, and she was thankful for that most of all.

"You're going to do the honors?" Ellie asked as she handed her a pair of bright red scissors bought specially for the occasion, and Gwen took them with a little laugh.

"I feel like we all should do it—"

"We're here," Ellie promised. "Cheering you on. This is a momentous occasion, Gwen. For you especially, as well as for all of us."

"I know." Gwen shared a smile of true affection with her daughter-in-law, whom she'd come to rely on so much. She didn't know what she would have done without Ellie these last few months—holding down the fort, keeping up with the housework and meals, driving her to chemo when Sarah couldn't, and all with unflagging good spirits. They'd come a long way since those first few difficult months, and Gwen was so very glad and grateful.

"I think we're ready," Matthew announced, and with a smile that was both determined and only a tiny bit wan, Gwen started toward the gate. She'd lost her hair thanks to the chemo, and it had only just started to grow back to a gray fuzz, making her feel like a newly hatched chicken. She now had a collection of colorful headscarves and knitted beanies; Sarah was often picking one up for her, saying how it would suit her. She was also a lot thinner too, but there was a wiry strength to her and a sparkle in her eyes that she had once wondered would ever return. Well, it had.

Everyone gathered round as she stood in front of the gate, the wide blue satin ribbon stretching across the lane. Matthew slipped his arm around Ellie's waist as Ava tugged on her hand. Sarah and Nathan stood nearby, and Gwen saw Ellie share a smile with Sarah before they both turned back to look at her, waiting for her to cut the ribbon.

Gwen raised the pair of scissors high as she looked around at everyone assembled, a trembling, thankful smile on her lips.

"The Bluebell Family Bed and Breakfast," she announced, "is now officially open for business!"

A LETTER FROM KATE

Dear reader,

I want to say a huge thank you for choosing to read *The Inn on Bluebell Lane*. If you enjoyed it, and would like to keep up to date with all my latest releases, just sign up at the following link. Your email address will never be shared and you can unsubscribe at any time.

www.bookouture.com/kate-hewitt

This story was inspired by my own family's move to a small market town in South Wales. As American ex-pats, it was a bit of a jolt but like Ellie and her family, we found a wonderful, warm community in our new home. I am looking forward to continuing her story in an upcoming sequel!

I hope you loved *The Inn at Bluebell Lane* and if you did, I would be very grateful if you could write a review. I'd love to hear what you think, and it makes such a difference helping new readers to discover one of my books for the first time.

I love hearing from my readers—you can get in touch on my Facebook group for readers (facebook.com/groups/KatesReads), through Twitter, Goodreads or my website.

Thanks again for reading!

Kate

KEEP IN TOUCH WITH KATE

www.kate-hewitt.com

 twitter.com/author_kate

ACKNOWLEDGEMENTS

I am always so grateful to the many people who work with me on my story, and help to bring it to light. I am grateful to the whole amazing team at Bookouture who have helped with this process, from editing, copyediting, and proofreading, to designing and marketing. In particular, I'd like to thank my editor, Jess Whitlum-Cooper, as well as Sarah Hardy, Melanie Price, and Kim Nash in publicity, Laura Deacon in marketing, Richard King in foreign rights, and Sinead O'Connor in audio. Most of all, I'd like to thank my readers, who buy and read my books. Without you, there would be no stories to share. I hope you enjoyed this story as much as I did. Thank you!